HEADZ

J. J. Colagrande

D0162250

BlazeVOX [books]

Buffalo, New York

Headz by J.J. Colagrande
Copyright © 2009

Published by BlazeVOX [books]

Printed in the United States of America
Book design by Geoffrey Gatza
First Edition

ISBN: 9781935402114
Library of Congress Control Number: 2008943140

BlazeVOX [books]
14 Tremaine Ave
Kenmore, NY 14217

Editor@blazevox.org

publisher of weird little books

BlazeVOX [books]

blazevox.org

2   4   6   8   0   9   7   5   3   1

The Party, though its flame may flicker low and all but gutter in these juiceless times, goes on forever.

—Lester Bangs

TABLE OF CONTENTS

HEADZ

Part One
New York Steez

Don't look at me! Thelonious already felt ticked off. It was a miserably hot day and he had missed the first downtown train to see Teflon by like a second. He had to wait ten minutes for the next train, and you know how hot the platforms get during the summer. All he wanted was to get on the subway and not hear some crazy person's spiel. He squeezed into an open seat.

A bottle of Gatorade, almost empty, rolled to his feet, next to his Gino Iannucci skateboard deck. He watched as red drops of Gatorade shook with the subway car. Then a woman began to sing along with her portable radio. The sound of the subway rumbled louder. So the woman turned up the radio. Thelonious stared at an advert for online education until he could no longer see it. Then, at Columbus Circle, a man entered with a white stubbled face. A cranky man, he spoke in fragments and spat. "Damn five horse! Didn't box Velazquez." Everyone without an iPod had to listen as the old man yelled nonsense about horse racing. The old man's spittle landed on Thelonious, and that caused his knees to tremble.

During rush hour, the train resembled the inside of a sardine can. And everyone appeared haggard, worn out. It was too much for Thelonious. This western Babylon. He wondered how long the world of consumerism could possibly continue. Take this, take that, buy, sell. It was way too much. Plus an intellectual subway hierarchy battle raged. The *Post* readers vs. the *Times* readers. Who's-reading-a-magazine vs. who's-reading-a-novel.

New York City often felt overwhelming. And at times a pressing need to leave arises, especially in the heat of summer, particularly if you're a spoiled Manhattanite with bipolar disorder.

Leave me alone! Thelonious wore the New York City evil eye, a hardened squint designed to keep people away, and then he flared his nostrils. Of course the woman cranked her radio so the subway car filled with the summer crooning of a teen pop star.

Thelonious shook his head real fast and a mop of black greasy hair covered his eyes. The subway suddenly felt very hot and he felt fear. He feared the people around him. He feared himself. More important, he feared losing his inspiration. What happened to his kung-fu grip? He should definitely get away. Escape the city.

Where could he go? He thought of Oracledang in only three days. One music festival would inspire him. If only he could hold on.

Then he looked up and two inches from his face he saw a fist. Someone's fist held on to the metal subway bar for support. The fist appeared chafed and cracked, like the sidewalks in the city above the tunnels. The fluorescent lights in the subway flickered. Thelonious placed his hand on his forehead and closed his eyes. To the old man who stood above him, it looked like the scraggily kid forgot how to breathe. Thelonious opened his eyes and screamed.

"Get me outta here."

Hurricane Clout

Thelonious Horowitz sang in a band called Hurricane Clout with three friends, all deejays. He sang under the name Monk. Jonah's moniker was Chopshop. Diamonds used Diamond D. And Lee spun records under Leroi Jones. Three deejays and one MC. They had a unique sound. Some could argue Hurricane Clout represented the next big thing. At least twice a month, they played decent city venues, like the Mercury Lounge. They've opened for bands at S.O.B's, Irving Plaza, and even BB King's. They've toured the country. And they played other local shows too. Skate parks out on Long Island, house parties in Queens, warehouses in Williamsburg, open mics on the Lower East Side, art galleries in Soho. If they could get drunk for free it was copasetic. Thelonious wrote most of the songs, but his buddy Lee wrote as well. Thelonious wrote lyrics all the time. Most of the songs didn't make the cut, but free-writing was a part of his process. Hurricane Clout would inevitably get signed. The first full-length studio album sounded good. The self-produced record neared completion, and they were garnering interest from some majors, according to their manager. This wasn't the time for Thelonious to lose inspiration. In three years, they'd come far, considering how often he traveled to music festivals. *The show in Chi-town's gonna be bananas. Word up!* One summer with Melody Rain he traveled around for weeks. But when in New York he lived for Hurricane Clout. The band operated like family. *Whatevs. I'll make it back for our gig, like always.* Maybe Thelonious should've never taken the subway to see Teflon.

Teflon Jones looked like a prince out there. The Yankees cap worn backwards was a crown. The Adidas tank-top, armor. The diamonds in both his ears were absolutely majestic. His very presence commanded the court, yet forever and always there were challengers. Watch Teflon dribble. Watch him work an opposing player. This opposing player hailed from Fort Greene. Fort Greene had tremendous talent. He wanted a piece of Teflon. In fact, everyone who played in the Cage wanted a piece of Teflon Jones.

"Richie Rich," Fort Greene said. "This ain't prep school."

"School his ass," Thelonious yelled, from the gallery.

"You ain't your daddy, boy," Fort Greene teased.

Teflon chewed his gum. "You talk too much, son."

Teflon glanced up to trick Fort Greene into looking up. Then Teflon quickly dribbled the ball between his defender's legs, bolted around him, grabbed the bounce pass, and elevated for an amazing 360° slam dunk. In the gallery, an ovation erupted.

"Owww," Teflon yelled, in pain. He came down awkward on his ankle. "Time out." The game stopped as his teammates ran over. Thelonious trooped inside of the Cage and helped his friend rise up. Teflon used him as a crutch and hobbled off the court.

"You aiight?" Thelonious asked.

"It's all-good," Teflon said, grimacing.

"You want to go to the doctor?"

"Maybe we better."

***

"*Gangstas contemptible, bitches act menstrual, we're dusted as hell, and still intellectual,*" Thelonious rapped. Teflon nodded his head. "We should work this hook. Keep it operatic. Except we don't want to sound like we're frontin on the ladies—" "Nah, never could we front on a lady. We're only frontin on bitches—"

"So we need to clear that up, you know, Jeru the Damaja style. Like *we're not frontin on the queens, the mammas, the young ladies, or the sistas*—" "Yeah, yeah, *we're just frontin on the bitches, the bitches*—" "word, *the bitches, the bitches.*" Thelonious laughed. "I hope we can remember this." Thelonious and Teflon always rhymed when they hung out. "Pick a play, Monk. You're getting a delay of game."

In Teflon's room at his father's Upper West Side pad, they played an older version of Madden on Xbox. The score was 0 – 0. The two had problems getting on the board due to the fact they were as stoned as the Adirondacks. They split six of Teflon's Percocets. Teflon also rolled a blunt while waiting for the prescription to fill. That's when Thelonious created the "gangsta's contemptible" hook. They sang it to the rhythm of an opera track playing on the pharmacy's speakers, Verdi's "La Donna e' Mobile" from *Rigoletto*. Now they worked the song more, always a process.

"Are you serious about leaving the city?" Teflon asked.

"Yeah, man. Music fests are the bomb." Thelonious saw a book on the floor, *The Eagle's Gift*, by Carlos Castaneda. He picked up the paperback. "You're into this guy?"

"My moms liked him. I'm trying to get into the New Age thing, you know, to understand why she did what she did. She was always reading Carlos Castaneda books."

"A lot of headz at the show like his stuff."

"I'd like to go to the show."

"It'd change your life like what."

"Where's the festival this time?"

"This one's in Chi-town, at Soldier's Field."

"Sounds dope," he said. "I wish I could go."

"But you can go," Thelonious said, smiling.

***

A few minutes later, while Teflon sat on the bed with his wrapped ankle elevated on a wooden chair with a pillow, someone knocked on the door. Thelonious was sitting on the floor, by the foot of the bed. "Can you get that for me?" Teflon asked.

Thelonious immediately lost his smile. "Mr. Jones."

Byron Jones quickly noticed his son's injury. He curled his bottom lip and shook his head. "Lower that music, boy." Teflon obeyed via remote control. "What happened to your ankle?"

"I sprained it. Dr. Dickerson says day to day."

"Thelonious, excuse us. I need to talk to my son, alone."

Byron "The Siren" Jones, five-time NBA All-Star, two championship rings on his fingers, a household name, and no matter how many courtside games Teflon and he had seen at the Garden, Thelonious thought Teflon's father was a phony. It seemed so obvious how he tried to manipulate his son for his own gain. Thelonious breathed deeply. "I'll talk to you later, bro."

Thelonious left and Teflon's father sat on the bed.

"Guess what Byron Jones did this afternoon while you played street ball? He spent the day convincing the New York Knicks you're worth their number one draft pick. They want you and will do anything to get you. They know our name is good for the fan base. The Knicks have been terrible. Know what it means? You'll be picked top ten. One year out of high school. I wasn't picked top ten out of UCLA, and we were a Final Four team."

"But we agreed on St. John's for another year—"

"Another year? Why? So you can blow something out in the Cage? You'd be throwing a multi-million dollar contract away. Is that what you want? Answer me, boy."

"No, sir."

Something hung in the air. Some nothing lay between them heavier than silence. "I want to talk about this, son."

"I don't want to talk about this, sir."

Byron Jones put his hand on Teflon's shoulder. "Your mother would want this. She always wanted this for you." Teflon jerked away. "All right, rest your ankle. We can't have you hobbling to the podium. You know I can set a conference up anytime."

"Let me sleep on it, all right?"

***

Four things about Teflon and his mom: one, she's dead, a couple of years already. Two, she killed herself. She soaked a small washcloth in ether, dumped it in a plastic white D'Agostino bag, and fastened the bag around her neck with duct tape. Asphyxia. Three, Teflon accidentally found the body, stiff and blue, when he came home early from basketball practice, in the tenth grade. On the nightstand, next to her body, he also found a short note, in an envelope addressed to his father. The note only had three words: "The shadow knows!" Four, Teflon didn't cry, not until the funeral, and then every sleepless night tossing in bed the first month he moved with his father into a new apartment. The shadow knows? What did she mean the shadow knows? Did it have something to do with the shadow nightmares that kept Teflon up at night as a kid? The dream he often spoke to his mother about? The nightmare where a dark shadow chased Teflon, eventually consuming him? Teflon's mother had a medicine cabinet filled with pharmaceuticals, and there were two botched suicide attempts. The first time she tried to kill herself she drove a leased Mercedes in the middle of the night into the Christmas tree at Rockefeller Center. Remarkably, no one was hurt. For that stunt, the courts gave her sixty days at the Kirby Forensic Psychiatric Center, a maximum security hospital. Byron Jones had to pull serious strings to keep her name out of the press. That's all he cared about. Teflon didn't care how crazy his mom acted, how delusional people thought she could be, how tragically herself she was, he didn't care—his mother was filled with love, and she had an awareness that Teflon recognized. An awareness that Teflon knew allowed her to *see* things. For example, she could *see* her husband didn't love her, and that he was a hopeless NBA adulterer. Teflon's father secretly kept an apartment with another woman, with whom he had two children. Those cheating ways eventually led to a divorce. And because of those cheating ways, Teflon tried his best to blame his father for his mother's suicide. Yet as hard as he tried, Teflon couldn't see why she'd kill herself, and he couldn't see what she meant when she wrote: "The shadow knows!"

'LUDE—*the rock star steez—a message from Thelonious Horowitz*

After chillin wit Teflon I decided to grab a coupla shwills. Teflon stays at 104th right on the park. I'm on 96th and Broadway. You might think I'd be the kind of kid who'd live in Williamsburg, but nah, I'm from Manhattan, and I'm not a bum. Teflon's the realest kid I've ever met. I know him from high school. We used to play basketball together at Trinity. Ask that nigga who gave him his nickname. Go on. Ask him. We're tight. Just nowadays I party harder than him. He only smokes weed. He ate that Percocet because he felt pain. I'll eat a Perkie because I'm hungry. That's my lifestyle, my steez. Teflon's ballin, I'm makin music, parlayin. On the Upper West Side, catch me at Jake's shwillin I.P.A., total good vibe, everything you need, fatty jukebox, pool table, foosball, they even have beer-pong. On beer-pong I'm nailin shots like John Starks, I'm on FI-Y-A, call me Joan of Arc. There are always some young birds chillin too. I hooked up a coupla times at Jake's. One time in the back room, an Irish bird from Galway rubbed one off for me. Wintertime and we had our jackets on our laps and she spit in her hand and it didn't take long. Hot spoons. Wha-a-at? Definitely dope. On the Lower East Side, I'll probably be at 7B, across from Tompkins Square. Catch me at the bar scribbling lyrics. I go through pens like scenesters go through trends. Two of my deejays live in the East Village, so we hang at 7B's. Place has a little *indie* vibe, yeah yeah yeahs, the joint is what it is. I try not to hang at 7B late cuz the freaks come out at night, and that ain't my steez, and that mos def ain't Tef's. Come to think of it, believe it or not, I'm not even a big fan of the Village. Too many artsy types.

Kristen Chastity McGovern lived in a Village studio.

Early morning light, fresh but faint, sliced through her blinds with the diligence of a baby being born. The lambent beams cut the shadows and illuminated particles of dust dancing gently in the sound air. KC stirred out of bed, careful not to disturb her sleeping boyfriend. She turned on her laptop, sauntered to the coffee maker, activated it, then carried her grogginess to the bathroom and plopped onto the toilet. She brushed her teeth and searched her milky complexion for blemishes. There were no pimples hidden among the freckles lining her nose. KC brushed her red locks until the hair lost its frizz, settling into its natural curl. "Work hard today," she said, her daily mantra. After her morning writing chores, she sorted through a stack of books in her library.

"Bishop to pawn—"

"What are you doing?" Dickie stirred. "Playing chess?"

"I'm thinking of hocking part of my poetry collection."

KC held *The Complete Poems of Elizabeth Bishop* in her hand.

"Oh, no," Dickie said, yawning. "You can't pawn Bishop."

"Why not?"

Dickie Fetters found his Upper East Side composure.

"You don't send classical formalists to the bargain bin."

"Classical formalists, huh?" KC mumbled.

"Metrics, iambic pentameter, come on, you-know-this."

"There are eleven *la's* in the theme song to *The Smurfs*."

"Eleven la's?" Dickie asked.

"*La, la, la, la, la, la, la la la la la,*" she sang, with a smile.

"Really, who has time, Kristen?" Dickie rose from bed. He scratched his butt through his underwear. "I have to go to work."

The next day in the park

In Washington Square Park, the arch remained under renovations. KC strolled through with eyes wide open. A Rasta lit a spliff. A Latino woman basked in the sun. A crew kicked a hack. What if the scene in the park were like a math equation? A scruffy white kid stroking a guitar plus two lesbians kissing is greater than or equal to a group lining up for street-meat minus a homeless man picking his toes? If five twenty-something women carrying shopping bags leave Macy's how fast must they walk before they become thirty-something women pushing baby strollers?

Of course KC wanted to write. She'd write on the subway. It felt too hot to sit down and scribble outside. If the fountains were on she might've jumped in. Instead, KC trekked to Fourth Street, then west to Sixth Avenue, where four out of six shops north of the old Waverley Theater belonged to tattoo parlors—the DragonFly, the Village Pop, the Kingdom, and the Whatever Tattoo. She thought about popping into the Kingdom to check out piercing prices, but it would've been moot since she knew she couldn't afford the nose ring. With a yellow Metrocard in hand, she stopped at the crowd of people gathered outside the basketball courts. She did not see against the screened cage the skinny rock star with the black messy hair or she might've recognized him as the lead singer in her friend Lee's band. She did see, before descending the stairwell into the subway, a flash of someone, who may or may not have been human, spinning through the air with grace and poise, in defiance of gravity, an inner-city, tornado-blown, black scarecrow yielding a pumpkin. Hmmm. She walked away. And like an overhead wave smacking a six-year-old, an ovation broke on her back as she descended into the subway.

**

KC looked up when the man on the subway started singing. She knew she missed the Times Square stop where Dickie now lived, but so what, she didn't want to stop writing. Things like that happened all the time. This paled in comparison to some of her previous digressions, shoot—she hadn't even passed out of Harlem. KC glanced the singer's way when she went to the exit door at the 125th Street stop and she held his eyes. She nodded, and the singer's lips pursed into a smile. Then she vacated the train, crossed the muggy dirty platform, and headed back downtown.

**

Goddamnit Midtown sounded obnoxiously LOUD everywhere nonstop the *vvrroom* of motors, Verizon jackhammers *d-d-d-d-d-d*, car horns *MEEP MEEP*, and what an unbearable smell near the Port Authority. Everywhere gas and urine and exhaust, the smell left her exhausted, you're in urine *Urinetown* KC combined with the humid heat summer swelter agghhhh she promised herself this would be the summer they'd take that long overdue summer roadtrip cross-country SHIT only now Dickie had a job, the stupid consulting gig at Merrill Lynch his stepfather had arranged for him, the six figure job he started only four months ago that enabled him to finally get his own apartment. Could he request a couple of weeks off? He took off today to get the apartment in order. She knew the roadtrip with Dickie was a pipe dream. Whatever, just get away from the Times Square area. Geez Louise. Who in their right mind would really want to live anywhere near Times Square?

***

Dickie Fetters saw his journey from the upper eastside of Manhattan to the westside as more than a change in tributary settings. The act constituted more than a switch from commuting on the FDR Drive to commuting along the West Side Highway. The trek involved more than having to look at vans and sedans with New Jersey plates rather than SUV's and coupes with diplomatic license plates. The journey would go beyond having to pass scruffy actors walking scruffy dogs rather than passing tiny manicured women with tiny manicured canines. This move represented a big statement to Dickie, and to everyone he knew. Don't perceive Dickie Fetters as an eastside bourgeois sprig no more. Check him out living in Hell's Kitchen. Hell yeah! And he hit the punching bag he recently finished hanging. The installation of his workout area was complete, some free weights, an ab-roller, the punching bag. All the furniture had arrived, and it looked official. He had his own place, a three-room railroad apartment, off Ninth Avenue. Dickie clocked the punching bag with a combo, yes, yes, yes. The idea of freedom combined with punching a bag made him horny. His phallus filled with blood and moved in a twitch. Dickie could hear moans coming from the unopened Jenna Jameson DVD that lay hidden in a box in the front room. He wondered where the heck KC was, but he knew she'd be there soon enough.

***

Kristen Chastity strolled toward Dickie's five-story brownstone. She walked past a laundry vent and it pounded her with warm air that smelled like fabric softener. At Dickie's front door, KC felt water drop on her head. When she looked up she realized the spray sprung from a humming air-conditioner unit. Then she rang the buzzer for Dickie and he instructed her where to go. Once inside, she made her way to his first floor unit.

"You're Midtown chillin, Dickie," she said, smiling.

"It's Hell's Kitchen," he corrected, "not Midtown."

KC entered, dropped her bag on the kitchen table, and walked through the middle room into the front room. She already noticed at least three things that needed to be rearranged. Meanwhile, Dickie wrapped his hands around her and started kissing her neck. "Stop." She slithered away. "I'm all sweaty."

"So." He came in for another strike. Scooping her up by the legs, he carried KC into the middle room, and threw her onto the bed. "The air conditioner's in here."

He started to unbutton her pants.

"Dickie," she complained.

"What? What's the problem? Isn't this cool? We can have all the sex we want without worrying about Mother walking in."

KC giggled. "Tis true." She relaxed and let her pants fall.

To KC, their relationship seemed very physical. If not fooling around or watching some movie, they were liable to start arguing. That's the way it went between them, lately.

Within two minutes, Dickie made his way inside her. He had her in the missionary, his favorite position. Eyes closed, she bit her bottom lip. Her dough was on the rise. She could smell a cookie. She could almost taste it. He might've delivered a cookie, except the stupid phone rang, until the machine finally picked it up.

"Rich-ard." Soon as Dickie heard the voice of his mother his erection softened and there went KC's cookie. "I'm on the porch. Please pick up before I'm accosted—"

"—For Christ's sake, Dickie. Pick up the phone."

"Hello, Mother," he said. "Okay. I'll buzz you in."

KC dressed. "Just the person I wanna see."

"I wasn't expecting her, Case."

Dickie threw on his workout shorts and answered the tap on the door. "Dah-ling," Mrs. Fetters kissed his cheeks. She looked at the room and sighed. "You couldn't have moved to Chelsea?"

"The furniture's all here."

"Well," Mrs. Fetters said, "give me the grand tour."

Dickie guided his mother around the kitchen and into the bathroom. He showed her the courtyard out back, pointing out the koi pond. Then he led her through the kitchen to the bedroom.

"KC's in here," he said, "just so you know."

"Where else would she be?" Mrs. Fetters said. "Working?" They entered the middle room serving as the bedroom. "Kristen."

"I heard what you said, Mrs. Fettas."

"You did?"

"You know damn well where I work."

"KC!"

"She started it, Dickie."

"Yes, shelving books," Mrs. Fetters said.

"Yeah, shelving books. So?"

"Quite a service to the community."

"Oh, screw you." KC bolted the room.

"Stay here, Mother."

Dickie caught up to KC in the kitchen. "I'm sorry."

"No, you're not."

"Come on. You know how Mother gets. She's only implying, you know, maybe it's time to get like a grown-up job."

"I have a job."

"Clerking at a bookstore is a dead-end job."

"I want to be a writer."

"What? You're going to be a starving artist?"

"It's better than a trophy wife."

"What does that mean?"

"Ask your mudda."

"Don't bring my mother into this."

"I wrote a book, Dickie. Don't take that away from me."

Park Avenue, from the Met Life building to forty blocks north, nothing but towering brownstones. All the buildings are about the same height. The effect obstructed the rest of Manhattan and the summer smog trapped in this configuration gave the block a strange hue. There were few commercial properties on Park Avenue (need diapers or batteries, trek over to Madison or Lexington) so there wasn't much foot traffic. Thelonious had no one in his way as he skateboarded on the sidewalk. He landed a backside one-eighty kickflip in front of his parents' building.

The skate maneuver echoed, and Mr. DeLucia, the doorman for as long as Thelonious was alive, shook his head the same way he always shook his head when he saw Thelonious. Then he opened the door, like he always opened the door. Thelonious made his way by elevator to the penthouse his family occupied.

"Yo." He entered using his own key. "Anyone hiz-ome?"

"In here," his father said.

Thelonious kicked off his Adidas Gazelles, as per custom.

In one of the parlors sat Mr. Horowitz. A cell phone and *The Daily Racing Form* lay on his lap. The sixty-inch high-definition plasma television broadcast live the last race from Belmont Park, an allowance event for non-winners of three, run on the turf at a mile and three-sixteenths. Thelonious stood idle as his father gazed at the television. Only upon completion of the horse race did Mr. Horowitz speak. "What a schmuck. I didn't box. That's the fourth winner Velazquez brought in today." Mr. Horowitz finally turned to his son. "Theo, what are you wearing? You call that a fashion?"

"Where's Mom?"

"The pharmacy." Mr. Horowitz opened his arms. "What, did we raise a derelict?" Thelonious walked over for the tight hug.

"You chillin?" Thelonious asked.

"Chilling? Chilling's for winter."

"Snowbirds are for winter, Pops."

"Pick up your pants. I can see your underwear."

Mr. Horowitz attended Columbia; his wife went to Sarah Lawrence; both studied psychology. They met at an old jazz joint called the Five Spot. Saul Horowitz and Adele Rubin couldn't keep their eyes off each other during one of Thelonious Monk's piano solos. At set break, he bummed a Pall Mall, and a cancer-stick led to a marriage void of children for twenty-five years until Thelonious popped out, named in honor of their first meeting. His parents belonged to the old-school. Thelonious's mother had him at forty-four. He grew up listening to his parents talk about the Fifties. Apparently, all they did was drink. All their stories set in some Village bar like the San Remo. Weird stories too, stories about drinking with abstract painters, method actors, musicians, writers. Their favorite story to recount was about the White Horse Tavern. Some famous alcoholic wrote Adele a poem on a napkin, but a jealous Saul Horowitz blew his nose with it. Every time Mrs. Horowitz tells that one, Mr. Horowitz says the same thing—wish I had the Thomas poem now, Adele. It'd be worth a fortune. Sometimes when Thelonious stumbled through the Village, he encountered one of their old watering holes and he felt nostalgia, but since they changed so much, Thelonious often thought their old days weren't worth respecting. In any case, the Horowitzes were big art collectors. They even owned an original Lichtenstein. Saul Horowitz paid more to insure his sculptures and paintings than most people made all year. He'd be the first to mention it.

***

Adele Horowitz noticed her son's sneakers as soon as she opened the front door. "Hell-o-o-o," she chirped.

"We're in here," Thelonious yelled.

Mr. Horowitz changed the television from the OTB channel to C-Span and he hid the racing form. He shot his son a look that said, I'm-too-old-to-argue-with-your-mother. Thelonious shook his head and smiled and rolled his eyes, and then the room suddenly lit up with an Upper East Side smile, held up with Botox. "Adele, have Chef Jay prepare some crepes for Thelonious."

Mrs. Horowitz handed a white Clyde's bag to her husband. "They only had your heart medicine, Saul. The pharmacist said for

you to call Dr. Goldstein if you want to refill your sleeping pills."
Mrs. Horowitz turned to her son. "I see you still haven't cut your
hair." Thelonious wore his bristles down in a long sloppy Caesar,
growing tresses over his ears. He hardly washed his dyed black
locks, and if he combed his hair he used his hands as a brush.

"This is the style," Thelonious said.

"Style," his father countered. "You look like Ish
Kabibble." Saul Horowitz loved referencing personalities from the
old days, personalities who had a sloppy sense of style. Either
Thelonious looked like Ish Kabibble or Man Ray or the Mad
Russian (in the case of the Mad Russian his father greeted him with
an obligatory how-do-you-do). Thelonious knew nothing of these
names; however, he never surrendered to their eternal calls for him
to clean up his act. One time, to shut them up, he brought over
magazines so they could see the models in *GQ, Esquire, Details,* and
Vanity Fair all looked like people they'd pre-qualify as degenerates.

"Have you considered registering for school in the fall?"

"Why would I do that, Moms?"

"Because your band notion is unrealistic."

"Ma, you do realize we're getting paid to perform?"

"Know how many musicians are out there with guitars?"

"Just in this city alone," his father ganged up.

"Luckily, there's no guitar player in my band."

"You're delusional. Are you taking your medication?"

"Son, in the Fifties the city didn't seem quite so big.
Everyone knew each other. You could eat off the sidewalks, damn
it. Today, in this monster, you haven't a chance." He took off his
eyeglasses and glared at his son. "You haven't a chance, son."

"Why did I come by again?" Thelonious said.

"Adele, please. Tell Chef Jay to prepare some crepes."

"No, it's okay. I have to go." He made a move for the
door, and then turned around. "I came to say goodbye because I'm
going to Chicago for a few days to get my head together. It'd be
nice, for once, if I could get some encouragement from you two."

"Saul," she sighed. "He's not taking his medication."

"Okay, Mother. Wanting to travel has nothing to do with
my bipolar disorder. Traveling sets me free. Traveling inspires me."

"Grow up," she said. "You're twenty years old."

They want to see bipolar? He shook until he knew his
black shag of a haircut would annoy them. He looked at his mom.
"If growing up means being like you, I don't want to be like you."

"Oy," his father said. "When will he grow up?"

"I'll never grow up."

"You will too grow up," she said.

"You can't make me."

"Yes, we can."

"You two should support me. I don't understand you."

"Oh, grow up."

"I don't want to grow up."

Along the way, Thelonious learned that being a grown-up entered one into a world of constant struggle. A world littered with sorrow, betrayal, sickness, death; a world of stress, anxiety, taxes, bills, and a job that one loathed. This is how the grown-up picture was painted for him. His parents held the brush. And the adults were so noble to bear it, to carry its weight, to shield it from the children. Even as a kid, Thelonious knew there had to be another way. He'd be like Peter Pan. He'd find a way to stay young forever. That's part of the reason why Thelonious aspired to be a musician. Rock stars didn't have to grow up. That's also why he loved going to music festivals. There were thousands of other kids just like him who carried the spirit of youth like a torch. No. Thelonious did not want to grow up. His classmates called him a punk. His parents labeled him a brat. But he saw himself as a kid. Sometimes, while waiting for a train, he even hummed the "Toys 'R' Us" theme song, a song he's been trying to clear a sample from for *Hurricane Steez*, the band's album nearly produced. "Listen, guys." He laughed. His parents could not understand why he was laughing. "I love you two but, *I-don't-want-to-grow-up*," he sang, leaving. "*I'm-a-Toys-'R'-Us-Kid.*"

Rebel Song (lyrics by T. Horowitz)

Doin flips in the pool / Don't tell me I'm a fool /
In eighty years I'll be done with school / Then I'll show
you who's the fool / What do you know? / Don't need
what you got / Don't need anything to take a shot /
We take shots / call me Monk / Don't need you /
fakin the funk / What do you know? / Nobody knows /
Nobody knows / Nobody knows / Nobody knows

Leave me alone

KC worked at Shakespeare & Co., on Broadway, off of Washington Place. Another bookstore operated a few blocks up. That gig would've paid better. That bookstore was bigger and a lot more crowded. That bookstore bought and sold used books. KC chose Shakespeare & Co. because she didn't like the idea of having to judge what one person's books were worth. Just like a worker at the vintage shop who puts a price on old threads, those characters acted like trend judges. The young writer couldn't imagine herself stranded in a place where she had to work as a trend judge.

Only recently had she transitioned into a full-time bookseller. KC used to work as an attendant at the Metropolitan Museum of Art. She scored a competitive four-month paid internship, extra impressive since she never claimed to be a student. KC was often hit on wearing the docent's outfit, the blue sports jacket and white buttoned down shirt complimented her pale skin and red hair. She eventually left the Met because she couldn't stand answering the same question over and over. It wasn't which dynasty do you think captures the purest and most essential aspects of Buddhism. Or even a simple who's your favorite Hindu goddess. No, Ms. McGovern left the Met because it annoyed her how many times she had to tell someone where the restrooms were. Do you know where the bathroom is? Talk about pet peeves. Same thing as a hostess at Diva, the Italian restaurant between Broome and Grand. There had to be in existence a better job than the intermediary between humans and their own waste?

KC liked the bookstore enough. She belonged there. For starters, the bookstore didn't have a public bathroom. And she could almost spit at the shop from her studio apartment. A three-minute walk to and from work is definitely a perk; however, on that particular summer's day, the three minutes felt like three minutes too long. The day was like a cannibal. It cooked, simmered, steamed, and drained the young girl. There, there, KC, almost, over, sweat, bullets, can't, breathe, get, out, of, New, York, City, in the summer. Beyond a shadow of a doubt, the day pleaded guilty to manslaughter to the tune of at least ninety-five degrees. When KC made it home she revved up the laptop. She turned up the air and put water on for a cup of freshly brewed iced tea.

On her answering machine was an unexpected message from Dickie's mom. Mrs. Fetters wanted to meet KC at six in the lounge of the Four Seasons. The message directed KC to come alone, it was important, and don't mention anything to Dickie. What could Mrs. Fetters want? KC wrote for an hour and sucked it up. She didn't want to stop writing, but since it sounded important, she sucked up the annoyance like a cold 7-Eleven Slurpee.

***

KC waited at a table with a red linen tablecloth.

A ginger ale in a tall skinny glass rested atop a white doily. She didn't notice Mrs. Fetters despite the wave of Givenchy perfume that preceded her. "Read a lot, do you?"

"Of course," KC said, closing the book.

"You know what they say," Mrs. Fetters sat down. She took off her amber sunglasses with the square frames and tapped her press-on nails on the table. "If you want a million dollars and you're into the arts, you better start with two million."

KC played with the edge of the red tablecloth.

"Thought you'd be in the Hamptons?"

"We're heading there shortly so let me get right to the point, Kristen." Mrs. Fetters went into her Gucci purse and whipped out a piece of paper. She slid it across the table. It was a check made out to Kristen Chastity McGovern. "I will give you ten-thousand dollars if you leave my son alone."

"Excuse me?" KC uttered. Mrs. Fetters stared at KC with a solemn look. Her face was caked in make-up. KC couldn't believe this woman's proposal. It certainly came out of nowhere. She picked up the Citibank check and gaped at her name attached to a number ending five spots left of the decimal point. KC came from a humble family in Brooklyn. Ten thousand dollars was a lot of money to a girl from Greenpoint. "Leave Dickie alone?"

"Yes, dear. Leave Richard alone."

"I'm not for sale, Mrs. Fettas." KC thought about the honorable way to behave. Henceforth, she would remain silent, raise a dignified brow, pick up the dirty check, rip it into fifty dirty shreds, and throw the confetti right into her adversary's eyes.

"Everyone's for sale, dahling."

She was so fake with those dah-lings. KC knew Mrs. Fetters came from Pittsburgh, and unless her maiden name read Mellon or Heinz, which it didn't, who did she think she was? No matter how hard Mrs. Fetters tried, no matter how rich she married, she could never get a blue-blood transfusion. To boot, in the five years KC has dated Dickie, his mom never showed more than an ounce of amicability toward her. "Well, dahling?"

KC slouched in the seat and sighed. She looked at Mrs. Fetters and thought about dignity. Pick up the dirty check, rip it into fifty dirty shreds, starve rather than eat her bread. Then she thought about what she could do with the money. She could self-publish her book, buy a car, travel. Did she care what this old bitch thought of her? She could self-publish her book! Wow. Imagine "Kristen Chastity McGovern" running along the bottom of its cover. No, no, no, no. NO. She thought about ripping up the check. She had her dignity and pride goddamn it. KC sat completely still. The one thing she didn't think about was Dickie. When she realized she didn't think about Dickie once, that's when it hit her, she didn't love him. She may have never loved Dickie. Had she been stuck? She had been stuck. The realization immediately unshackled her. So, it came too easy? Sometimes life comes easy. Their relationship was doomed. How could KC not have seen it? Everything they did lately led to a quarrel. Dickie didn't encourage or believe in her dreams. Maybe he loved her, but she wasn't the same person from five years ago. Mrs. Fetters anxiously continued to tap her nails. "This is the last time I—"

"Okay." KC perked up as she pocketed the check.

A perfect binding

As soon as New York got unbearably hot she began to dream about self-publishing, traveling, hitting up open microphones, selling her book, maybe catching a summer festival. Her buddy Lee from the bookstore always yapped about these shows one of his bandmates would run off to. In a perfect world, Dickie would've been about it. But no, she couldn't have even brought up the idea. He'd have just laughed. Dickie didn't believe in wanderlust. He had a new job at Merrill Lynch with new responsibilities. When they met, he had literary dreams like hers. But then in his own words he grew up. Gave up was more like it. Without Dickie she could do it. She could really follow her dreams.

First thing first, the collection of short stories. Since she was self-publishing she took advantage of her creative liberties, liberties some editor at a publishing house could snuff out. Using

Quark, she inserted .jpeg images that went along with the stories. In the back of *Poets & Writers*, she found a printing company up in Westchester. Because the manuscript was copy-ready in Quark, she haggled and cut a deal for a short-run printing of two hundred and fifty books at three dollars a pop. *Ms. Daisy Doolittle and Her Crew of Wascally Wabbits* came out to 160 pages on 20 lb. recycled paper with a full-color-coated semi-glossy cardboard stock cover, and of course, a perfect binding. In the meantime, regretfully, she took off from work. She told her manager at the bookstore she had a family emergency. Yeah, she lied. Sometimes things move fast, they move one, two, three. Like her apartment. On Craigslist, within minutes, numerous people responded to a one-month sublet in the Village available a.s.a.p. She chose an English woman, Annie Becka, a writer as well, who worked for a European edition of *Vogue*.

Finally, with thanks to the *Auto Trader*, she purchased a used car, a 1996 Camry with 55,000 miles. She trekked out to Astoria on the N and bought it from a sweet old Greek guy with bushy eyebrows who lived off of Ditmars. He wanted thirty-five hundred, but KC knocked him down to three. The next day she went to a tag place and received plates and a temporary title. The title would arrive in three weeks. Three was her magic number.

***

KC double parked her car outside of Dickie's apartment.

At the front door she pressed the buzzer. Three drops of water from the humming air conditioner above dripped onto her neck. When Dickie buzzed the door, she walked in. He met her in the hallway. "Oh, my," she said. "What happened to your face?"

He had a big black eye and a swollen lip with what looked like a herpe attached to it. "Some guy at the *bodega* around the block flipped on me for looking at him funny," he said. Dickie sounded dejected. "Where have you been?" They entered his apartment.

KC blocked the door when he tried to shut it.

"I gotta run, Dickie. I just came to say good-bye."

"Where you going?"

"I want to give you this." She handed him her book.

He raised his eyebrows. "What's this?" Dickie sounded tired. He sat down at the kitchen table. "Does your behavior have something to do with your writing?"

"Of course it's about my writing."

"Why don't you let me fix something up with Jonathon Pomper?" Dr. Jonathon Pomper, MFA, Ph.D., tenured professor of English, NYU (friend of the Fetters family).

"Pomper's a kook. I can do it on my own. The times are changing, Dickie. We don't need the publishing industry. We have the Internet. I want to be my own publisher."

"Dr. Pomper's a scholar."

He sounded like his mother when speaking of Pomper.

"I need experience, Dickie." She looked away.

"You leaving me?" he asked.

"You know I saw your mother."

"She's sick."

"Oh?"

"Bad eel in the Hamptons. They pumped her stomach."

"Hmph—"

"Are you really leaving, KC?"

KC's leaving came to him without surprise. The way his week unfolded it seemed fitting that his girlfriend of five years would walk out. Still, he didn't really believe it until he looked at her. The look of pity in her eyes and the awkwardness of her body language told Dickie what he needed to know. Damn. He couldn't believe this hot girl was going to leave him. "Don't you love me?" he pleaded. Dickie would've married KC. She knew that. He was starting to make good money. He would've taken care of her.

She knew that too, but so what? "Love?" She took a breath. "I've felt love a hundred times, always through a book, and never once with you, sweet Dickie." She stroked his swollen face and kissed his cheek. "I have to go. I'm double parked."

"KC, wait."

KC's plight, told in a Smurfy eleven-syllable verse

> She left him in his Hell's Kitchen apartment
> with a punching bag, a Jenna Jameson
> DVD, his job at Merrill Lynch, and a
> swollen lip with a quasi herpe attached.
> KC headed strait for the Lincoln Tunnel.
> La, la, la, la, la, la, / la la la la la

When summoned, Teflon entered the expansive living room of his father's apartment. His two half-brothers, both also named Byron, eight and five, lay on the floor playing with GI Joes, their mother out shopping. Byron Jones, Sr. sat in a huge black leather recliner. No one else was ever allowed to sit in that seat.

"Check this out, son," Byron Jones said. They had TiVo, and he recorded part of an ESPN telecast. The television paused on a picture of Teflon, smiling. First time his image was ever broadcast to a national audience. His picture had made it into the local papers many times before, but never nationally. This moment likely predicated the beginning of the end of his anonymity.

It was weird for Teflon to see his head shot in the upper left corner of his father's gigantic flat screen television. ESPN had imposed him over a red background. He thought he looked like some devil in the corner up there on the screen. Teflon thought the smile made him look greedy. Like a kid hungry for money. He didn't recall where and when the picture was taken. He wondered if a computer created the image from scratch.

Teflon knew what his father prepared to show him. It wasn't a surprise. Teflon agreed to it, but he still wished they used a different picture. Like a picture of him shrugging a defeated smirk, his palms up, his facial expression saying, hey, none of this has to do with me. Byron Jones turned up the volume and pressed play:

> College basketball phenom Byron Jones, Jr. is planning a press conference tomorrow where it is expected he will declare himself eligible for this year's NBA draft. Jones, Jr. set records across New York's high school landscape leading Manhattan's Trinity Tigers to four consecutive State championships. The 19-year-old shooting guard, son of NBA great Byron "The Siren" Jones, is projected to go late in the first round of the draft. In more NBA news, Rasheed Wallace... *click*

Byron Jones shut off the television. "NBA great Byron Jones," he said. "And his son a first-round draft pick."

"That's me."

"Your mother would be so proud."

"Sure she would, dad."

***

The morning of the press conference, Teflon practiced free throws in the Cage. His injury felt better, but he didn't want to play a game. He wanted to shoot free throws. No lay-ups, no dunks, no crossovers, no three-pointers, only free throws, hundreds of free throws. No rolling cameras, no bright flashes, no dirty money, no loud cheers, no horny groupies, only hundreds of free throws, inside of the Cage, alone. A lot of action unraveled outside of the Cage, but Teflon stayed inside, and concentrated on free throws. A little startled, he heard a familiar voice call to him.

"How'd I know you'd be in the Cage on the morning of your big day?" Thelonious Horowitz entered the courts and approached Teflon. They grabbed hands and pounded each other on the shoulder, the half-hug. "So check it. I'm goin to OD soon."

"What?"

"I'm off to Chi-town for Oracledang. I'm leaving soon."

Thelonious positioned himself under the rim to throw the ball back to Teflon, who continued to shoot free throws. It was dark. Because of the tremendous skyline, the sun seldom shone down on the Cage, and the basketball court was often covered in shadow. "Are you cool with entering the NBA?" Thelonious asked.

"Conference is at four."

"You'd be crazy walking away."

"Crazy," Teflon muttered.

"You'd be a true head."

Teflon had a decision to make. Thelonious could tell he needed to be alone; besides, Thelonious had to hook up with Lee and Diamonds to go over some band business before leaving. "What they do?" He approached Teflon. "I wanted to give you a shout before I bounced." Thelonious and Teflon hugged. The tightness of the embrace transferred the love, faith, and confidence between them. "No doubt. You'll make the right call, brethren."

Teflon's furtive gaze followed his shaggy friend out. Then the young athlete shouted from inside of the Cage. "Thelonious, wait a sec. What exactly is the music like at this Oracledang fest?"

"It's jazzy, man. You'd dig it."

"Jazzy? That's it."

"They'll be all sorts of music at Oracledang."

"But is there going to be hip-hop at the show?"

"Of course there will be hip-hop at the show."

Thelonious tossed his friend a peace sign and a smile.

Meanwhile, Teflon stayed inside the Cage and shot hundreds of free throws. Free throw after free throw. His stroke sizzled. At one point he nailed seventy-five free throws in a row.

***

All-eyes-on-Teflon. A bunch of microphones on a podium, station names and channel numbers: Fox 5, NBC 4, ESPN, WFAN. Look at the technicians, reporters, and hanger-ons. Hanger-ons like his father Byron Jones, and his father's old slimy Greek agent Phillip Mitanko, picked to be his son's agent as well. Look at the lights and the camera lenses pointing right at the kid.

Young Teflon appeared poised. He wore an Allen Iverson jersey and a white headband. If he thought about millions of people watching him, well, he had zero desire to think about millions of people watching him. "Good afternoon. I'd like to thank all of you for coming out. Let me begin by mentioning a few names. Kevin Garnett, Kobe Bryant, LeBron James, Jermaine O'Neal, these talents, also personal role models, are of an elite class of athlete. They're a few of the players who've bypassed college and entered right into the National Basketball Association. They entered the NBA, and not all of them found success right away. But for all, success came, sooner or later; not only success, but dominance. It would be an absolute honor to join that elite class." Teflon paused as a slew of cameras lit up the room with shuttering lenses and bright flashes. "After heavy talks with my father, he decided it would be best for me not to let opportunity pass. That's why, after careful consideration, and this decision was by no means easy, I've decided to take a year off from basketball-related activities." The room changed. Something unfolds according to routine and then the old twist, accompanied by the usual gasps and rigid shift in posture from all. "This isn't to say I'm renouncing basketball. I truly love basketball. But the NBA is not going anywhere." He looked around the room, until he found the eyes of his father. "The bottom line is I'm not ready for the NBA, and I know I will never have the opportunity to be a teen again."

Teflon stood firm, filled with conviction.

"What are you going to do, Byron?" a reporter asked.

"People call me, Teflon," he said, pausing. "Well, I have a serious love of hip-hop. I wouldn't mind pursuing musical avenues. In the interim, maybe perhaps travel. You know, enjoy my youth."

Byron Jones, Sr. looked livid. A few photographers turned their eyes on him, but the old man was too image savvy to make a scene, especially with the cameras rolling. But, oh boy, did he want to scream! Byron Jones wanted to scream so bad he had to leave the room immediately, like in the old Warner Brothers cartoon, The Three Bears, when Papa Bear, not wanting to wake the baby, holds in his cry of pain, and runs into the hills to let it all out.

Kill your father

On the corner of Sixth Avenue and Third Street, atop the entrance to the subway, lay a wooden green booth. Inside, a Middle Eastern man sold candy, drinks, magazines, and newspapers. Byron Jones could hear his son's voice coming from inside of the Cage. He walked to the gated entrance of the basketball court. As Teflon dribbled, he noticed his father and stopped. Neighborhood kids gathered, circling Byron Jones, Sr. He handled their adoration by smiling, then someone presented him a basketball and a Sharpie.

"Do you mind if I borrow this ball, son?"

"Sure, Siren," the autograph seeker said.

Byron Jones threw the ball at Teflon.

"You embarrassed me, boy. You tainted my name."

"I didn't—"

"Shut up and play." People in the Cage stepped back. They stood behind Byron Jones. Teflon stood alone. "You think you're hot shit. Remember where you came from?" He grabbed his jock.

"You want to play me in basketball? This is wack."

"You're wack," Byron Jones began. "You walked away from millions of dollars. You walked away from the Knicks, from this fucking city." Everyone watching the heated exchange whispered when Byron Jones mentioned the Knicks. "I bet everyone in this here cage thinks you're wack." Teflon's head went down. "Want to talk about wacked with Byron Jones? You're as wacked as your mother. Byron J certainly ain't make you like this."

"As wacked as my mother."

A piercing *shrill* traveled down from a maple tree in the Golden Swan Garden behind the courts. A hawk perched on a branch. Teflon *saw* the hawk. He had just enough time to wonder what a hawk was doing in the city (rat control?) before it flew away.

Meanwhile, the gallery cleared a path to let Byron Jones walk through. That's when Teflon threw the basketball at his father. "Game to three," the son said. "Let's end it. Loser's out."

Teflon let his father have the ball first. Byron Jones threw up a quick shot that went in. Three quarters of the gallery expressed their allegiance by cheering. Unfortunately, that simple jump shot was the last whoop they would whoop. Teflon banked in a fade away shot. Then he stole the ball from his father. This time he laid it around Byron Jones. After his father missed a jump shot, Teflon grabbed the rebound, cleared it, and prepared to drive to the rim. In the city skyline, the sun temporarily crept past a building, and light shone down on the Cage. Inside the courts, the player's individual shadows became accentuated. As he drove to the rim with authority, Teflon could *see* his shadow precede him. Then Teflon dunked on his old man, who wound up on the asphalt, falling into his own silhouette. Teflon looked down at his father, covering him in shadow, until the sun again fell behind a building, and all the shadows dissipated into one big shadow.

Teflon marched off, leaving his father inside of the Cage.

Once outside of the Cage, Teflon turned around to speak. "Recognize this. The only thing I'm walking away from is you."

Part Two
Flori-duh Steez

A high-intensity discharge lamp hung in the walk-in closet. Aluminum foil lined the ceiling and walls. Reflecting off the foil, illumination from the fluorescent light bulbs radiated the inside of the closet. The light in the grow room bathed Curtis and the plants. In the grow room, he could hear the *shhhh* sound of the fan, the grumbling of the water pump, the soft trickle of water through the hydroponics system, and the rustling of the plant leaves. Other cogs of Curtis's efficient hydroponics system included a twenty-gallon bucket, PVC pipes, epoxy, clamps, hoses, a nutrient solution, and rock wool. His homemade hydroponics system had arms jutting from the bucket, the plants grew wildly out of the rock wool slabs, and the concoction looked like a white octopus. Curtis, as he did every time he entered the grow room, took a deep breath and smiled. He wore black sunglasses. The light reflected off the glass beads wrapped around his sandy dreadlocks. The five-month-old plants had been receiving eighteen hours of light per day. More light equaled more time to mature before flowering; maturation equaled better quality and a bigger harvest. Curtis knew five months was a long time for a plant to mature before budding. He could've forced the plant to bud in three months. But he cut the light cycle in half only a week earlier. With the light cycle cut on a mature crop, the flowers bloomed with monster buds. Curtis's colas looked out of this world. The buds were white and sticky and littered with nasty purple hairs. The leaves were covered in kief.

As he shut the lights in the grow room, the apartment's front door opened. "C-u-u-u-r-r-tis," Geri called out. She stood by the front door, and her black dreadlocks fell to her shoulders.

Something else brewed in the tone of her voice.

Curtis walked into the living room.

"Hey, baby," he said, smiling. "It's harvest time."

"I'm pregnant, *papi*."

"You're what?"

"You heard me."

"That's great, Geri."

"Think?"

"Absolutely," Curtis said.

Geri walked to the dining room table and sat down.

"How can you be so sure?"

"Because we're already family."

"I'm scared, Curtis."

Curtis massaged Geri's sweaty shoulders.

"Why?"

"We're too young."

"Too young?"

"You're twenty-three. I'm only twenty-one," she said.

"We'll always be too young."

"But can we afford it?"

"Can we not afford it?" Curtis asked.

Geri walked to the wall air-conditioner unit and turned it all the way up. She stood in front of the window and the rumbling air conditioner chilled her sweaty skin.

"I don't want to live in Miami if we're going to do this."

"Then we'll move."

"The waters are too shallow in Miami."

"Are you listening to me?"

She looked out the window and saw a butterfly.

"Move where? To the country?"

"We'll move to the country. Buy a place with some land."

Geri walked to Curtis and hugged him. "Oracledang's in a couple of weeks, babe," she said. "Between your summer harvest and all my clothes, we'll have plenty of product for this festival."

"We'll work the festival good."

"I don't want to live in Miami if we're going to do this."

"We'll disappear. It'll be like we were never even here."

"Like we were never here?"

"Like we were never here."

***

The Little Haiti apartment had two months left on the lease. That gave Curtis and Geri until the end of August to get it together. To figure out where to re-locate, to pack, to say good-bye to Geri's family, and the few friends they had. In the meantime, they had a harvest and a plethora of patchwork overrunning the apartment. As Oracledang crept closer, the apartment became even more jammed with product. They had more clothes then they could possibly sell at the festival, yet there sat Geri at the cluttered kitchen table working on a pair of patchwork pants as Curtis walked into the room butt-naked. Geri spoke without looking up. "I should be sewing more than ever the next eight months."

"Open a website," Curtis said. "Threads will go fast."

"I was thinking the same thing."

Geri glanced up, not surprised to see Curtis naked. Neither was she surprised to see him dancing a little jig. Ever since she told him about the pregnancy, he started to dance these little silly jigs. His reaction helped a lot. Geri wished she could dance a little jig.

"I ordered a vegan from Andiamo," she said, referring to the local pizzeria.

"I'll postpone my custie."

"Custie?"

"Mikey the taper wants an elbow."

"You know," Geri paused. "I was thinking—"

"This should be the last crop."

"I mean it is illegal."

"You're right."

Geri pleaded. "There are places we could go—"

"—California."

"Well, yeah. But the question is can we leave the—"

"East Coast—"

"—East Coast?"

"I know what you're thinking before you do, hee-hee."

"I know you do, *papi*." Geri smiled and laughed. Then she leaned forward and gave the tip of Curtis a tap from her lips. He laughed and danced and laughed and went so far in his joviality that he accidentally slapped Geri in the shoulders with his nut sack.

"Watch yourself," she said, pointing the needle his way.

***

Mikey the taper sat in his South Beach condo biding the time before he met Curtis. He listened to a bootleg he recorded and stared at the taper ticket that recently arrived in the mail. The Soldier's Field ticket, printed with a graphic of an army battalion walking toward the stadium, ensured him a place in the designated taper zone, a place where he could record the concert. Mail-order tickets looked different than box-office or Ticketmaster clones, mail order tickets had graphics, mail-order tickets were collectibles.

A show will creep up like Christmas or a birthday, holidays that are planned for, looked forward to, and then land upon you in the blink of an eye. And everything's good, the preparation, the gathering, the celebration. It was all-good. In preparation, Mikey needed to get his car checked—done and done—he needed to make sure all his audio and videotaping equipment were in order— a work in progress—and he wanted weed for the excursion.

Mikey the taper didn't attend half the shows in his collection, he traded for many. Still, all of the tapes were of the best possible sound quality. When bored, he liked to stare at his collection. A lot of the concerts he did record, and soon enough there'd be one more addition to his prized set, that with the label:

Oracledang, Soldier's Field, IL.

Each festival had thousands of stories to tell

Bonnaroo, Manchester, TN
Coachella, Indio, CA
Langerado, Ft. Lauderdale, FL

Each and every show a novel itself

Bumbershoot, Seattle, WA
Joghorn Candlejar, Deer Creek, IN
Burning Man, Black Rock City, NV

What lengths were traveled to get to

Reggae on the River, Piercy, CA
South by Southwest, Austin, TX
Vegoose, Las Vegas, NV

How many heads lost their mind at the

Voodoo Music Experience, New Orleans, LA
Athens Popfest, Athens, GA
Sasquatch Music Festival, the Gorge, WA

How many memories were created at the

Siren Fest, Coney Island, NY
Jazz & Heritage Festival, Fairgrounds, New Orleans
Telluride Bluegrass Fest, Telluride, CO

How many lives altered one way or another?

Mikey the taper drove on 395, off-the-beach, west to downtown. So he had to drive ten minutes to appease Curtis. The sun shined, the sea glistened. Three pelicans flew above the bay, almost parallel to his car. Mikey rolled down the windows and welcomed the breeze. The wind refreshed his skin like toothpaste refreshed his teeth. It was a no-worries Sunday. The bootleg on his radio, first-rate quality, front of the soundboard, a master he recorded. Soon old and majestic downtown Miami, silhouetted against the bay, came into view. This was the Magic City.

Mikey made his way to N. Miami Ave. and 2nd Street. He parked in front of the New World School of the Arts, ten stories high, the windows barred and rusted. Why did the art school look like an asylum? He arrived at the spot and wondered about Curtis.

Mikey picked up his cell phone. He received a text message. A change in plans. He was to meet Curtis on the beach.

***

Back on 395, toward-the-beach, he headed east.

The sun disappeared behind a thick patch of gray cumuli. The sea no longer glistened. A pelican dropped a bomb. The white rocket soared through the wind, landing on an arm that dangled from a car. What the heck? Mikey moved his hand inside, rolled up the windows, wiped the dung on the seat, and put on the air conditioner. When he looked in the rearview mirror, construction cranes distracted him. Miami looked sick with condo fever. He cursed Curtis. That's exactly when the taper's back tire blew out.

Mikey leaned up in his seat. The car began to rattle and swerve as he maneuvered to the emergency lane. When the car came to a stop, it ground along the cement barrier that prevented a fall into the bay. Mikey shut off the car, put on the hazards, and jumped out to survey the flat. Cars zoomed by. No one stopped. He didn't have a tire jack, but he did belong to a roadside assistance program, AAA. He also had his cell phone, but technology failed him. He couldn't get a signal on the Nokia, only a busy tone—the phone wouldn't allow him to dial out. He resisted the urge to throw the phone into the bay. Instead, he grabbed from the car a backpack with Curtis's money. He wiped remnants of the dung on the side of his pants, and he began the long walk along the emergency lane toward the beach. Every fifty feet he tried in vain to call AAA. Then he turned around to see how far he walked. A Lincoln Navigator swerved in and out of the emergency lane. The car headed toward Mikey, only forty feet away, then twenty. What the. . . . Mikey noticed a look of ecstasy on the driver's face, a brown skinned man. The driver's head turned upward, his eyes rolling in his head. The car was ten feet away. The last thing Mikey saw before he tumbled over the side of the bridge into the intracoastal was the outline of a girl's head rising from behind the steering wheel. During the fifty-foot fall into the bay, he flipped twice, his cell phone soared, and he screamed like a girl.

Vaya a la playa

On South Beach, at Third Street, the locals spot, a soaking wet Mikey sat in the sand, his bag beside him. The sun played peek-a-boo behind the clouds. The tide looked low with the East Coast's waves only knee high. Surfers appeared awkward paddling in shallow water. They stood on their boards for a second before the weak waves gave out. Then all of a sudden Curtis popped-up out of nowhere. He wore a Cubs hat atop his dreadlocks, an old Sammy Sosa T-shirt, and baggy jeans. Strapped to his back was a green Jan Sport bag, old and torn, with a Steal Your Face patch stitched on the front pouch. "Why are you wet?" he asked.

"Why didn't you just come to my house?"

"You know, six-up."

"There are no cops at my house."

"That's what they want you to think, Mikey the taper."

"Fucking, Curtis—you're such a trickster."

"I ams what I ams."

"You and Geri going to Oracledang?"

"We'll be around."

"I got my tickets already. Mail ordered through the web."

"Yeah?" Curtis was distracted by a man filming on the beach. He wasn't a fan of tourists filming locals. "You taping?"

"DAT and probably video."

"Hold on," Curtis said. "I'll be right back."

The man with the video camera had the pasty skin tone of a tourist from New England. The girls he filmed were exotic beauties tanning topless. Curtis walked over to the invading tourist.

"Excuse me," Curtis said. He walked in front of the lens.

"Eh, what's the deal?"

"We don't like that down here. Film this instead."

Curtis dropped his baggy jeans and underwear. He fell to the sand and began to break dance, doing The Worm. Dreadlocks fell all over him while his genitalia flopped. He finished with a headstand, and then landed upright, quickly pulling up his pants and underwear. "Hee-hee-hee," Curtis laughed. The girls tanning topless also laughed. The embarrassed voyeur put away his camera, but not without filming Curtis. He'd get his revenge on the rascal by uploading the scene at YouTube. Meanwhile, the sun returned.

On Miami Beach, seagulls dodged footballs, while people tossed Frisbees, and everyone's fleshy, tattooed, tan, international skin looked very tight indeed. Curtis walked back to his customer.

"Dude," Mikey said. "Don't attract attention."

Curtis opened his backpack and retrieved a pillow.

"The weed's in a bag inside. Geri sews em in old pillowcases now. At the crib we got Scooby Doo, Transformers, GI Joe, Dora, hee-hee-hee. Cut it open when you get home."

"You're slinging a pound of weed in a kid's pillowcase and you give me Strawberry Shortcake? What the fuck?" Mikey handed over the wet brown paper bag that held four thousand dollars. "Why didn't you just come to my house?" Mikey sat on the ground clinging to a Strawberry Shortcake pillow stuffed with the kindest crippy bud in South Florida. Mikey looked sour and wore a pout. "Dude. I could've burned you the latest show. I just traded for it."

'LUDE—*the rock star steez—a message from Thelonious Horowitz*

Like what! I know Curtis and Geri a long time. I met those kids at a show on the West Coast, maybe at the Gorge in Washington, or at Red Rocks, or was it Shoreline? I can't remember. Shows blend together for me. Whatevs. Curtis and Geri are two of the most beautiful headz in the world. They're family. When I'm in Miami, I always holla at Curtis and Geri, and they come through with a smile and a hug with everything always kicked-down. What they do? That's family. I've been down to Miami just to chill with them. They're private people too. We rarely went to any bars or clubs. On Thursdays, I'd have to drag them to Little Havana to peep the Spam All-Stars. Of course I snuck away to chill at the Pawn Shop. All skatin on the half-pipe outback yo the ladies seen me land a fakey 360 heel-flip and it was on in like twenty minutes in that VIP room made from a school bus. That club probably closed down by now. Miami always be flippin the script on that shit. Anyway, one other time Hurricane Clout came back to Miami for Winter Music Conference. That's the deejay scene right there. But that was strictly business—kinda. Like Leroi Jones went to all these workshops. He deejays and writes, but he also makes beats from scratch, programming sequences into Abelton Live; so Lee was taking classes, while Chopshop and Diamonds had their own separate poolside day gigs. I was the only kid in Hurricane Clout just sorta chillin, mad networkin, tryin to meet peeps on the front end, A&R stuff. We all gigged out together at Vagabond, dope night, mad industry headz. Curtis and Geri came through, like always. I love Curtis, the crazy trickster. It's like he's from a different planet. And Geri yo, well, she's just so full of love. And that girl can sew like what, I'm tellin you. Her work belongs in Art Basel. On the real for real! We're all motherfuckin rock stars!

Nemo Rosenbloom, notorious local musical promoter, lived at 2540 Biscayne Boulevard, above a vacated video rental shop. Mikey the taper, wearing a burgundy backpack filled with a quarter pound of marijuana, repeatedly buzzed the apartment.

"*Oye*," the voice came from above a torn, weathered worn canopy, the video rental store's awning. A kid with a blue Mohawk stuck his head out of the window. "Nemo's out promoting."

"Can I come up?" Mikey asked.

"You better wait, *daawg*. He'll be back."

Mikey walked toward the corner. The sidewalks were littered and a sudden breeze from the bay blew the trash in circles. He noticed a Snickers wrapper, probably bought in the *bodega* on the corner, and a torn white Wendy's bag, the nearest chain ten blocks to the north. A dilapidated Styrofoam cup was stained with espresso tar. One ounce *colada* cups were scattered about. The nearest joint that made such coffee the Costa Rican shop a block to the south, *Alimento con Sonrisas*. Mikey decided to grab a newspaper and hit up the diner across the street. He went to a red vending machine and settled on a *Miami New Times* because the green *Street Weekly* bin was empty. He cursed Nemo and rolled up the newspaper. As if Nemo Rosenbloom knew someone was thinking a negative thought about him, he entered the scene, sitting shotgun in a Bentley. Nemo jumped out. As the Rolls Royce drove away, Nemo started singing to Mikey with the projection of an actor in a Broadway musical. *"That'll be the day when you get your money back / that'll be the day when the Pope smokes crack / that'll be the day when I won't tell a lie—"* The mohawked man stuck his head out of Nemo's apartment window and yelled, *"when's that Nemo?"* The music promoter finished the ballad off with, *"that'll be the day that I die."*

***

"What a dump." Mikey entered the den of Nemo's lair.

The floors were covered in flyers promoting upcoming concerts, as well as a bunch of clutter. The walls were painted olive green. On the eastern parapet hung a poster of Al Pacino in *Scarface*. On the opposite side of the room, next to the window, lay a shrine to PeeWee Herman. Along the north wall, there was a gallery of pictures. Nemo's exhibition included an autographed photo of Bill Clinton, a Polaroid of himself in a banana costume, a poster of The Smiths from the cover of *The Queen is Dead*, a pinup of Woody Allen holding an umbrella along the Seine, and a plaque from the Hitachi Foundation. The plaque honored Nemo Rosenbloom with the Yoshiyama award for exemplary service to the community, presented on October 18, 2005, in Washington D.C. "I was on C-Span for this, you know," Nemo said. An oak desk ran along the eastern wall and Nemo relaxed in a large mahogany chair. "Sit down, sit down."

Mikey settled on a milk crate, forced to look up at Nemo.

"So, whatchugot, Mikey the taper?"

"A q-per, right? A quarter-pound. Twelve-hundred."

Nemo's left brow raised when he saw the popcorn crippy nuggets. He immediately, without hesitation, fetched the appropriate amount of money from a compartment in the desk.

"Are you going to Oracledang?" Mikey asked.

"The show in Chicago? Are you kidding? I am the show."

"What do you have coming up?"

"Glad you asked," Nemo said. He perked up. "This one's going to be huge, the biggest one yet, on October 30th, I already have eleven bands signed up. I'm going to need a half page, no, a full page ad in *New Times*, 'Nemo's Hell-or-Ween Celebration.' Listen to these acts: Ween, Otto Von Schirach, Humbert, Council of the Sun, Fitzroy, Fashionista, Suenelo, Brendon O'Hara, Rachel Goodrich, the Lynx, Monkey Village. I got Ween to headline! They'll be deejays, a pumpkin fashion show, a haunted house. I want orange fireworks. Are fireworks expensive?" "Halloween? It's only summer—" "I'll be the host. I'll put on a body suit made of bones so's I look like a skeleton. I'll come out on stage and sing *I-I-I-ain't got nobody*. No body? A skeleton costume? Do you get it?"

***

Thelonious Horowitz knew Nemo. Many indie rockers who've been through Miami knew Nemo. Everyone knew Nemo, just no one liked him. Nemo promoted a Hurricane Clout gig like two years prior. The show was at Señor Frogs, on the beach. Unfortunately, Thelonious and the boys never got paid. They did get their airline tickets taken care of. Nemo had them on a flight leaving out of a JFK terminal none of them knew existed. Gusto Airlines [think Spirit Airlines with a chicken on your lap]. They arrived at MIA, crashed at Curtis and Geri's crib in Little Haiti, played the gig, and didn't get paid. Poor Diamonds caught something on the plane ride and couldn't even make the show.

***

Ray Ray Rodriguez was fresh off a ten-hour stint at the University of Miami Law Library when he decided to pay Nemo a visit. Word on the street whispered that Nemo had the dank bud. See Rodriguez had three weeks before he took the Bar exam, for the fifth time, and he needed to relax after reading through ten hours of constitutional law. Outside his destination, Rodriguez looked in the rearview mirror, traced the thin mustache that ran along his upper lip, and hit the midnight Biscayne streets.

Nemo's door stood unlocked. Inside it appeared so dark Rodriguez didn't even know if his eyes were open. "*Oye*, Nemo." He flipped the light switch and nothing happened. Then a match ignited, fire sparked, and water bubbled. Nemo sat in the corner of the room, behind his desk, a bong hit blowing from his mouth. A digital scale lay on the desk, as well as a pile of weed. The poster of *Scarface* behind him in good contrast to the current scene, except Montana's pile looked white. Nemo exhaled a cloud of smoke.

"Man," Ray said, "you're a fool. Pay your electric bill."

"I will, right after you give me $375 for this." Nemo lit a match and found two candles. From his desk he retrieved a baggie and threw it at Rodriguez. "One big o' fluffy ounce of weed."

"Three seventy-five? No taxation with representation."

"Life is like art history, my friend. And this here is what my biographer would consider my Baroque period." Nemo said. "However, I expect a Renaissance, starting with $375 from you."

"You're driving a taxi. I'll give you $350."

"For you?" Nemo rose. "Three-fifty it is."

Rodriguez produced three hundreds and one fifty. As Nemo attempted to put the money into his pocket, he swung his arm out to the side and knocked one of the candles on the floor. "Eeek!" He bent down to pick up the candle but he slammed the desk and knocked the other candle onto a stack of fliers piled next to a bunch of the crippy weed. The fliers, printed on a non-laminated light-weight paper, the cheapest sort available, promoted a hip-hop show at Churchill's, featuring DJ Immortal, Seventh Direction, and the Secondhand Outfit. The adverts caught fire.

Nemo's weed lay close to the blaze.

"I'll just let myself out," Rodriguez said.

Only the burning fliers lit the room. Nemo ran in circles around the desk. Cawing high-pitched *ahhh* and *gawww* noises, he sounded like a momma bird protecting her eggs from a snake. Nemo Rosenbloom wasn't quite sure what he was looking for.

A teenage wasteland

Rob Base told everyone how he wanted to rock right now.

Ladies night at Roy's, two-dollar cosmopolitans, and Ray Ray Rodriguez was in the house for a drink. He sat alone at the bar and checked out the scene. He preferred to be somewhere else, like Blondie's in Ft. Lauderdale beach or Georgio's in Hollywood or the Cove in Deerfield. Anywhere but a bar in suburban Coral Springs, but he lived in Coral Springs. He didn't want to drink and drive outside of Coral Springs, and when in South Florida, you drive everywhere you go. Rodriguez had a blasé attitude about living at home with his parents at twenty-six, but he was on a tight budget. So poor he even had to pull hustle moves. The reason he frequented Roy's in the first place was to sell a quarter-sack to Miguel Caruso. Rodriguez managed to squeeze five quarters out of the ounce he bought from Nemo. The weed was like fluffy popcorn, the sacks didn't look light. Caruso paid a hundred dollars for the quarter, outside in the parking lot, no qualms. In the end, Rodriguez would sell four quarters, recoup his money, plus fifty bucks, and get a free quarter-ounce out of the deal. He felt like a monkey, but at the same time he thought the world one big zoo, and there were worse animals to be than a monkey. Rodriguez stuck around Roy's for a drink because the Princess said she'd meet him there. The Princess, his gal for the past month, was late, again.

When the Princess entered the bar she obtained notice; her marble skin and curly strawberry locks; her blue eyes danced when she invaded a room. The Princess wore a short white ruffled skirt and a pink top with two words printed across her breasts: Boys Lie.

Walking to Rodriguez, she took a route so as many people as possible could see her. "You're late," Rodriguez said.

"You can't rush perfection," the Princess said.

Outside, a brawl broke out in the alcove where one had to go to smoke. "You see that fight outside?" Rodriguez said.

"Hmmph," the Princess shrugged. "Must be New Yorkers. Broward County is to New York like Australia was to England."

"What do you mean?"

"New York sends all its monsters this way."

"I'm from New York, originally."

"Exactly." The Princess raised her brow and threw Ray Ray Rodriguez a patented princess smile. She smirked without showing her teeth, and tilted her head forty-five degrees.

"I need to bust a power move into a city," Rodriguez said.

"You need to buy me a drink."

"Granted, in Coral Springs, all the girls look like strippers—" The Princess slapped Rodriguez in the face. "Excuse me. Everything looks like a strip mall, the, the, monotony of suburban sprawl, it's very frustrating. On top of which, who wants to live in a place that crazy terrorist Mohammed Atta called his American home? Coral Springs. Who could possibly imagine?"

"What do you want?" The Princess asked. She paid more notice getting the barkeep's attention than to her date's ramblings.

"I want to pass the Bar exam. I want to get out of the suburbs. I want to take you to Disney World." She laughed. They had plans to go to Orlando the following night.

"What do you want to drink, boy-toy?"

As Rodriguez looked around the room he noticed how cocky everyone looked. "These people think they're Johnnie Walker Black, but they're really watered down Dewar's."

"Bartender," she said. "Johnnie Black on the rocks."

"Anything else?"

"And a double Patrón margarita, on his tab."

"Let me tell you, Princess. When things get spoiled they rot, the suburban epitaph, if and when the suburbs ever die. Mark my words. When things get spoiled they rot."

The deejay at Roy's saved the day and threw on a booty song. The whole place erupted. Every man in the bar paired up with a girl. Heavy bass boomed out of the speakers, and almost everyone in the establishment started to dance to the booty music.

"What do you want, Princess?"

"Me? I-want-it-all."

I used to hate booty music like what! I remember when I heard Trick Daddy on that Uncle Luke track. Shit was like so far from what I thought hip-hop was about. Now, stoops. I love booty music. Booty's the bomb. The ladies love booty music, that's all I'm sayin. We got a booty track on our LP, *Hurricane Steez*. Actually, Teflon collaborated on that joint with Hurricane Clout. Booty lyrics are easy like what. *Get on the floor and shake yo booty / don't matter if the girl's a cutie / don't matter if the girl's a slut / get on the floor and shake that butt / shake it slow and shake it fast / get on the floor and shake that ass / don't stop / shake it shake it.* Leroi Jones produced a heavy bass beat. He used M-Audio fingers hooked into Abelton Live, then with the finger pads Lee set off the bass, drums, and samples. Chopshop and Diamonds constructed scratch sequences from old school booty tracks and they cut it up like what. *p-p-p-peanut butter jelly time j-j-jelly time.* Technology is making this music thing sick. "Bootie Time Across the USA" came off dope. It's one of three songs on Hurricane Clout's MySpace page. Track has four hundred and seventy thousand hits and counting. I'm sayin. The ladies love the booty. You can front on booty music all you want, until you get a shortie all rubbin up on your dills—until you can lean back and throw your hands in the air and let the shortie get all crazed. Until that happens, you have no idea what youse missin.

Rodriguez knew the best route to Disney World, the best on his pockets. Take I-95 up to Fort Pierce then bounce on the Turnpike for another hundred miles into Orlando. Seven dollars cheaper than taking the Turnpike all the way to Orlando from Commercial Boulevard. The Princess insisted on taking the toll ridden Turnpike, she'd have it no other way. "The trucks on I-95 make me nervous. There are no trucks on the Turnpike."

"Not true," Rodriguez said. "And it's cheaper to take—"

"Cheapy, cheapy, cheapy."

Rodriguez waited behind four cars at the Commercial Boulevard entrance ramp to the Florida Turnpike. He didn't have exact change or a SunPass, so he had to wait in line.

The toll plaza collector wore dreads, nametag read Curtis.

"Can you break a hundred?" Rodriguez asked.

"Nah, you need something smaller," Curtis said.

"Do you have a dollar?"

"I didn't bring any money," the Princess said.

Rodriquez sighed. "You look like a reasonable man."

"Fifty-cents," Curtis yelled. "Holla, hee-hee."

"Don't have it, man," Ray said. "What's the procedure?"

The Princess was frustrated with the delay. She rummaged through the glove compartment. The Princess helped herself to one of Rodriguez's nuggets and showed it to Curtis. "Will this do?"

"Off to Oracledang with that stuff?"

"Now wait a minute," Rodriguez said.

She reached across and handed the nugget over. "We're going to Disney World, Mr. Bob Marley, white dreadlock dude."

"Now wait just a goddamn minute," Rodriguez protested.

***

Rodriguez and the Princess drove north on the Florida Turnpike. "Feels good to get out of Dodge," Rodriguez said.

Once past Jupiter, the scenery opened up into nothing but trees and cow pastures. It was already dark. His plan was to get to Orlando before midnight, bounce around Orange Avenue, find a nice cheap hotel near Kissimmee, fuck like bunnies, and spend the next day hanging out with Goofy, Mickey, and Donald Duck.

Between Hobe Sound and Palm City, a bored Princess allowed Rodriguez to finger her, while she stared out the window and looked at a cloud blocking the moon. She could've sworn she saw Pegasus in the cloud, as she approached an orgasm. Rodriguez, fully erect, soon realized the Princess wasn't going to return the favor, and he gave up. The ensuing silence bothered them both.

Eventually, they fell behind an 18-wheeler.

No trucks on the turnpike, huh?

Rodriquez looked at the Princess, and his eyes turned into beady little balls. He couldn't pass the truck for the next twenty miles, due to construction. When they approached the town of Yeehaw Junction, after they left the truck behind and the road opened back up into a three lane highway, the Princess's boredom increased. She rested on her middle finger, her elbow on the door. That's when a Florida State Trooper crept up from behind, attempting to pass them on the right. Except the State Trooper caught the Princess's middle finger, slowed down, and moved back behind Rodriguez. Soon blue and red filled the night sky.

"Shit." Rodriguez pulled over. He rolled down the window and shut the car. "Stay cool, Princess. I'll take care of this guy."

"Whatever," she said.

The Florida State Trooper wore tight brown pants, a green shirt, and a big brim hat. His lips moved slowly behind a groomed moustache. "License and registration."

"Sir, was I violating any laws?"

"Y'all young ones always violating laws," the officer said.

"Being young is not probable cause to be pulled over."

The cop took a moment to survey Rodriguez. He laughed. Then he rocked back and forth on his heels. "Son, what do you know about probable cause?"

"I hold a law degree from the University of Miami."

"You an attorney?"

"No, sir."

"Out of the car."

"Sir?"

"Out of the car, now, City-boy."

Rodriguez shut the car and slid the keys into his pocket.

"You stay put," the cop said to the Princess. "You, against the hood, spread your legs." The cop forcefully began to frisk Rodriquez's ankles. The officer slowly moved up to his calves.

"Wallet's in my back pocket."

"Maybe you can bribe the law in Miami-Dade County."

"I'd never bribe an officer. I'm merely clarifying—"

The cop reached Rodriguez's groin and quickly grabbed a hand full of testicles. "Clarifying?" Rodriguez squeaked while the State Trooper began to fondle. "You like that, City-boy?"

The natural reaction was to swing around.

Rodriguez clocked the officer in the nose with his elbow. The cop lost his balance, fell, and then quickly rose. Blood trickled from his nose as he placed his hand on his nightstick. "Right there's assaulting a police officer." The cop raised the nightstick.

In the dark sky, barely lit by a quarter-moon, the nightstick hung. Then it fell. It swooshed the air until it met Rodriguez's face. The officer hit him in the stomach, head, and shoulders. The blood of Rodriguez splattered across the car windshield.

"What are you doing?" the Princess yelled.

"I'd stay put if I were you."

The State Trooper threw handcuffs on the pulpy Rodriguez, dragged him toward the squad car, and tossed him in the back seat. The officer called for K-9 backup. Since they were in the middle of nowhere, it would take awhile. In the meantime, he'd bring Rodriguez in and destroy the surveillance tape, so as not to complicate matters. He'd tell the Sarge the camera was on the fritz, again. It seemed to happen all the time in Yeehaw Junction.

The cop walked back to the Princess.

"I'll need the keys, Officer."

"You'll need more than that," the Florida State Trooper said. "Wait here. Another officer will be by shortly. For your sake, there better be no drugs or contraband in this vehicle, young lady."

***

The mosquitoes were out in full force. She swatted bugs that came in through the open window. No radio, no air conditioner. No way to roll up the window, no way to start the car. Her cell phone had no signal. She looked for a spare key, under the floor mats, under the front and rear bumper, in the gas gasket, no can do. The only illumination came from the blinking hazard lights. Except for that, nothing existed but darkness. Where were the cars? How did this happen? The Princess sighed repeatedly.

The Princess wanted to cry, except she felt too annoyed, too hot, and she hungered. Why didn't she get a bite to eat when they stopped before? How far was Yeehaw Junction? Could she walk? Wait a minute. She couldn't leave the scene. There'd be another cop arriving soon. Where could she go on foot? They'd definitely pick her up. Oh my god. She thought of the marijuana in the glove compartment. The Princess had to get rid of it. Where? How? If she threw the weed away, what if the cop brought a dog? A dog could sniff it out. What could she do? Ugh! Why would her boyfriend do this to her? She slapped her neck and squashed a mosquito. Her back felt sore, her neck tightened, her legs cramped up, and her knees ached to no end. The Princess stretched along the side of the road. She was abandoned only five minutes.

Thunder rumbled from afar.

***

Mikey the taper noticed the car with the blinking hazard lights. "I'm pulling over." He and two of his taper buddies were on their way to Chicago for the music festival. Nobody objected to helping the damsel in distress. "You all right?" Mikey asked.

"No," the Princess said. "Do I look all right?"

"You look fine," Tommy the taper yelled. "Need a ride?"

"What took you so long?" She walked to the car window.

"We're going to Oracledang," Richie the taper said.

"You're welcome to come."

"I have nothing to wear."

Her overnight bag was locked in the trunk.

"You can get clothes at the festival," Mikey said.

"I don't have any money."

"Is there anything of value in the car?"

"There's marijuana."

"Grab it. That'll be better than money at the festival."

The Princess thought about it. If she took the marijuana at least the cops wouldn't be able to lay a drug rap on Ray Ray. She grabbed it from the glove compartment. She shut the hazard lights, walked back to her new ride, and opened the passenger door. She cleared her throat until Tommy jumped into the back seat.

The Princess hopped in.

"Now, what's all this crap about a festival?"

Late afternoon summer and South Florida dim with rain.
Rain fell on the Turnpike, I 95, and A1A.
Rain fell on side roads causing puddles the size of ponds.
Rain fell on loblolly pine and buccaneer palm.
Rain on lizards and iguanas and possums on the ground.
Rain on pelicans, sea gulls, and parakeets in the trees.
Rain fell like thick teardrops in the lakes and canals.
Rain in Wellington, Boynton, Stuart, and Deerfield Beach.
Rain in Miramar, Opa Locka, Cutler Ridge, and Hialeah. Rain in
Oakland Park, Davie, Sunrise, and Plantation.
Rain raged down on the horse barns in Parkland.
Rain raged down on the Coral Springs Ale House.
Rain raged down on Curtis and Geri *putt-putting* north in
their magical 1984 Volkswagen Jetta known as *The Jedi*. The back
bumper of their car sported one sticker: Are You Kind? Soon as
they crossed into St. Lucie County, the summer rain subsided.

Inside Oracledang it'll be on and on and on till the break-a break-a dawn. They'll be lighters scattered across the scene like a vigil. They'll be cherries flashing like lightning bugs from the tips of cigarettes and bowls. Music festivals are the bomb. You should see me on stage. I'm my own hype man, pumpin up the crowd like what, throwin my hands up, choppin the air, bouncin around the stage all buggin out, kickin the mic stand down, then bringin it back. See me doin the wet noodle all wiggily wiggily. I let it all hang out. Check me running behind my deejays when they're soloin, all cuttin it up. Lee, Chopshop, and Diamonds all spin and scratch on two turntables, plus they run Serato and Abelton Live on dual laptops where they feed beats and samples through a mixer and use foot pedals to load new loops for continuous playback. On the front end, I'm always wearin some ripped T-shirt like a punk, sometimes throwin a sports jacket over that shit. That's my steez. Hurricane Clout's all about takin styles and sounds to the next level, combining elements, and gettin headz to surrender to the flow. When everyone feels the flow then the pulse begins to really pulse and the flow becomes like light. Everyone's energy is charged like one big grid. Get the audience to surrender to the flow and it elevates everything. That's what happens at music festivals. It's mad inspiring. I realize I'm just telling you, but there's no other way. You need to see it for yourself. Everyone disconnects from space and time. For a few hours there's no identity but one, no age but one, no space but here, no time but now. Oracledang! I'm going to O.D. I can't wait. It's like staying young forever. Word!

Part Three
San Francisco Steez

Sky Tyler's violin lessons were going well. She worked on fingering techniques, on trills, vibratos, harmonics, pizzicatos, glissandos, things as such. Her left hand was really starting to feel the instrument, really starting to feel the correct placement on the neck along with the proper way to stretch the fingers. She started taking lessons a month previous. For $300 off of Craigslist, she found a full-size Cremona, including the bow, a case and canvas, rosin, a shoulder rest, a digital metronome, and an extra pair of strings. She had jumped on the offer, trekking cross-town to Noe Valley to pick up the instrument, and the next day, in the same classifieds, she found the services of Mrs. Mellows, $25 an hour, walking distance from her house. Her teacher originally hailed from the Louisiana Bayou and never lost the Cajun accent. She pronounced her *shins* as *shones*. Sky loved it. "Why, Ms. Sky, your ears do have a natural inclination toward intonation," Mrs. Mellows said, as her student completed a listen-then-play exercise.

Sky Tyler didn't have to take violin lessons. She wanted to take violin lessons. When she wanted to get involved in a Buddhist cause, she joined the Bay Area Friends of Tibet, helping to organize grassroots projects and events designed to educate the public about China's occupation of Tibet. On March 10th, the anniversary of the Tibetan National Uprising, she trooped, with hundreds of others, from Yerba Gardens, to the Civic Center, to the Chinese Consulate on Geary and Laguna. That's Sky Tyler. She who volunteered for the Save-the-Redwoods League, giving eight hours a week to the San Francisco chapter, helping around the office, while assisting the development team by gathering information on potential grants. Not to mention her monthly internship at *PNN*, an online magazine dedicated to the poor and homeless community in the Bay Area. Sky Tyler cared. She cared about the world. If she really wanted to save the world, the world better watch out. But she didn't want to save the world. That's a lofty goal, even for her. She was happy with her easy restaurant job at the Askew Grill. She had no problem taking a couple years off from school after graduation. Sky wanted to have fun. And to her, violin lessons served as one part of the equation equaling fun.

"Practice, practice, practice," Mrs. Mellows said, finishing up their weekly lesson. "Repetition breeds convention, Ms. Sky." "Sho you right, Mrs. Mellows," Sky said, smiling bright, as she packed up her things. "I'll definitely see you next week now."

***

Melody Rain loved to look at people on the city trams, especially when they had no idea. She pretended to stare out the window, when really she immersed herself in the reflection of the person across the way. She sat in her seat, twirling a pack of American Spirits, staring. She saw them in all forms and colors, but some women held her glance longer. She often wondered how Jah could create something so beautiful. Melody Rain loved the N Judah, for not only did the tram deliver her to Sky Tyler off a voyeur's aphrodisiac, the tram's very name rang with her beliefs, the N Judah, the lioN of Judah, respect. Melody Rain, the conquering lion on the N tram to Judah. Jah love. Rastafari.

***

Sky lived on the first floor of a large purple Victorian on Cole Street. The Victorian divided into four railroad apartments. Like everybody in San Francisco, Sky had roommates. Her roommates were hardly home. The strange thing about Sky's abode was that the front door remained unlocked. At least Melody Rain thought it was strange. She always locked her doors. Melody Rain found Sky in her room, on the computer. "How was your lesson?"
"Good, I learned some new fingering techniques."
"Fingering techniques, huh?"
Melody Rain moved to the bed.
"Listen to you," Sky said, giggling.
Sky minimized the computer and swiveled the seat around. Melody Rain lay on the bed with her legs spread wide. Her pheromones splashed the room with vigor. Melody Rain wore on her face a lustful look, very appetizing. The diner looked open.
Sky hungered for her girlfriend. She loved her mulatto skin tone, and her body; half-Jamaican, with the hips and bottom to prove it, and half-German, efficient in other proportions. She went and planted a sticky kiss on Melody Rain's caramel stomach.
As Sky's head and kisses moved up Melody Rain's torso, so did Melody Rain's shirt move upward, until it fell on the floor. Sky put Melody Rain's breast in the cup of her hand and gently

stroked little circles. She pursed her lips against Melody's hardened black nipple and drew from it the imaginings of divine nectar. Then Sky leaned up and took off her own shirt. Melody Rain in turn lusted after Sky's coated marble skin, smooth and milky, bleached in California, tainted by a handful of freckles and beauty marks, complemented by the thin brown dreadlocks that fell past her petit soft chin. When their naked flesh touched for the first time that day, a sanctified communion was once again performed.

Slowly, their hands explored each other's bodies, rubbing, scratching, lightly and lovely, pressing little buttons, buttons over valleys, pressing, but taking their sweet time. Their tongues took the exploration further, down the soul, down the moist valley, down the slope, down the valley. Further down the valley, further through the valley, pressing buttons, buttons over soppy valleys, pressing, but taking their sweet time. The valley they roamed and explored. The hills were alive with soft pants and moans while somewhere on this planet a symphony approached its crescendo.

The life saver?

What Would Jesus Do?

It was written on a flyer promoting the S.F. Baptist Church on Powell. Two eleven-year old Chinese girls were running around Stockton, giving away free LifeSavers attached with Scotch tape to the flyers. Sky and Melody Rain were walking along Stockton toward North Beach, where they planned to spend the day. In one of Melody Rain's hands an American Spirit cigarette, in the other, the palm of Sky Tyler. They stopped at a fruit and veggie stand, releasing each other's hands to fondle the produce.

A young missionary bounced on Sky. "Want a LifeSaver?"
"What?" asked Sky, her attention on cherries, only 79¢.
"LifeSavers?" the young missionary offered. "Take two."
Sky looked at Melody Rain, examining bananas.
"Take em," the missionary said.
Sky took the two pamphlets and read the promotion. "What Would Jesus Do?" She pondered. "The only Jesus I know is the dishwasher at the Askew Grill, but he pronounces his name Hay Soos. He'd probably mumble something like *pinche puta*."

The eleven-year old Chinese missionary shrugged, and then walked away to do more of the church's grunt work. Melody Rain came up and pinched Sky's butt. "Whatcha got there, girlie."

"LifeSavers," Sky said. She looked at Melody. Sky's clear blue eyes sparkled with appreciation. "But I have my life saver."

Sky stole a kiss from Melody Rain's lips.

Melody Rain smirked. "Don't you forget it."

***

It went down in Berkeley, two months prior, at a place called the Irie Café. The type of café that sold smoothies, tofu burgers, and veggie sandwiches; a café where hummus and sun-dried tomato could tie for the Most Frequent Ingredient in a Platter award. While Sky waited for a tofu burger, a black man with dreadlocks walked in and immediately began to grill her. She could feel his eyes pulling at her, a vampire's lure, some energy trap. You Rasta? No, sir. You no Rasta then why you wear dreadlocks? A lot of people wear dreads. What do you believe in? Tofu. Sky had hoped to end the conversation, but the Rasta wouldn't give it up. He started screaming something about the Bobo Ashanti and Prince Emmanuel and Bull Bay and Kingston town and fuck Golden Gate Fields. She tried to ignore the situation, but he wouldn't stop. That's when Melody Rain came to her rescue and started yelling. Jah is about love and guidance, not hate. You bad Rasta! This sister got white skin but it's only paint, brethren. Then the Bobo dread started Ras-clotting and bumba-clotting at both of them. Then he whipped out a nine millimeter. Oh, no, he didn't; right in the middle of the restaurant. But crazy Melody Rain told him to take it to the street. She kept yelling at the bad man, and eventually he ran out of the café. When Sky thawed, she mumbled something about the East Bay getting crazier and crazier, until Melody Rain opened up her arms for a hug and told her everything was all right. They've been together every day since. Shoot. Sky thought Melody Rain saved her life by diffusing a near fatal racial hate crime. Melody Rain and the Irie Café workers thought the same thing. The truth is Melody Rain did not save the day. Her interfering only made it worse. The Bobo Ashanti dread belonged to a sect of Rastafarians that looked down on women. For him to receive a lecture from a woman was too much, especially after gambling away his rent at the racetrack. He entered the café with the intention of sticking the joint up. Melody Rain did not save the day. A camera had saved the day. The camera the Bobo dread noticed in the corner of the café. The Bobo dread saw the camera, knew he'd be caught, and decided he had enough risk for the day.

Keith Lipsiznowaz tried to get off the bus, but the back door jammed. The green light indicated the door was ready to open. It did not. He stood in the little exit cove and pushed. The driver began to pull away. "Back door," Keith yelled. The driver looked in the rear view mirror. "Back door," he yelled again, along with three other MUNI riders. The door opened and out jumped Keith Lipsiznowaz. Walking along Haight, he passed the Ben and Jerry's, crossed Ashbury, and paused under the clock stuck at 4:20.

His plan was to venture to Stowe Lake and rent a canoe for some cardiovascular exercise. He had a few hours before he taught his yoga class. Even though the skies were gray, and the wind acted up, he wanted to get out and exercise. He could've stayed on the bus, its route went up Haight Street, then along the park, but one of the riders smelled really bad, and Keith wanted fresh air. He already regretted the move to walk through the Haight. There were too many hippies. Okay. There were murals on the sidewalk of Joplin, Hendrix, Morrison, and Jerry Garcia. That's great. A wonderful piece of history. Except that's what it was, history. Why were hippies still walking the Haight? What did they currently have to offer? Solicitations for spare change and marijuana? Keith had no change, and he didn't smoke marijuana. "Nuggets? Who needs nugs?" a dirty hippie said, right on cue.

Keith shook his head, looked up, and temporarily lost himself in the grid of MUNI wires overhead. Those wires fueled the city's electric trolley buses. Those wires sometimes sparked. Keith regretted abandoning the bus, stinky passenger and all.

Again, he made eye contact with a hippie who walked the Haight. "Want some headies, brah?" asked the hippie.

Keith looked more like a head than a customer, with his beard and simple garb. He looked like someone who would buy weed off the Upper Haight crowd. "This isn't a music fest, dude," Keith said. That's it. He took out his phone and called Sonia. If he were talking on the phone, he thought no one would bother him.

"Sonia?" The wind rose. "Can you hear me?"

Keith bounced inside a coffee shop to get better reception.

He invited Sonia to the park, but she had school work to do. Maybe he would hang low too. The conditions weren't ideal for canoeing. Maybe he'd order a tea. Shake off the negativity he felt.

Inside the coffee shop, Keith stood in line. When he looked outside the café, he noticed the lady with the dog.

No way, it can't be.

Sky Tyler, his lady with a dog.

Don't be seen. Keith moved deeper into the café, into the shadows. He sat at a table, picked up a *Chronicle*, and hid behind the sports section. Keith peeked out from behind the newspaper.

Sky, standing near the doorway, played with her dog, a puppy Golden Retriever. Keith rose with the intention of approaching her. He wanted to talk, but instead of heading toward Sky, he made a beeline to the bathroom. Inside the restroom, he looked in the mirror. Keith had a sunflower seed stuck in his beard. He hadn't munched a sunflower seed since the previous afternoon. He picked at his teeth and combed his hair with his hands. There was an ashy stain on his faded blue jeans. He washed it off with a wet paper towel, and then straightened his red flannel shirt. He looked at himself in profile, one more dusting off, one last fluff of the hair, a smile. Keith swallowed a capital-sized GULP and exited the bathroom ready to talk to Sky Tyler. Then a young girl with pale skin and gothic clothing smiled at him. All right, his mojo was on the rise. He felt even better when two ladies with white Steve Madden shopping bags smiled at him. Confidence level high, his walk morphed into a semi-strut, until he looked down and saw something white. He realized why the ladies were smiling at him. A long streaming piece of toilet paper attached itself to the bottom of his sandal. Keith jumped up, contorted his torso, and wiggled his legs. He shook, shucked, juked and jived; he danced crazier by the second, providing more entertainment to those around by the moment. He felt more frustrated than embarrassed. A girl with a nose ring and a long, hand-sewn dress, an eye sparkling goddess, she walked over to Keith. "Let me get this for you, brother."

Keith glanced at Sky, by the front door. Look, she's glowing. Inside the coffee shop, it was always dark. Outside, the sun rode the wind and broke through the gray clouds. Sunny outside. Dark inside. And there stood Sky Tyler. And she smiled at Keith, as she hung in the doorway of the dark coffee shop with the sun at her back. And she glowed. Keith did the only thing he could think of. The one thing that made sense. He ran out the back door.

Keith, what are you doing to us? *We can't go back to the coffee shop. That girl throws our mind for a loop.* What if she was there first and we walked in? *Would it have made a difference? We'd have run.* There are things we run away from and there are things we chase. You know this. *We ran like we ran two years ago.* We didn't have a choice then. Sky was pregnant with another man's baby. *We're not healed.* Maybe we should've stayed in Los Angeles. *Love is a torture chamber.* You know how the gods operate. Fortuna sometimes rolls with trick dice. We were bound to run into her. *I don't understand what happened at the coffee shop?* Our heart and our mind were at different ends and we ran from the thing we once chased. *Should we listen to our heart or our mind?* Listen to our heart. *We're obsessing.* We're running and chasing at the same time. *It's been two years.* Time is the only thing that wins. *We're not alone.* Keep saying that. *We're not alone.* It's a part of life. If we want to hold on, sometimes we have to run. *Most of our obsessions we can put aside by focusing on the yoga.* This stupid love thing's another story. Our heart has its own one-way express lane into a part of our mind we can't control. No matter how hard we try to break free and take control, our thoughts are like a bunch of bugs caught in a sticky geometrically complicated spider-web. *We're a slave to the spider, and our spider is Sky Tyler because that's the only girl we've ever loved.* When we think about Sky, obsess over Sky, see clouds configured like the face of Sky, see strangers shape-shift into the form of Sky, we can't silence our mind, not a chance. Almost nothing can deter us from falling victim to the unfortunate solace of our own pain, so we run. *We can function if we're able to get past our crises.* Things aren't good right now. We better not be alone, Keith.

Keith had picked up two pounds of asparagus. He stood in the kitchen of Sonia Maria Chow's Nob Hill apartment. Her roommates studied in their rooms. Coltrane played on the stereo. Two bottles of Chianti on the table. "I love our neighborhood."

"Me too," Sonia said. She sat at the kitchen table. "You grew up in the Richmond?" Keith chopped off the chunky asparagus stems and ran the tips under the faucet. "Close to the park," he said. "The park was like my office in high school."

Sonia Maria Chow was half-Chinese and half-Italian. A native of San Francisco, she was born on the cusp of North Beach and Chinatown. She was conceived the night of a big soccer game, 1986, Italy versus China. The game ended in a 2 – 2 tie, and for a single night, the two neighborhood pubs were as one. Like dim sum stuffed into a canoli, crazy things happen. "The park is nuts," Sonia said, rubbing her finger around the rim of her glass. "Last week I saw a group in pirate costumes, drinking, playing croquet."

"Sounds par for the course," Keith said.

Keith boiled some water and used a thin flat sieve on top of the pot as a steamer. He threw the asparagus on the sieve to let the steam work on the vegetable. "You have to let the vapor get inside every pore of the asparagus. I know some people like to keep it raw. But I say cook it, soften it, give it time, and make it tender. Let the vapors make love to the organic." After he steamed the asparagus, he put it in a baking pan, topped it with butter, breadcrumbs, and Parmesan cheese, then he threw it in the oven on Broil and joined her at the kitchen table. They sipped Chianti.

"So how long were you in Los Angeles?" Sonia asked.

"Two years."

"What did you do?"

"Studied sweaty yoga with the master. Tried to act."

"You tried acting?"

"It was what it was."

Keith met Sonia at work. She took a class he taught and had liked his style. He was very patient with his students. And his voice was so calm, so deep and relaxing, very meditative. And the way he sweated. Like he didn't sweat at all. He glistened. It'd be 105° in the studio, and everyone else dripped trickling streams, yet Keith the yoga instructor stood in front of the class and shined. She started going to yoga only when he taught. One afternoon class she found herself distracted. It had happened very suddenly. His ass. In the reflection on the mirrored wall. She couldn't stop looking at his ass. One day, after class, she asked him out for coffee. They've hung out a couple of times since, very casual.

Keith opened the oven. Whatever he cooked came out burnt. "Check-it-out," he tried to play it off. "Asparagus au rotten."

Sonia laughed. "Cook for me anytime you want, boy."

***

The next morning in his own room, Keith worked out with yoga. He liked to listen to hardcore music when he did yoga, bands like Minor Threat and Operation Ivy. He hated the New Age crap the studio made him play during lessons. The house rule for the instructors was either play Enya now, or we'll Cya later.

At home he had his own routine. He didn't make up the poses, but he made up the order to fit his style. He started with the *vrksasana*, the tree pose, for eight minutes. Then he dropped into *adho mukha shvanasana*, the downward dog. Hands stretched forward on the floor, tailbone up, shoulders and head stretched down, heels down to the floor, a nice resting position. Five minutes. Then out of downward dog into the *dhanurasana*, or bow pose, for four minutes. After working out, Keith turned on the computer.

As he waited for the Dell to boot, he felt the burden of routine. Keith felt too connected to time, too connected to space, to technology. A sick sort of dependence he felt, like a slave afraid of freedom when offered. What could he do to break this feeling of routine? He could hike Big Sur? Go scuba diving in Monterey? Pick strawberries in Watsonville? All those things would remind him of Sky, having done them all together, especially the strawberry fields. He didn't need to think about Sky and the first time they made love, losing their virginity in the strawberry fields, way-out, beyond even the migrant workers. There was a looming show in Chicago he could sneak off to, Oracledang, but the windy city seemed too far away, besides, he was done with the festival scene. He thought most of the heads in the scene were immature and reckless.

When Windows finally opened, Keith made his way to Hotmail. There waited one message in the inbox and four in the junk folder. Junk first. Do you need your penis enlarged; Great mortgage loans pre-approved; Generic Viagra cheap; vhgsssre dhjhgsss. You sure you want to erase everything in the folder? Yes.

On to the inbox. After the comprehension of her name, a distant voice charged to the front of his mind. The voice that wanted to see the name every time he checked e-mail. The voice sometimes heard, but never allowed to enter. Upon seeing the name Sky Tyler, the voice validated itself, and then took control. See, I told you. I knew she'd e-mail us. He fought off the voice. Breathe. Breathe. A deep breath kept the voice from swelling. Another breath and Keith Lipsiznowaz could click open the e-mail.

What's up monkey,

You know I saw you at Rockin Java. You didn't have to bolt. It would've been nice to talk. It's been awhile. When did you move back to San Francisco? Everything in my world is nuts, as usual. I'm seeing a sister now. She's a hottie. You'd like her. ;) I got a dog. He's so cute. Did you see him at the coffee shop? Listen, I'm writing because it's BAY TO BREAKERS TIME. You have to run it with me, Keith. I have the perfect idea for a costume. And I know you're the only one who can pull it off. You're not still mad, are you? We can be friends, right? Call me. My number changed.

It's (415) 948-3022.

Later skater,
ST

Hmm. Keith read the e-mail over and over, maybe fifteen times. What did she mean you're the only one who could pull it off? He wondered if he should write back. He started to write her with the intention of declining. Yeah, we're still friends, but it wouldn't be right. He canceled the message and decided to call her. Call her later. *I want to call her now.* No, call her later. He wondered what costume idea she had in mind. Bay to Breakers with Sky, hmm. No, totally impossible. Not an option. He'd e-mail her later and make up an excuse. He had to work. He had to go out of town. He had the gout. *Maybe I'll ask her about the costume idea.* No, don't even do that. There was no way he'd go to Bay to Breakers with Sky Tyler. He wouldn't even call or respond to the e-mail. How could he? Four out of five Keiths agreed: the last thing he needed on God's green planet was to go to Bay to Breakers with Sky Tyler. It wouldn't happen. *Nope.* No way. Not a chance.

Keith could hardly see out of the veil. Sky kept insisting he keep it down. She certainly didn't look like a male groom in her baggy tuxedo, her dreadlocks bouncing off her neck while they jogged. Sweat stuck to her forehead and her breasts clung to the tuxedo shirt. Keith couldn't help but notice; they caught his eye when he raised the veil. He didn't like the veil. Keith hit Sky with the bouquet every time she tried to put it back down. At least she yielded on the heels issue. He had insisted on wearing Reeboks.

Bay to Breakers is San Francisco's annual mini-marathon. Usually seventy-thousand people run in the less than eight-mile event. People are known for wearing wacky costumes. Some people wear nothing. The first time Keith and Sky raced, they dressed as superheroes, her Wonder Woman to his Flash Gordon. The next year, they ran as Tweedle-Dee and Tweedle-Dum. The third time they raced together, they dressed as Siamese twins, but on that occasion their costume fell apart and they never finished the event. And now, in weird gender swapping roles, Sky Tyler played a groom, while Keith Lipsiznowaz dressed to the hilt as a bride. The wedding gown felt surprisingly comfortable to Keith. It fit right on, a size 12 with a thirty-inch waist. The gown was a Jessica McClintock, tagged by a sewn in label, a cute, white, Italian, sleeveless bodice, with a pearl clustered neckline, a dropped waist, and a full skirt. Lucky for Keith, the dress had a detachable train so no one would trip him. In any event, their costumes were a success. Almost everyone had a smile for the young bride and groom.

As usual, the race was a spectacle. They came across a lot of characters. Of course they came across naked people: naked pirates, naked tennis players, naked Dr. Seuss characters, painted red and blue, Naked Thing # 1 and Naked Thing # 2. They saw eleven Elvises and a plethora of Elviras. Jogging bulls and jogging matadors. Jogging Starskies looking for jogging Hutches. Most of the field consisted of regular joggers, running along.

Five miles into the race, they approached the big duck pond in the park. "Only two miles left." Keith slowed down and looked behind for Sky, who made her way to the benches by the pond. She looked visibly exhausted. Keith went to her. They sat down and caught their breath. "Sky, did you stop doing yoga?"

"I don't do it as much as I should. Where are you teaching? Maybe I'll come by." Sky scrunched her nose like a cute little mouse and then grabbed his hand.

Keith's heart skipped a beat. He felt scared. "Don't." He moved his hand. "And don't come by. It's not really a good idea."

The moment of silence is a son of tension and a father to awkward. They looked around. Old people fed ducks stale bread.

"Are you ever going to forgive me?"

"I'm here now," Keith replied.

"I never meant to hurt you."

"I don't want to talk about it."

"You were the one I loved—"

"Talking only ruins it."

"I wasn't a possession, Keith."

"Please, please, please, please," he said. "Let's not talk."

What didn't Keith want to talk about? Maybe he didn't want to talk about how his girlfriend of four years, his one and only love, became pregnant after hooking up with another man following an insignificant quibble that resulted in a break Keith never wanted to take. Maybe he didn't want to talk about how he ran away to Los Angeles because it hurt so badly, and he didn't know how to forgive her, even though he thought about her every day, and leaving her was the hardest thing he ever did. Maybe he didn't want to talk about how he loved her, and always would love her, and could never say no to her, no matter what she asked, even if it hurt him, and he knew it could never be the same, and he knew they were no good for each other, and it would never work out.

Sky looked at Keith, but he lived in the pond, on a ripple.

"I had it." Sky went to the pond. "And I gave it up."

Keith came back from the ripple. "You give up too easily."

"Story of my life." She managed a chuckle.

There was still a race, and joggers, determined to reach the end, breezed by them. "Finish the race. Then take your honeymoon," yelled a cranky jogger dressed like Oscar the Grouch.

"It's hard for me to think about *it*." Sky felt empty. She dug in her pockets. "Do you remember this?" In her hand, she held an amber crystal. Keith recalled the stone. He gave it to her when they started hanging out, in the ninth grade. "I've held this rock in my pocket every day for six years. Maybe you'd like it back."

She held the amber crystal out as a peace offering.

Keith let the stone stay in her hand. He didn't want the crystal. In fact, he didn't want to be there anymore. He could barely see Sky through the scar tissue of his old wounds. The old pattern spun. It was time for him to run. Keith lowered the wedding veil.

"I would've suffered for you."

"Keith, wait."

Sky watched him run away, a bearded man in a wedding gown, wearing Reeboks. He didn't even turn around once. Not once. The yoga instructor jogged right out of Golden Gate Park.

Zombie love

Sonia Maria Chow was depressed. The heat she felt in her chest when she thought of Keith. Her mind raced with thoughts of him. The realization that she'd sacrifice her dreams, her plans, all her freedoms, for just a chance, just a kiss. She didn't have the slightest clue what to do. Should she call him again? Was she supposed to wait? Should she be serious or funny? Should she be herself? What did that mean? Sonia felt too smart for this. She was a Stanford girl, goddamn it. What good were her wits? She felt as if love took the form of a zombie, a soulless creature of the night, direct from a George Romero movie. Love was a zombie devouring her wits and brains. Sonia thought there was no way it could work. She thought she'd fuck it up. She felt scared. It was all so utterly crazy, not sound, it made no sense. Was she an invalid at love? She had been hurt before. Sonia felt more depressed. Should she call him again? Why did she leave such a stupid message?

Um, Keith, it's Sonia. Just calling to see what you're doing. I had a really good time with you the other night. Yeah, um, it's like one in the afternoon, and I hope everything is copasetic in your world. I was thinking about asking you if you'd like to maybe go to the symphony with me tonight. MTT's conducting Chopin's Etudes. Should be a blast. Call me back if you're not working, okay? What a stupid message. Then, kismet, her phone rang.

"Hey, Sonia. It's Keith. I'm returning your call."

Washington Square Park and the surrounding streets were jammed with people for the North Beach Fair. Sky sat under a tree eating cherries. She looked around the park for her girlfriend. Melody Rain had wandered off to enter a contest to win an Alaskan cruise. She said she wanted to take a holiday. Did the North Beach Fair constitute a holiday? Sure, for the city. Then Sky's thoughts drifted to her own family. Every Thanksgiving, she sat with her two brothers in front of the television, watching football. Her brothers would wonder why the Lions were rewarded a game every year when they sucked to kingdom come. And Sky would wonder why the Redskins were called the Redskins. Isn't that a little derogatory, especially on Thanksgiving? And the television would take on static lines every time their mother in the kitchen used the electric carving knife. The sound had bellow, like the blow dryer their mother used when getting ready for one of her dates.

Melody Rain returned and plopped down near Sky's stomach. "You should've brought Bodhi-dog to get blessed." She was referring to the animal blessing at St. Francis of Assisi, where as part of the fair, Sky could have her pet recognized by the church.

"Are you kidding?" Sky said. "Bodhi's not a Catholic."

Melody Rain nodded. "It's hella crowded here."

"You want to go? I have a violin lesson at four, so—"

"Some heads are throwing a little barbecue in Sonoma."

"I have lessons today, honey."

"Oh, come on. Skip one. We can stop off at Muir Woods."

"I don't know," Sky said. "I have a violin lesson, babe."

***

Getting off the 101, on state road 116, the girls trekked west through downtown Sebastopol, passing mini-malls with little markets and artisan shops. Sky's old Honda whipped the narrow corners of the countryside, and they arrived at the barbecue, parking near a big blue barn. When Melody Rain said some heads in Sonoma were throwing a little barbecue, she understated the occasion. What transpired looked like a full-out jam. Inside the barn, there was a glassblowing contest called a flame-off. Eight glassblowing stations were set up along the walls of the lodge. Torches, oxygen and propane tanks, four kilns to share, plenty of glass, fans, light, and ventilation shafts in the windows. Everyone, including the blowers and spectators who stood behind them, wore glasses to soften the glare from the torches. And little tables next to the torch stations were scattered with all kinds of goblets, marbles, paper weights, one piece pipes, Sherlock Holmes pipes, chillums, glass scraps, little beads, man made crystals, half-completed pieces, used supplies, old rods, there was glass everywhere. Toward the back of the barn, a stage played host to a reggae band. And during the band's breaks, a deejay spun hip-hop and funk. Sky brought along her violin, hoping before the night was through she could have a chance to jam. And of course, a full sized keg held its own in each corner of the barn, and the dankest microbrews flowed: amber ale, nut-brown ale, black stout, and golden pilsner.

Outside, the jam spread. Behind the barn, a hill dropped a hundred feet into a flattened mini-valley. A homemade Slip and Slide looked like a giant yellow tongue as it set down the decline and rolled along the flattened ground. Water from the barn hose kept the plastic concoction slippery. On the bottom, a little jump ramp launched heads into a kiddie pool, and all the easy riders flew down the summer slide headfirst with their cold beers in hand.

Three hundred people were scattered throughout the compound. In the mini-valley, on two tables, lay the food. Potato salads, egg salads, green salads, fruit salads, strawberry rhubarb pies. A roasted pig sat on another table, sliced up. And there was fish on the grill, all kinds, salmon, ahi tuna, tilapia, grouper. Of course a keg flowed outside, too. And what about the babies? There were tons of babies, and the mammas were taking care of the babies. "I like how this is a family affair," Sky said.

They walked around the compound. Past the mini-valley with the food, another hill existed. On the other side of that hill, a lake with a diving board. Kids flipped into the water. If there's water, then you know where the Labradors were. "We definitely should've brought Bodhi-dog," Sky said. "It's beautiful here."

At dusk, Melody Rain and Sky found a private grassy spot off the lake. They watched night come to them slowly, as the blue hues darkened, then turned darker. "We should stay out here."

"Yeah," Sky agreed. "Let's stay outside, not inside. Who knows? Maybe tomorrow we can go to town, buy a raft, and float down the Russian River to the ocean. I haven't done that since—"

That time with Keith in eleventh grade, during Spring Break. She let the thought fade. A little cuddle session erupted on the hill with light kisses. Melody Rain's finger found Sky's thigh.

There were stars up above. Night came, and then night comes. And then the girls placed themselves in the hands of darkness.

***

Darkness led the girls to a huge fire in the mini-valley and a drum circle. A dreadie head named Dimitri waved the girls over.

"Want to smoke some DMT?"

"What's DMT?" Sky asked.

"It's interesting," Dimitri said.

"You have DMT?"

"I don't know, Melody."

"It only lasts for a little while."

"Well," Sky said, shrugging, "I'll try anything, once."

The DMT chalice was a cylinder glass pipe with a bubble on the end. There was a little hole near the bottom of the bubble. Dimitri put the white dust DMT powder in the hole, and then he lit it. "Don't puff it. Let the smoke fill, then hit-it," he said.

The silver smoke built up slowly. The pipe looked foggy, deluded, and fantastic, like San Francisco at seven in the morning. The pipe looked like a cloudy crystal ball. Sky felt nothing as she watched the smoke build. Then she inhaled all the smoke.

Sky looked around. She had no idea what to expect, and for a moment she felt nervous. Then her pupils dilated, and the wave crushed her. The DMT hit hard and fast and hard. She raised her hands in front of her face. Her appendages looked funny. They looked terrestrial and scaly. The middles of her fingers were up to something strange. The wrinkles in the middle of her fingers. The wrinkles in the spots where the bones met. The wrinkles in the middle of Sky's fingers had turned into eyes. The wrinkles turned into eyes, and the wrinkled eyes began to open and close and blink.

"Are you all right?" Melody Rain asked.

Sky held her hands up to her face. "It's interesting," she mumbled. On both sides of her hands, twenty bulbous eyes were blinking and watching her. Even though she couldn't say it at the time, she felt the watching eyes were Mayan. They looked like the eye on the dollar bill, but the eyes had nothing to do with the Freemasons, no, the eyes on Sky's hands were Mayan, definitely Mayan. "It's interesting," she mumbled, again, to herself.

Dimitri turned to Melody Rain.

"Are you going to Oracledang?" he asked.

"Is it Oracledang time again?"

Melody Rain took a hit from the DMT chalice.

"Chicago's a long drive." Sky scratched her dreads. "I'm a little faded, Melody. We should go back to the city and just chill."

"Come on. We'll make it a road trip. It'll be like a holiday."

"I guess I could blow off work."

"You need to experience a festival. You're always talking about experiences. Do you trust me, luv? I won't lead you wrong."

"Can we experience *it*?"

"I'll find a glassblower to front us some product to work."

"Experience *it*." Sky was up all night and a bit off.

"We can bring your dog. They'll be dogs at Oracledang."

"All right, Melody-monster. Let's experience *it*."

Melody Rain had little difficulty finding someone she knew to front them glass. She scored two bubblers, two Sherlocks, five hammers, and five chillums, for $350, to be paid upon their return. To keep the glass safe, they padded Sky's violin case with Styrofoam egg crates. During the course of the night, someone at the party plastered the violin case in *God Bless the Freaks* stickers.

The girls left Sebastopol toward San Francisco at eight in the morning. Sky drove. Tired from sleep deprivation, she ate up the white divider lines on the highway like Ms. Pac-Man, *wakka-wakka-wakka*, looking for energy, looking for a Power Pellet.

They arrived outside Sky's pad by nine o'clock.

"I'll be back," Melody Rain said. "Get ready to head out."

"Where are you going, sweetie?"

"The drug store," she lied, sort of.

Melody Rain made her way down Cole Street. With every step, a deep, demanding, and tortuous need grew on her, like algae. She felt like pond scum. It didn't bother her. She didn't care. On Haight Street, her feet felt heavy, her pace slowed. A wave of hatred and loathing filled her. She hated. She hated what exactly? Her mind raced with one thought, and it ran over and over. Go, get, it, go, get, it, get, it. She walked past the Cuban restaurant. Past the coffee shop. The record store. The disco. The supermarket. The fast food establishment. Across the street, she entered the park. Melody Rain knew where to go, what to get, and who had it.

***

Sonia Maria Chow rested her head on Keith's chest. Her straight black locks lay sprawled across his ribcage. To be naked under a down comforter. To have your head and shoulders compressed in a mountain of goose feathered pillows. To be next to someone. To be young. It all felt good. "What is this thing called love?" Keith had his arm around Sonia, and he lightly scratched his nails along her porcelain back. "I mean, who can solve its mystery. I know I'm not going to let it make a fool out of me, no way—"

Sonia started to crack up in laughter.

"What?" Keith asked.

"You're paraphrasing a Billie Holiday song, you goof."

"Oh." Keith rolled his eyes. "Well, I like Billie Holiday."

***

Melody Rain's outstretched hand held a pink pill.

Bodhi-dog, sitting on Sky's lap, licked Melody Rain's hand.

"This isn't for you, dog," Melody Rain said. "Here, Sky."

"What's this?"

"A vitamin. It'll wake you up."

"Will it wake me up more than a Red Bull?"

"A little bit more," she laughed.

Sky popped the pill and washed it down with water.

Melody Rain unconsciously stroked the pockets of her jeans, to make sure. The pill wasn't the only thing purchased during her excursion into the park. "Ready?" Melody Rain kissed her girlfriend on the cheek, and roughly turned the key in the ignition.

Melody Rain's mad secretive. I first met her at a show in Orlando. She wore this baggy patchwork hat with "JAH LOVE" printed on the front. She liked the way I hugged. That's what that tricky girl said when we first met. You give good hug, baby. Whatevs. She's a hottie. We stayed together through New Orleans and Austin and Phoenix and Denver, peepin shows and catchin rides, until we landed in Frisco. All I'm saying is Melody Rain's got secrets she keeps from people. I know because in the middle of the night she used to toss and turn and kick her legs. I've been around, son. When they kick their legs, they got secrets. Whatevs. I had an aiight time in Frisco. It's just soft out there. Frisco needs some balls. I spent a lot of time in Amoeba Records looking for vinyl to send back to the boys in New York. I felt bad for leaving the band for six weeks. I wrote a song for Melody Rain. It actually made the cut, it's on *Hurricane Steez*. It's not a rhyme. I don't bust it, I kind-a sing it. Song's about this spot she took me to in the East Bay. It was a huge space, like an abandoned warehouse, on the second floor of a mall. One night we were drinkin at the spot and I passed out cold. The sound of laughter woke me up. I came to learn a comedy club operated under the spot. Check this! I had mad ducats, like over a grand, because I was hustlin these roofies. Anyway, when I awoke, Melody was ghost and my pockets were empty. No ducks, no Melody Rain, nothing. I had nothing. Only laughter echoing into an empty abandoned warehouse and me. Got it? I had no idea what happened. Was the girl arrested, kidnapped, did she rob me and split? I have no idea. I loved that girl. She didn't have to rob me. If she needed money, all she had to do was ask. Stoops. It's history. Girl's hella crazed. Monk made his way back east and rebounded just fine because you know this hurricane got the clout, for-shizzle.

THE SPOT (lyrics T. Horowitz)

I know a spot
Where we can rot
Nothin but pipes
Old fluorescent lights

The dust is real
The rot is real
The real is a wheel
The wheel is real

Empty / abandon (4x)

The spot is real
Just under construction
Someone will fix it
Fix the malfunction

Ha, ha, ha, ha, ha, ha
Ha, ha, ha, ha, ha, ha (fade-out)

Part Four
On The Road Steez

The ceremony's about to begin

Chapter 11—Melody Rain and Sky's on the road montage

(in a Smurfy eleven-syllable verse)

Out of San Francisco: I 5 south, south, south,
Ms. Pac-Man *wakka wakka wakka wakka,*
south to 58 east. Camel hump hills, grass
like old straw, dry and a little desperate.
I 40 east, east, east, east *wakka wakka*
wakka wakka wakka wakka east, east, east.
East, east, two beasts, to a summer sunset, Grand
Canyon style. Clouds spread wide and thin and long—
cloudy spirits haunt the bridge between the West
and Midwest. Sidetrack south on I 17.
Sidetrack 89A nature-nature, yea.
Red-faced canyon walls—red rock like fire burns,
red rock burning summer glare. Red fire rock
clay temple chisel, chisel, chisel mountains,
crown kingdom Montezuma meet Sedona.
Red rocks stick out like appendages. Red rocks
like garden of middle fingers, red garden
of middle fingers. "Place is like God saying
fuck you—you wish you were this beautiful," Sky
says. Melody sits behind the wheel. In the
twists of 89A, in the fading light,
Sky sees weird faces in the rocks. The girls
zoom by red mountains and random rock patterns
continue to take the form of strange faces.
"Baby, these rocks don't like me. They're judging me."
"Don't get paranoid, now," Melody Rain says,
wide-awake, appreciating the sunset.

red rocks that judge Sky as they zoom by

I 40 east, east, east, east *wakka wakka
wakka wakka,* a stop in New Mexico.
The native at the gas station in Ramon
who sold the mescaline to the girls referred
to it as *mescalito.* Melody ate
one. Sky gobbled two and called the brown pellets
Scooby Snacks. A sign with an arrow reading
"alien crash landing." The sign points into
the desert along a beaten path. They drive
down the path until nightfall. On their backs in
the desert. A star turns colors: red-blue-green-
yellow-red-blue-green-yellow. "You see that, Sky?"
"Uh, huh." A star turning colors: red-blue-green-
yellow-red-blue-green-yellow. "We have to tell
them," Melody says, a little scared. "Mid-dle
nowhere," Sky says. "We're not in the desert, hon—
we're lying in the La Quinta parking lot."
Sky points at the weird star: red-blue-green-yellow.
"We should really report this. You call em, Sky."
Sky used her cell phone to dial 9-1-1.
"In--heavens," she says. "Red-ba-lu-green-yell-oh.
May-be ex-tra-ter-re-str-ial. Understand?"
"Where you calling from?" asks the operator.
Sky quickly hangs up the phone. "Think they know now."

Wrong turn at Albuquerque

After running around all wacked out on Scooby Snacks,
without any golf shoes, Melody Rain somehow found sleep, easily.
Sky Tyler could not sleep. She ambled into the La Quinta
bathroom. Thirsty, she couldn't bring herself to drink the tap
water. Her thirst intensified, and she felt an urge to brush her teeth.
She rummaged through her toiletry bag, discovering a nice surprise.

The amber crystal Keith gave to her in the ninth grade. Years ago, she asked him what he played with in his pockets every time they passed in the hallway. Keith, to her surprise, produced the amber crystal, and gifted it to her. He said he carried the rock every day in his pocket for a year and a half, and it was amply charged, and it belonged to her, and would bring her good luck. He said he knew the crystal belonged to her, but he'd been waiting for the right time to give it to her. It was the first gift a boy ever gave Sky. She now sighed, scratched her dreads, and looked parched.

Pocketing the amber crystal, she stumbled into the La Quinta hallway, in search of a soda machine. She wanted water. Sky walked along the red hallway carpet. The red carpet surged with shifting patterns. She tried to focus so the patterns would stop shifting. The patterns did not stop shifting. Sky came to terms with the shifting patterns on the red carpet. And she walked on down the hall. And she came to an office door. And she looked inside.

The office had glass doors and walls. It appeared empty and dark, except for a computer. A green light glowed from its hard drive. Despite the blank monitor, the computer had life. Then she caught her reflection in the glass, and when her dreads hissed like Medusa's snakes, she looked away. Sky could feel the amber crystal against her thigh. She missed Keith. No one knew her better than Keith. So what if Melody Rain saved her life in Berkeley? What about Keith? What was the harm in dropping him a line?

The office door opened. Sky approached the humming computer and hit the keypad to wake up the dormant monitor. After navigating over to Yahoo, she ignored all the unopened messages, and went straight to the composition of a new e-mail.

Subject line: AHHHH!!!!!!

Keith—

I'm in New Mexico. There's a hole in my head. Transmissions from the mothership have been disconnected. Left San Francisco daze ago. Made wrong turn at Albuquerque, been chasing aliens in the desert, and ate two too many Scooby Snacks. Who knew? Lol. Wowzies. Now off to Oracledang in Chicago. This is *it*. Experience *it*. Remember your eyes on me at SAKE? Seeing eyes I am. U.I.R.B.Y. Keep chopping wood and carrying water. I love you. st

Keith checked his e-mail the next evening. The voice, finally at bay, sailed back. The voice that stayed on the ship when his boat docked at Sonia Island and he debarked; the voice that let him have a meditative vacation. The voice roared back. *This isn't the Sky Tyler I know.* First he felt disgust. Then he felt irate. But all the while there was sympathy. After reading the letter he knew Sky faced trouble. Keith could feel an inorganic energy seeping through the computer. He could almost taste the chemicals that were altering her mind. She knew better than to do drugs. It must've been her so called girlfriend's influence. Why else could Sky have sounded so messed up? It didn't even matter. The last thing Sky wrote made up his mind. Three simple words could alter his destiny over and over as long as he carried around the body he was trapped in. Three words constructed and tangled his spider's web: I love you. *Did she really write that?* Three monosyllable words led Keith to Expedia.com to buy a ticket to Chicago. *What did I just do?* He decided rather expeditiously that he would chase after Sky. *There was no other choice, dude.* He obsessed like never before. *Shut up.* It might not have been the best idea. *I'm going after Sky.* There are things you chase and things you run away from. *I'm a chaser and a warrior stalker.* He was obsessing and his obsessions were strong. *I want Sky. Tell me what she's thinking?* No. *Does she love me?* You don't belong in this point of view, Keith. *I need to think this thing through.* He wasn't thinking about Sonia. *What about Sonia? We never put a label on our thing.* You had an unspoken bond, at least in her mind. *Sky needs me.* Keith tried to delude himself. Even if Sky still loved him, she was not a possession, and he knew that. *Shut up. Sky loves me. It's love, not obsession. It's love. I'm not possessing. She loves me and I was right all along.* Unfortunately, Sky still spun the web of his life, and the Sonia situation, however deplorable, was a rebound situation. *Shut up, dude.* Keith Lipsiznowaz was absolutely a glutton for punishment. *That's absurd.* Keith liked being a masochist. *No, I don't.* He really did enjoy the pattern, the loop, and the circle. *I don't care. She needs me. I'm going to Chicago to save her.* He felt as happy as can be.

Keith's hasty e-mail to Sonia

Subject line: it's not you it's me

Sonia--this is weird. I'm writing to let you know I have to leave town. This has nothing to do with you. Believe me. You're wonderful. My friend Sky is in trouble. I have to protect her. I might be exaggerating things too. I'm not sure of her situation. A part of my head says let her take care of herself, but my heart says go to her. I have to listen to my heart. And I would be lying to myself, and to you, if I said I didn't love Sky. I'm not sure how long I will be gone. I'm sorry I have to do this by e-mail. I know it's selfish and I'm sorry. This is where I'm at right now, and all I really know is the now. We'll cross paths again, I'm sure, and I hope you can forgive me. Yours truly, Keith Lipsiznowaz

Sonia's thought out rebuttal e-mail

subject line: love sucks

Why is it that you always meet someone and then they leave? You're supposed to be a guru, answer me that one, huh? To tell you the truth, Keith, I hope we don't cross paths again. I will do what I can to avoid it. For starters, I think I'll start doing hatha instead of sweaty yoga. I'm glad I didn't let myself fall too hard. I had a sneaky suspicion you were the flake you turned out to be.

Best of luck on your path.

Sonia

At one of those horizons in Central Florida where the hills
rolled and the grass was wet from a summer storm. North of
Orlando, still on the Turnpike, before I-75, near Leesburg. The sun
looked like a fading portrait of red Hermes over a tropical sky.
Curtis was behind the wheel of *The Jedi* like a young Neal Cassady,
as Geri sat shotgun, rubbing her belly, sewing a patchwork apron
tee, while staring out the window. She saw a pelican, an out-of-
place pelican, far from the sea. She wondered if she would miss
Florida. She would not miss it. There was no looking back. Not for
that *hermana.* Beyond the pelican, an executive-jet streamed a line in
the tropical sky, a line like white chalk. The chalky cloudy line said
everything there was to say about Florida. What side are you on?
This side of paradise, or this side of decadence? Is the chalky white
line powder for Hermes to sniff on his western trek across the
Florida sky, enabling the deity to visit some strip club like Mons
Venus in Tampa? Or are you down with the spirit? Are you ready
to ride the Holy Chariot as far as it can take you? That's Florida:
choose or lose. Whatever the case, buckle up because it's click-it or
ticket country. And no matter what, the ride will be crazy, and filled
with turbulence. Curtis and Geri would be leaving nothing behind
in Florida, because the state had nothing to leave behind. It will be
like they were never even there. Want to know a secret? Curtis and
Geri don't exist. *The Jedi* doesn't exist. Their old crib in Little Haiti
doesn't exist. Geri's grandmother in Hialeah doesn't exist. Look at
the pelican. Fly pelican. The pelican is the only thing that exists.

From Athens to Asheville, through the Appalachians and the Smokys

The Jedi made it into Athens, Georgia, in time to meet up
with some old heads Curtis and Geri knew. They all went out for
pizza at the Mellow Mushroom, and then played Texas Hold'Em in
a tournament at the Last Call Saloon. They spent the night drinking
dank beer until they fell out, a pit stop on the road to the next pit
stop, on the road to Oracledang. At a Shell in South Carolina, Geri
locked the keys to *The Jedi* inside the car. Did they stress? No.

Curtis went through his cell phone and dialed friends until he found someone with AAA (Mikey the taper), and they borrowed his account number. They went off into the brush behind Shell and made love while waiting for the AAA man. After being tipped ten bucks, the man didn't care what he opened with the slimjim.

***

Asheville, North Carolina. If you don't know a single person, within five minutes you still feel at home. They spent the day in Asheville antiquing. Curtis picked up a vintage McDonald's thermos with a graphic of the Hamburglar, one of his alter egos. He also bought a Fat Albert lunch box. Often on the way towards Chicago they stopped briefly to rummage through small town thrift shops. It was a good trip through the South for a fabric addict like Geri. In the full glory of thrift shop passion they scored. In Gainesville, Florida, at Flashbacks Recycled Fashions on University Avenue, Geri found My Little Pony pillowcases; she found Wonder Woman bed sheets at Cillies on East Clayton in Athens, Georgia; and the Cabbage Patch Kids pajamas and Rainbow Brite pillowcases both were found at Make Me on Lexington Avenue in downtown Asheville. And of course before they left Asheville, they stopped to eat lunch at Rosetta's, always feeding the family right.

***

Out of Asheville, in the valley of the Appalachians, small creeks trickled over smooth rocks. In a place where the story is that of the lonesome pine, Geri made Curtis pull *The Jedi* over to wander through a meadow, and they pulled each other's daisies.

***

From Rocky Top, Tennessee, to the Bluegrass of Kentucky, to the haze over the Smokys, to the Daze Inn hokies, Curtis and Geri were glazed like the continental donuts from six to ten in the morning, as they lunched at Waffle House for hash-browns, scattered all the way, priced right at $4.20. With this, Curtis and Geri pushed their Volkswagen *further* toward their new Home.

The National Mall played host to families picnicking on the lawn, old senior couples walking hand in hand, scattered groups of unarmed soldiers, and the pleasant chirps and flutters from a motley of birds, most notable to KC, a retarded sparrow that tried to eat pebbles and an oriole who bathed itself in a puddle.

Interestingly, the Smithsonian Institution was not one big museum like KC always thought, but a collection of eighteen museums and galleries, most of which lay along the National Mall. KC also found relief when she learned the National Mall was actually a park, and not like she imagined, vandalized with kiosks owned by Sunglass Hut, Cingular Wireless, and Auntie Anne's.

The young writer left her car near Georgetown University where the previous day she sold five books during a late afternoon impromptu reading on campus, the ends to which resulted in a place to crash in an undergraduate's dorm room, where she played chess and drank chamomile tea until eleven o'clock. Ms. McGovern left New York ten days prior and never looked back. Bookstores, coffee shops, poetry readings, college campuses, spoken-word slams, art galleries, outside the symphony, the opera, the theater. Trenton, Princeton, Philadelphia, Wilmington, Baltimore, now Washington. So far the experience was well worth it. She sold fifty books, paying for all her expenses, and then some.

***

A bald, stocky, Asian walked down the street carrying a bulky backpack. He approached that classic image of the White House from one-quarter of a mile away, glorified by Hollywood, the front lawn, the fountain, the fence. Here, dozens of tourists snapped pictures from a street Hollywood doesn't name. Tinsel Town never shows dozens of cops on mountain bikes patrolling the unnamed street. Washington calls the road E Street (is the e for easy?). Expressionless, the bald, stocky Asian walked past the cops, looking them in the eye. He trekked across the path of those taking pictures. He didn't yield to let the tourists snap; no detour, he cut across, slicing the air filled with foreign tongues: Castilian, Chinese, Valley Girl, and German. Two weeks later, a shaved head will appear in four different rolls of pictures, picked up at four different pharmacies: Barcelona, Beijing, Anaheim, and Hamburg. Four tongues will curse the shaved head that ruined their picture of the White House. Shore Morris, if he knew, would've said, fair, indeed.

***

Later, KC came upon the stocky, bald, Asian. He was politicking on a microphone near the metro stop for the Smithsonian Institute. The man had a deep voice, and at times it reverberated. "You get off at Shady Grove. I prefer Friendship Heights. Go ahead people. Take the Metro to Suitland. I'll hang in Greenbelt." He had nothing to throw money in, not even a petition to sign. He used a karaoke system similar to the one KC used when doing an impromptu reading. And an oversized American flag, like a picnic blanket, lay under his feet. KC interpreted the bald man's rhetoric as using stops along the Metro Mover as euphemisms for an aesthetic platform. "Dear, sweet, people. Don't corner yourself in a Federal Triangle when Union Station is but a few stops away." Shore Morris yelled without the use of the microphone. He raised his arms and signaled everyone in the area. "Come unity! Community! We need a gathering not a crowd." Gathering not a crowd? KC wrinkled her nose. She didn't know about that guy.

***

There existed neither a gathering, nor a crowd, but instead a handful of people, minus one, as KC McGovern chose to continue on her quest of conquering Washington's museums. At first, she found the Washington galleries, in her own words, rinky-dinky. After all, she was a New York girl, an ex-attendant at the Met, a young Frank O'Hara true, a culture whore through and through. She needed something huge because she found herself comparing Washington to her birthplace. With a certain level of pride in New York and prejudice toward DC, her thoughts reeked of politics. She needed to be set free. The Freer Gallery did it, particularly one exhibit titled *Hanuman Returning with a Mountain of Healing Herbs*. It took an exuberant monkey-god in silk boxer shorts to set KC free from the politics her mind made of the art in Washington. She then whistled her way through the Whistler Gallery, moody night scenes and all. Inspired by the Peacock Room, she even scribbled copious notes, outlining a story where after a series of escalating calamities, a vacationing Flannery O'Connor finds herself masturbating in the ornate cove. By the time KC completed a lap around the Freer Gallery, she didn't even mind the young Capital Hill intern who tried to pick her up with a hollow promise of a tour through Supreme Court Justice Antonin Scalia's chambers, then dinner at the Two Quail. Instead, she kissed the intern on the cheek, leaving her bipartisan amber smell and a strand of her red hair on his Brooks Brothers suit. After shedding a tear at the National Museum of the American Indian, KC collapsed on a bench outside the Botanical Gardens. She was exhausted, worn out, in her own words, too pooped to pop. She needed a nap if she wanted to hit up an open microphone in Georgetown. The skies, cloudy and gray, were as tired as KC, and it started to rain. Without an umbrella, she dashed in the direction of the Metro Station. There, again, she saw the bald, stocky, Asian man.

Shore Morris stood atop his American flag. He yelled, speaking with his hands. "Where is justice?" He paused, looked around, and pointed at KC. "It's just us, hungry and poor. It's just us, lost and blind. It's just us. A community of just us. Come unity and justice. The revolution will not be televised. Live and direct—"

"Why you screaming?" asked KC, not minding the rain.

"If you yell, you might get heard."

"But there's no one here."

"No one, nothing, zero. There's something to it all."

"What's your name?"

"Shore Morris," he said, smiling.

KC smiled. She decided she liked Shore Morris. She liked his dedication and his style. She wondered if he worked for Barack Obama with all the grassroots talk. "Doesn't seem fair your boss has ya out here in the rain," she said, heavy with the Brooklynese.

"Fair's foul, foul's fair. Let rain fall in the Washington air."

"You're paraphrasing Shakespeare. Are you in trouble?"

"No trouble here."

"Who do you work for?"

"Shore Morris, LLC. Boss is a real tyrant," he winked.

"A tyrant?"

"A petty one of course."

"You want to go to a poetry reading, Shaw Morris?"

"I'm trying to get to Soldier's Field for Oracledang."

"Me too! I'm driving to Chicago for the same festival."

"Need a rider, I got gas," Shore Morris said, awkwardly.

KC looked at him funny.

"I mean money for gas."

Rain seemed to collect on his shaved head. KC contemplated the situation. She could use a rider with gas so expensive. This guy seemed articulate enough to provide good company. It was hard to tell how old he looked. She thought he had to be at least thirty-five. Whether it was his overtly serious nature, or his physical and mental presence, something about him made her feel safe. Based on what she heard from Lee at the bookstore, music festivals were where the counterculture came together. Why couldn't she help someone get to the festival? From here on out she'd go with the flow. "I'll tell ya what. Come with me to this open microphone, we'll talk some more, then we'll see."

'LUDE—*the rock star steez—a message from Thelonious Horowitz*

Getting your health on at the Green Star Co-op in Ithaca, New York, with that nigga Cornell, yell, rock the bells, if I'm gonna do it, gonna do it well, afraid of heights, looked down and I fell, if you kiss me, most likely I'll tell, well, well, well. Check it, when you're on the road there's no need for college, listen to what I said cause I'm droppin knowledge. That nigga Zappa said, "If you wanna get laid go to college. If you wanna learn go to a library." Well, Horowitz says, if you wanna get laid form a rock band. You know my steez! If you wanna learn, well, damn it, travel. Wha-a-at? No ducats? It's better to do it in style, with nice Hilton hodies every night, but that's just an excuse. You don't need money to travel. I'm sayin, been there, done that. Sittin on the curb, no enthusiasm, all hobbs like roy, The Natural, bottle of Dr. Bronner, all scruffy, spare changing like a gutterpunk, total slave to the Greyhound to catch the next show, cause the last show put me in the tank for a flask of dank, fifty-dollar-fine-for-disturbing-the-peace, jeans all creased, breathe in, breathe out, release. Yeah, yeah, this is how we do it, this is how it's done, from the rising of the moon, to the setting of the sun, yo, don't talk to that kid, that kid's spun. Get out! Get on the road! Keep it real! You're a natural born leader. Lee and Diamonds and Chopshop are always wondering how I can leave the city with little money, travel around the country, and then return with more money than I had when I left. They could do it too. I wish they could drop everything and come with me to a music festival. I always said in Hurricane Clout, I'm the eye, but they're the storm. I'm always coaching them to trust their instincts to keep them out of harm's way. They would do just fine on a last minute mission. Trust. It's all-good once you get on the road.

95

A Telephone Conversation between Teflon Jones and Thelonious Horowitz

Teflon: Where you at?

Thelonious: I'm on a train. What's the dilly?

Teflon: I'm coming to Chicago. I arrive at O'Hare tomorrow.

Thelonious: W-h-h-h-a-a-a-a-t!! You're coming to Oracledang?

Teflon: I want to hear live music. Cept I don't have a ticket—

Thelonious: Yo, don't even worry. I don't have one neither.

Teflon: What will we do? Buy em from a scalper?

Thelonious: Nah—funk that, scalpers are wack.

Teflon: Then how will we get into the show?

Thelonious: I'll get us a miracle. It's what I do.

Teflon: What's a miracle?

Thelonious: Don't even sweat it, dude. So, what happened wit you?

Teflon: I flipped the script. Decided to pass on the NBA.

Thelonious: W-h-h-h-a-a-a-a-t!! Pops must be trippin.

Teflon: I left him on the floor in the Cage.

Thelonious: Holy, Holy, Shiite! I wish I seen that.

Teflon: Yeah, so how do you want to do this? How will I find you?

Thelonious: Oh, it's all-good. Just holla at me when you land.

Teflon: A-i-i-ight. I'll holla at you tomorrow. Mos definitely.

Thelonious: Ni-i-i-c-e. And Teflon. It's showtime, bro.

Part Five
Oracledang!

The first thing Teflon noticed when he exited the airplane at Gate 22, the very first thing he witnessed out of the great dome windows of Terminal 1 was the wind. It whipped up three giant American flags and three City of Chicago flags in parking lot B. Teflon watched the flags. A plethora of hipsters milled around the general vicinity. They seemed to flow from the gates, a parade of scenesters, a few on that flight from Denver, a couple in from LAX, a few more from Las Vegas, even more arriving from Seattle.

As the sun filtered through the translucent roof windows of Terminal 1, Teflon lowered the brim of his Yankees cap, and began to move. Terminal 1 looked like a mall, with a Chili's here, a Wilson the Leather Experts there. Add in the pilots abound in pilot regalia, stew the stewardesses wheeling luggage, cue the CNN on the video screens, and you have yourself an airport. Near Gate B8, next to the information desk, by the huge replica of a Brachiosaurus altithorax, a giant advertisement for the Field Museum, Teflon paused. In lieu of the cool looking dinosaur, he dropped his Puma bag and called Thelonious. "What? You're walking to the stadium from Union Station?" As Teflon's ear pressed against his cell phone, his wandering eye fell on a beautiful lady bending over to adjust something on her luggage. "Yeah, it was straight." Teflon kept his eye on the lady. She picked up her belongings and walked toward him. He smiled at her and nodded. "Nah, I'm fixin to rent a car." She smiled back. "Probably in like an hour or two." Teflon played with the back stud of his diamond earring then pulled up his pants. "I can't hear you. The phone's breakin up." Teflon switched the receiver to his other ear. "Hello."

***

Keith Lipsiznowaz noticed the vase of daisies. They were yellow, yellow gerberas, and they looked like the eyes of a sun deity, as golden as the state he just flew in from. The vase rested on the counter of an information desk. Keith needed to know how to get to Soldier's Field. The yoga instructor's sense of direction was bad. When in a foreign location, he could have a map and a compass, and he'd still get lost. "Greetings," he said, great eye contact, benevolence on his face, a grin, like the smile of the Buddha. "Can you tell me *the way*—" Keith leaned his elbows on the counter. He inched closer as if to reveal a secret, except he knocked the vase of daisies over. The vase fell on top of a mug that spilled hot coffee all over the information desk and the man minding the booth. The gray-haired man was one of those old airport hounds, hardened by the pace of the scene, disillusioned by its transience. He didn't look happy. "Whoa, how'd that happen?" Keith bowed quickly and began to walk backwards. "Sorry." He continued to back away, bowing in apology. The information-desk worker dealt with his smoldering testicles, cursing in an accent with Polish undertones.

Keith did not see the black Puma bag on the ground. Walking backwards + black Puma bag = *thud* Keith on the floor.

"Yo," Teflon said, "you all right, kid?" He wanted to laugh but he had to ask this question first. Wasn't that the rule? Keith, scratching his head, looked up at the stranger towering over him.

"I'm functional if I can get past my crises." His face lit up when he saw Teflon holding a copy of *The Eagle's Gift*. Teflon was reading the book on the plane. "I *see* you like my favorite author. Maybe you can you tell me *the way*—" The old actor in Keith tried to make the scene dramatic. "—to the festival, Oracledang."

Teflon smiled. "I happen to be going to Oracledang."

Keith rose. "Want to finish the journey together?"

Teflon took a good look at the funny guy with the beard. He looked innocent enough. They could go to the stadium together, yeah, why not. With heads it was all about helping each other out. A fellowship of brethren. At least that's what Thelonious always yapped about. Besides, this Keith dude loved Castaneda books, as did Teflon's mom. Teflon was beginning to also.

He looked at the Californian and chuckled. "You got something in your beard." Peanuts in his facial hair, presumably from the flight. Teflon used his hands to mime the location. Keith rubbed out the crumbs then smiled a beautiful crescent moon.

"So what do you say?"

"Let's do it. Let's go see what this Oracledang thing is all about." Teflon picked up his Puma bag. "Carrying any baggage?"

"That's an interesting question."

Mikey the taper and the Princess sat in bumper-to-bumper traffic. Lake Shore Drive was in the midst of another renaissance as its landscape appeared dotted with cranes busied in the erection of condominiums. Later on, Thelonious will recognize the acronymic value of the avenue. In the meantime, Lake Shore Drive could have been the yellow brick road leading directly to Oz, to a golden place, or in this case, Soldier's Field. The entrance to the parking lot was backed up for a mile, a sign the circus had indeed come to town. The gridlock congested with headie cars, old vans and buses, SUVs covered in stickers, and fuel efficient rides like Mikey's Corolla with Florida plates, a proud indication that they had come a long way.

Mikey, in a state of bliss, cranked up a tape he'd recorded, a recent show from Red Rocks, Colorado. Although listening to live recordings all during the road trip, no bootleg sounded as sweet as the album played while waiting in line to enter Oracledang.

"I'm hungry," the Princess whined. She lowered the radio.

Mikey sighed. "Get food on the lot."

"I have to go the bathroom," she said.

"Again?"

They were four when they left Florida. Tommy the taper dropped out on a side trip to New Orleans. He grabbed his stuff when they were in the French Quarter for lunch, said he'd skip the festival and wait till one came South. Said he knew some heads in New Orleans, and he was feeling the Big Easy. Said it had nothing to do with anybody in the car, he had a change of heart, that's all. The other dropout, Richie the taper, did not leave with such subtlety. It happened in Missouri and started as soon as they entered the Show Me State. From the first exit on Interstate 55, the Princess began a two hundred mile rant. Oh my god . . . this puts the bore in boring . . . I want to see the arch in St. Louis . . . this state is faker than Alicia Goldman's chest . . . where are the cities . . . I have to pee . . . let's swim in the Mississippi . . . my neck's cramped . . . you mean we're not seeing Kansas City . . . I have a problem, all right. The defector, after calling the Princess words unworthy of a princess, grabbed his backpack, jumped out at a traffic light when they stopped for gas outside St. Louis, and ran.

"I'm bored—"

"Listen to the music."

Mikey turned the volume back up.

The Princess immediately lowered it.

"You take my privacy without bringing me company."

"If you're bored, Princess—*you're* boring."

"Mikey, look at that." The Princess pointed to a shabby dressed man on the side of Lake Shore Drive. He held a cardboard sign advertising tickets. "Let's ask him how much he wants?"

"I have mail-order tickets."

"What about me?"

"What about you?"

The Princess rolled down the window.

"Do you have tickets?" she screamed.

Mikey utilized the control he had on the power window. He locked her ability to use the switch on the passenger side door, and then raised her window from his side. "Don't talk to that guy," he said. "You don't want an overpriced ticket from a scalper."

"I want a ticket, Mr. Window-nazi."

"You're incorrigible—"

"I'm not corruptible, beast." She pinched Mikey's knee. "That tick..l..e..s...S-t-t...o...p."

Mikey the taper hit the accelerator with his spastic leg. They bumped the car in front of them hard enough so the air filled with the clumsy bungled noise of glass breaking. Not quite sure what glass broke where, they looked at each other and cringed.

"Oh-my-god," the Princess said. "What did you do?"

At the supermarket

The supermarket looked like a giant ant colony as heads shuffled in and out. Before every show, supermarkets in the surrounding area are overrun with heads picking up supplies for the concert: soda, beer, water, a variety of foods, cigarettes.

"Go get the dog food," Melody Rain said. "And get me a pack of cigarettes too, hon. I'll stay here and clean out the car."

"No, no, no, you stay here, clean out the car," Sky said. "And I'll go get the dog food. After all, he's my dog. Aren't you Bodhi, yes-you-are." Sky turned and played with Bodhi-dog.

Melody Rain sighed. "Why did I give you that other pill?"

"To the batcave." Sky skipped towards the supermarket.

Melody Rain sighed again. What a mess! The car looked totally cluttered. There was a lot of loose change. She picked up the coins and deposited them in the console under the radio, below the overflowing ashtray, next to the cell phone charger plugged into the lighter socket. A tan bag from Whole Foods lay on the floor. Melody Rain began to deposit trash into it. The granola bar wrappers, the box the disposable camera came in, the life section of *USA Today*, an empty container of organic orange juice, a matchbook from the La Quinta Inn, an empty pack of American Spirits, tissues, a crushed Diet Coke can. A half-consumed Peach Snapple rested in the cup holder. Why did Sky leave half-empty drinks? That girl never finished anything. The Snapple was tossed away. She found her blue lighter. The backseat looked more cluttered with Bodhi-dog there. Melody Rain lit an American Spirit and began to deposit more trash into the Whole Foods bag.

"Your mamma's fucked up, pup."

***

At the show, the first thing Sky did upon exiting the car was fling her body around Melody Rain. "Give me a hug, baby." Sky wrapped her up like leftovers. Like a piece of Saran Wrap, she clung to her nourishment with total transparency. "We made it." Melody Rain patted Sky on the back and looked down at Bodhi-dog. The retriever sat next to them, looking up with little black button eyes, panting like a wolf chosen to lead a crew in the Iditarod, the animal as happy and excited as its master to arrive at the festival. Melody Rain, to her discredit, let Sky's hug overwhelm her. Instead of stepping up to the powerful embrace, instead of countering the hug with a hug just as strong, Melody Rain surrendered to the hug, and quickly deflated. "Yeah, we made it."

They parked in the South lot, between the football stadium and the convention center. The cars, after paying twenty dollars to park, trickled into this place like drops of water from a leaky faucet, one after another, after another. The South lot could and would accommodate most of the heads arriving to the concert by car. Melody Rain knew there would be cars from all over the country. She knew there would be a party with plenty of goods to consume. And then there would be a concert where everyone could lose his or her mind for a few hours, before getting on with it all. Understanding this, she also knew the drill. Work first, and then play. And they too had work to do. So as Sky Tyler jumped up and down, clapping her hands, Melody Rain dug through the trunk looking for the old violin case holding their glass product. Meanwhile, Sky continued to busy herself with hugs. She introduced herself to four college kids from Tucson, Arizona. Sky hugged them all. "Keeper," she said. "It's like one big family."

"Do you have any mushrooms?" asked a college girl.

Melody Rain turned in time to see Sky embracing an Arizona boy. Melody Rain gripped the violin case with the *God Bless the Freaks* stickers. "Come on, baby." Melody Rain mixed baby with a hint of annoyance. "It's time to go to Shakedown Street."

Miracles

Shakedown Street is the heart of town. Town in this situation is the parking lot outside of the concert. At the beginning of each concert, Shakedown Street represents un-chartered territory. No one owns Shakedown Street. If one sells wares on Shakedown Street, no permits are issued. There are no reserved spots, or vending fees. Curtis and Geri made sure they arrived early, to lay claim to a prime piece of parking property. They drove the last ten hours nonstop, pushing *The Jedi* to its limit, ninety-five miles per hour. They had a miniature boutique to vend, more than enough gear to warrant a spot along the heart of Shakedown Street. Curtis unloaded the gear from the trunk. A fold-up table, two fold-up metal chairs, two racks, divided by dozens of hangers, plus boxes of clothes, multiplied by their special pillows, all of it equaled more enterprise than ten *Star Trek* episodes. Curtis thought maybe *The Jedi* should change its name to *The Enterprise*. While Curtis put together the racks, Geri sat down on a chair and began to unpack the boxes. Starting with patchwork dresses, she then unloaded the rest of their wares: patchwork pants, spinny skirts, apron-top shirts, tams, hemp backpacks, sock monkeys, and glass-pouches. Their setup quickly transformed into a conglomerate of clutter.

"We're in business," Curtis said.

Geri rummaged through the backseat of *The Jedi* and found her sewing gear, along with the bags of new fabrics she scored on the way. She rummaged for a certain pillowcase. "The Care Bears," she said. "I've been looking for the Care Bears for years." She found them at the Silvery Moon vintage shop in Nashville.

"Make sure the bears dance, sugar."

"We'll all be dancing bears in a few hours," Geri said.

Curtis began a version of the robot dance.

"I'm going to troll Shakedown. Stretch the legs."

Geri nodded. She picked up her fabrics. Curtis's robot dance sprung into motion. He disappeared. Geri settled in with a needle, thread, scissor, and a Care Bear pillowcase. In less than a minute, a custie came along. "Welcome home," Geri said, smiling.

***

The first thing Thelonious did was run around Shakedown Street with his index finger in the air. "WHO'S GOT MY MIRACLE?" he yelled. He had the inspired energy it took to will a miracle ticket. He couldn't stand still. Every bone in his body tensed with what he would call a boo-ya-ka boo-ya-ka buck buck energy. He charged a group of people playing hacky sack to see if anyone had an extra ticket. They needed a ticket, and had weed to trade, but they had no extras. Thelonious didn't care. He was happy to just be at Oracledang. He felt thrilled to see all the cars pulling into the lot, to see heads setting up coolers and barbecues, blasting radios. At one point he even found some heads freestyling, and he joined in the circle, making up rhymes, the valve of his mind feeling completely open. Still his top priority was getting two tickets for the festival, for him and Teflon. Thelonious knew if he really wanted a free ticket, a free ticket would receive him.

"I need a miracle," he screamed, along Shakedown Street.

In the center of Shakedown, Curtis materialized. He held a ticket in his hand. Curtis grinned. Thelonious smiled. Curtis smiled. Thelonious grinned. Their smiles and grins burst into laughter, and then they hugged each other. "I knew I'd see you here, Curtis."

"I wish I could miracle you, hee-hee."

"My nigga," Thelonious said. "Who's the miracle man?"

"You are," Curtis said.

Thelonious has never been shut out of a show. Eighty for eighty were his numbers, and more than half of the concerts he's seen were with free, miracle tickets. "You know I'll get a miracle, no worries." Thelonious smiled. "Where's your girl, Geri?"

"We're vending up Shakedown." Curtis pointed.

"Servin anything?" Thelonious asked, nonchalantly.

"I'm serving nugs. Want to see the new crop? It's sick."

Thelonious was so excited to see his friend from Florida. His head started to shake, as if a Charlie Parker solo carried his thoughts from synapse to synapse. Then his whole body began to quiver. He looked like a popcorn kernel on the verge of its pop.

"Give me another hug, C-love."

***

Geri sat on a fold up chair, a needle in hand. A few heads browsed her wares. An unopened Sammy Smith Oatmeal Stout lay on the table in front of her. "Thelonious!" She walked around the table and hugged him hard. "You made it." Curtis joined them in the embrace for a few seconds, and then he walked through the display of racks. Maneuvering around the customers, he ventured into the back seat of *The Jedi*. Geri and Thelonious stared at each other with wide smiles. "We didn't think we'd see you here."

"Yo, I had to get out of New York."

"Are things cool with Hurricane Clout?"

"Everything's straight. We have a show in three days."

"And you're in Chicago? Is the band cool with that?"

"It's all-good. New York was taxing my inspiration. A good festival and traveling will always charge my batteries. Besides, the album's almost finished. Girl, if things go right, this time next year, we'll be playing Oracledang. What's new with you?"

"*Papi*," she said, rubbing her tummy. "I'm pregnant."

"Thelonious," Curtis yelled, from the backseat.

"Congratulations, Ma. That's wonderful news."

Thelonious hugged Geri and joined Curtis in the backseat of *The Jedi*. He walked right into an atomic dank odor of nodule. Then a cumulus ganja cloud. Curtis was coughing. "Try this," he mumbled, passing Thelonious the chillum. Thelonious huffed, then exhaled a big happy Bob Ross-afro cloud of marijuana smoke, and he too coughed. "Here, kick-down," Curtis said, handing over half an ounce in a Ziploc bag. It looked like a fluffy pillow filled with green popcorn. "Don't forget the little guy, Monk, hee-hee."

"You rock, C-love," Thelonious said, still coughing.

"We're family."

"Yo." His coughing fit ended. "Geri told me the news."

"Crazy, huh?"

"What are you going to do?"

"We want to get out of Miami, buy some land."

"In the country?"

"We'd rather be on *our* farm than the king of New York."

"That's all you," Thelonious said, shrugging.

Kristen Chastity McGovern never experienced a show. Now KC could see all the hype for herself. "Look at the potential here. Wowzies. Let's definitely trow that open microphone."

"Let's trow that open microphone," Shore Morris said, laughing. He was absolutely amazed that such a pretty intelligent girl like KC could possess a voice like Tony Danza.

They found a parking spot in the South lot, more toward the front, on a corner. They could vend where they posted. Traffic would pale in comparison to Shakedown Street, but hey. Once settled, they spread a blanket on the floor, so KC could lay her books out. She had a beach chair in the trunk. And just like that they built a bookstore. Shore Morris could deal. As long as the operation had nothing to do with Barnes & Noble, Waldenbooks, or any corporation, he'd lend his support, independent all the way.

Really all they needed was a storefront sign. That's why Shore Morris went to work to set his flag atop KC's car. He attached the American flag to a plastic rod they picked up at a local hardware store. The plastic pole stretched thirty feet into the sky. The bottom hooked to the side of KC's roof. Their spot marked the only American flag on the South lot. Other flags blew in the panoramic winds, the pirate skull and crossbones, the rainbow gay pride, the Boston Red Sox logo, all symbols for someone to follow, and with the American flag a-flying anyone could find their way to an open microphone, all they had to do was follow Old Glory. The two heads admired the flag. They felt warm and nodded.

Shore Morris knew things. He had experienced many shows. He knew what to do when they arrived. "If we're really going to have that open microphone, let's make up some flyers."

They took it to task and created flyers to promote. Using black Sharpies, they wrote on the unlined side of index cards: OPEN MIC. Underneath that: SOUTH LOT 6:00 PM. Underneath, they wrote: LOOK FOR THE AMERICAN FLAG.

After they made a flyer, they placed the cards in a pile between them. They smiled and giggled, like two kids in art class. Shore Morris noted KC tossing her red tresses over her shoulder every time she finished a card. In a little while their pile grew.

"Head over there." Shore Morris pointed across the way. "I'll stay here, make more flyers, and hold down the fort for a bit."

"Cool beans," she said. "Be back in a few."

KC grabbed her backpack and filled it with books.

One summer day Keith Lipsiznowaz was asked to remove himself from his place of residence. That request came from a voice. Deep down, he knew the voice was right. But he also knew that someday he would return to himself. With nowhere else to go, he arrived at the airport and met a new friend, Teflon Jones. Sometime earlier, Jones also removed himself from his place of residence, vowing never to return. Can two displaced men share a car ride to Soldier's Field without driving each other crazy?

Can you hear the theme song from *The Odd Couple*?

Of course they got along. When it came down to it, both had friendly dispositions. They spent the car ride in conversation, chatting about the circumstances that led them to Chicago. At Soldier's Field, Teflon parked his rental car in the South lot. Keith insisted on paying for parking. As they walked toward Shakedown Street, the line to enter the parking lot still stretched south along Lake Shore Drive for as far as the eye could see, yet people were already scattered everywhere throughout the parking lots.

"So you forgot your phone?" Teflon said. "And you came here chasing a girl? How on earth do you plan on finding her?"

"I'll find her."

"How?"

"It's useless to plan on anything, except the now."

"Wack."

"You've never been to a show," Keith said.

"And you have?"

"I've seen a few," he said, "along *the way*."

They parked about fifty spots deep into a lot that seemed to stretch way further. As they walked past a bunch of cars, all with different state license plates, Teflon looked around and realized exactly how expansive the area was, particularly with the monster stadium in the foreground and the gigantic convention center behind. He felt relieved that he and Thelonious had cell phones, or how else would they find each other, by magically feeling out vibes like his kooky friend from Cali? Yeah, right, he didn't think so.

Once upon Shakedown Street, Teflon's world changed.

SHAKEDOWN STREET

```
        2b              2c              2d              2e
 *   car /\ car     car /\ car     car /\ car     **  car /\ car

    *:=:/\:=:    *    :=:/\:=:    **    :=:/\:=:   **      :=:
 *   :=:/\:=:  ****:=:/\:=:* *     *:=:/\:=:       **      :=:
     :=:/\:=:   *   :=:/\:=:* ******* :=:/\:=:      **     :=:
     :=:/\:=:  ***   :=:/\:=: * **** * :=:/\:=:    ****    :=:
 * :=:/\:=:   **  :=:/\:=: ******** :=:/\:=: **      * :=:

  *      ***********************************  ***  ** **
***********   ********* ***** **** ********* ****   *   * *
 * * *****  * ***** * **** ****** *************** *  *** *
***    ***    ** ***    the heart of town   ***** ***   ****
 * * *****  ***** ******  **  ** ** * *** ***    *  **   *
 *  :=:/\:=:      :=:/\:=:***********:=:/\:=:       * :=:
    :=:/\:=:  **   :=:/\:=: ******** :=:/\:=: ***     :=:
 *  :=:/\:=:      :=:/\:=:********** :=:/\:=:       * :=:
    :=:/\:=:      :=:/\:=: ******** :=:/\:=:   **    :=:
    :=:/\:=:  ***  :=:/\:=:***********:=:/\:=:       :=:
    :=:/\:=:      :=:/\:=: ********** :=:/\:=:       :=:
              row2              row3              row4
```

* represents a head

row 3 is Shakedown Street

:=: Kurtis and Geri's car The Jedi

** Teflon and Keith

"This is it," Keith said. "The mecca for heads."

"Damn," Teflon said, "this place is off-the-hook."

Shakedown Street. One aisle filled with thousands of heads. All the vendors. The overwhelming sounds and commotion. Everything came together in one big chaotic chorus of *who's-got-my ice-cold kind-gooey veggie-head-nug Molly-burrito doses*. Teflon felt dizzy.

"I've never seen anything like this."

"Where did your friend say to meet him?"

"He just said, 'I'll be on Shakedown.'"

"You kids want some doses?" asked a shirtless head, a log afloat in the river. "You don't want any doses, Teflon. Do you?"

"Nah," Teflon said. The kid with the doses floated away.

Keith's eyes were set on one thing, finding Sky. There were tons of dreadlocked women, but no Sky. He knew he'd find her. What interested Keith was that the closer he came to finding Sky, the less he obsessed. In fact, ever since he fell upon Teflon, he hardly thought of Sky. Why was that? He looked up at his new friend. There was something about that guy. Teflon walked in a state of open-eyed splendor. At first, he thought the festival scene might be filled with a bunch of hippies, a group often slovenly and too white for his comfort, but as he looked around, he realized there were people of all colors, cliques, and crews. Thelonious would've given him a big phat stoops for not trusting his friend's assessment, and for having pre-conceived judgments in general.

The two heads then came to a spot on Shakedown Street where on one side of the aisle a vendor sold drums and on the other side of the aisle a merchant worked posters and art prints.

"Yo, Keith. I wanna peep these drums, straight?"

"Cool. I'll be here," Keith said. He pointed to the vendor who sold posters. "I want to look at these." He paused and had an after thought. "Maybe I'll buy a poster for Sky or something."

***

Teflon always wanted a drum, like a bongo the people from the Caribbean played. At the drum vendor's stand, for sale or trade were a variety of ashiko and djembe drums, and an assortment of long wooden instruments in the shape of a cylinder. "What are these?"

"Didgeridoos," the vendor said.

"Didjerrydowhat?"

The vender explained that the didgeridoo was a long conical horn type-instrument used traditionally by the Aboriginal of Northern Australia. His didgeridoo's were carved from different woods like walnut, ash, maple, and redwood. Teflon picked one up and noticed how light it felt. Then he stuck his eye down the center of the instrument. "Are they hollow on the inside?" he asked.

"The insides are sealed with a liquid epoxy to provide extra strength and improved sound," the drum vendor pointed. "Then each end is wrapped with a rawhide sleeve sewn on with sinew."

"Bless you," Teflon said, pretending the vender sneezed.

"Try and play it."

Teflon blew. The resulting sound resembled a whoopee cushion. "Circular breathing, it's not easy," the drum vendor said. "Let me show you. It's very meditative." Teflon passed the didgeridoo over, and the head played it like magic: *EEEEEEEE JJJJJJUUUU AAAAAA*. The instrument produced a constant vibrating drone. Teflon relaxed. His feelings resembled a calm pond. His mind felt like a rock landing in the pond. And the drone was a ripple spreading across his waters: *EEEEEEEE JJJJJJUUUU AAAAAA*. If Teflon were a dog, his ears would've perked up, like the retriever who rolled up beside him. "Check it out, Melody Rain," Sky said. "Bodhi-dog likes the didgeridoo."

"I like em too," she said, looking Teflon up and down.

Bodhi-dog started to bark. "What up, dog?" Teflon placed his hand out for Bodhi-dog to sniff. He felt a little apprehensive. "Your dog ain't got a thing against black people, does he?"

Sky rubbed the dog behind the ears. "No, no, no. He hardly barks. Be cool, Bodhi. Find your center." The dog stopped barking. "I think he barks when he sees a ghost or an angel."

"I'm ghost if the dog makes a move," Teflon said. He bent down to pet the golden retriever. Bodhi-dog smiled, lifted a paw for a high-five, and licked Teflon's hand. "I think he likes me."

"What's not to like?" Melody Rain said.

Teflon noticed for the first time how attractive the two girls were. The girl with the dog was cute but a bit uppity on the energy, she couldn't keep still. But the caramel skinned girl. In an apron-top shirt, Melody Rain's breasts sent a shiver through him.

"I'm Teflon," he said, extending his hand for a shake.

"Melody Rain." She gave him a long hug.

Teflon enjoyed the ten-second embrace with Melody Rain. Her breasts covered his pectorals like honey. And she smelled sandy, like the beach at night. Once again, Teflon was feeling the vibe at the show. "Yeah," he said, smiling, "this is my first show."

"Well, you give good hug," Melody Rain said.

"Do you like to pound skins?"

Melody Rain looked to see if Sky was paying attention, and then she winked at Teflon, before answering the question. "Drumming is hella important here. It raises the spirit, it energizes the body, and it releases stress. There's unity in drumming."

Melody Rain jumped on a djembe and came with a slap:
PA PA GO PA PA GO
Sky started to play an ashiko:
GO GO GOON GO GO GOON
Teflon grabbed a drum and hit the middle for the bass:
GOON GOON
The vendor started back up with the didgeridoo:
EEEEE—JJJUUU—AAAAA
They had a nice little rhythm going, until Sky noticed Bodhi-dog wandering. "Shit," she said. Sky chased after him.

Everyone else stopped playing. "Guess I better follow my girl," Melody Rain said, with a regretful tone. She hugged Teflon.

***

Teflon Jones rejoined Keith Lipsiznowaz at the poster shop. He never received Sky's name, or he would've put one and one together and grabbed Keith immediately. "Yo, I met some hotties at the drum stand," Teflon said. "We were all jammin out."

"I heard," Keith said. "I was just about to come over."

Reunite on ice

It started when KC found herself a funky little boutique. "Look at this splat of a display," she said, her Brooklynese very evident. "I like this one a lot." KC held a mint-green apron-top shirt with strips of green cotton and patterned corduroy. The shirt had "peace" appliquéd across the bodice. "You make this?"

"Sure did, Red," said Geri, at work sewing a Care Bear on a pair of pants. "I'm Geri," she put down the patchwork, threw her

dreads over her shoulder, leaned forward, and hugged KC tight.
"That's Thelonious." He was sitting on the floor scribbling lyrics.

"I think I know Thelonious," KC said.

Thelonious looked at the pretty pale redhead. "You do?"

"I work with Lee at Shakespeare's. I've seen ya perform."

"Leroi Jones," Thelonious said. "That's my boy."

Thelonious and KC hugged long and hard.

"Lee speaks highly of you," she said. "Remember me?"

Thelonious shook the mop of black locks away from his
eyes. "Yeah, yeah," recognition drifted upward through the soil of
his mind like the roots of a sunflower in the spring. "At the
Bottom Line. You were with some dude who bought us shots."

"My ex-Dickie." KC laughed. "You have a good memory."

"Only when I'm on point," Thelonious explained. He
began to jump up and down. "Da-a-m-n, I wish you brought Lee
to Oracledang. I'm always trying to get him to come to a show."

"You like to read?" KC grabbed a paperback from her bag.

"You wrote this?" Thelonious leafed through the book.

"Read the book," KC said. "No point leafing through it."

"If you're sellin them," Geri began, "drop some here."

"Right on," KC said. She counted out ten books. "That's
like super cool beans. You know, I really like your patchwork. This
is quality stuff. How much do you want for this 'peace' shirt?"

"Keep it." Geri smiled a curve and everything was straight.

"You're kickin down a sixty-dollar shirt?" Thelonious said.

"Redheads bring luck," explained the superstitious
brunette, rubbing her belly. "Ain't nothing wrong with a lil' luck."

"N-i-i-i-ce," KC said. "Except I insist you keep the books.
Whatever money they bring you, just keep it. We'll call it a trade."

Shore Morris tapped KC on her shoulder.

"Hey," KC said. "Who's watching the set-up?"

"Our neighbors, fair people. I wanted to pass out flyers."

"Where'd you pick up this old dog?"

"Thelonious, good to see you again, brethren."

Curtis returned with Sammy Smith beers. He handed
Thelonious a Nut Brown Ale. The beer caps did not twist off so
Thelonious whipped out a blue lighter and popped the cap. Curtis,
with his own blue lighter, performed the same trick on an Oatmeal
Stout. "Can we drop off some flyers at your table too?" KC asked.

"Word, an open mic on the South lot," Thelonious said.
"I'll represent." Then he became overly excited. "Holy, Holy,
Shiite." He noticed Teflon. Thelonious put his beer on Geri's table
and ran full-throttle. He dodged random heads walking along

Shakedown. "W-A-A-S-S-S-U-P." He jumped on Teflon. They both fell to the floor. Teflon's Yankees cap fell. Thelonious picked up the hat and slapped his friend with it. "You made it, kid."

"This place is bananas," Teflon said. "Monk, meet Keith."

The three of them walked over to Curtis and Geri's booth.

When Keith first laid eyes on the smiling KC, something happened like the Fourth of July. "The marble statue of your smile," Keith said. "Like, whoa, you're made of pure ivory."

"Thanks," she said. Her pale cheeks turned blush. If she could've written a story about the moment in her Mead notebook, she would've probably named the character playing her Beringer.

"Four-Twenty," Curtis yelled. He held a nugget in hand.

"Definitely time for a 420," Thelonious said.

"Word," Teflon agreed.

"What's a 420?" KC asked.

"Time to smoke," Shore Morris replied.

"Oh," KC said, "I don't wanna smoke."

"I don't smoke, either," Keith said.

"Shaw," KC said. "I'm heading back. You staying here?"

"For a bit." Shore Morris grinned. "Then I'll flyer."

Curtis passed the bowl. "Do the honors, your honor."

"Nice meeting you," KC said. She looked around at her new friends. When she came to Keith, she stopped. "Wanna walk?"

Keith looked at Teflon. Teflon nodded.

"You know, since you don't smoke," KC resumed.

"Um, sure." Keith looked around. "Be well, everyone."

"That Keith guy straight?" Thelonious asked.

"He's straight," Teflon said. "He likes Castaneda books."

One man gathers what another man spills

It happened on the road where none are homeless: Shakedown Street. Melody Rain and Sky stood on the side of the market near a vendor selling quesadillas. Teflon and Thelonious walked along Shakedown after leaving *The Jedi*. They felt pleasantly high. Teflon lost himself in the sensory cacophony of the area. It was Thelonious who approached Sky. He thought she looked cute.

"Whatcha got in the case?" he asked. "Your Tec nine?"

Sky shrugged, limply holding the black violin case covered in *God Bless the Freaks* stickers. Then Thelonious looked hard at Melody Rain with squinted eyes. His face lit up in recognition. "Well I'll be damned," he exclaimed. "If it isn't Melody Rain."

"Hey." Melody Rain recognized Teflon but not Thelonious. She looked at the skinny white kid with the messy hair waving a finger at her. "Do I know you, dude?"

"You're kidding, right, bitch?" Thelonious said.

"Who you calling a bitch, suck-a?"

"Easy," Teflon said. He needed a striped shirt to ref.

"Thelonious, from New York. It's been a minute but yo."

"Thelonious, no way. I didn't recognize you."

"Excuse us for a minute."

Thelonious grabbed her by the arm and led her away.

Teflon felt awkward left alone with Sky. The girl seemed so out there. And she was too fidgety. "Maybe you should keep your dog on a leash," he said, in an attempt to make conversation.

"No way, man. Bodhi's free," she said. The leash dangled off her shoulder, next to her purse. She twirled the leash in the air.

Meanwhile, Thelonious led Melody Rain about twenty feet to the side of Shakedown Street, half-way between one aisle and the next, in an area between two cars. "Thelonious. Slow down. You're grabbing my arm hella hard. What's the deal, brother?"

"You left me in a warehouse," he yelled. "That's the deal."

"I didn't leave you, sugar. You left me."

"I woke up minus a thousand dollars and no girlfriend."

"I don't know anything about that."

"Don't give me that shit."

Melody Rain slid up to him and poked his chest. "Listen to me. You were nodding out. I went to the comedy club's bathroom. They let me into the showroom. Two hours later I went upstairs and you were gone. We were wasted remember? You had roofies. I said I was going to the comedy club. You're the one who left me."

"I don't remember eating any roofies," he whispered.

"This was two years ago, Thelonious. What do you want?"

"Someone jacked me," he said.

She looked at Thelonious with soft brown eyes. "Don't think I robbed you." She walked back over to Teflon and Sky.

She lit up a cigarette.

"What's the dill?" Teflon asked. "Is it all-good?"

"It's-all-whatevs-is-what-it-is," Thelonious said, rejoining them. "So, what's the word Melody, bird? Y'all working glass? I want to give my boy here a pipe. Want to trade for some nugs?"

The Shakedown Street crowd moved beside them like a tributary leading to Niagara Falls. The four sat down along its banks, removed from the flow. Sky opened up the glass case for Thelonious. A few pieces remained: two hammers, a sidecarb, and two chillums. "I like this one." Thelonious held a cylinder chillum.

"But it's broken," Melody Rain whined.

"Let's fix it." Thelonious dug into his head sack and grabbed a popcorn nugget. The girl's violin case stayed open and soon customers sauntered over. Thelonious dunked a nugget in the pipe and passed it to Teflon. Teflon took a monster hit and handed it to Melody Rain. The Pyrex glass already began to change color.

The christened pipe shared itself with anyone who asked. Sky packed the next one. After two bowls, everyone felt extremely lifted. In the process, Sky and Melody Rain sold out of glass. With work out of the way, the girls were free to enjoy the scene.

"You seem tense," Teflon said. "Relax."

"Yeah, we got good music coming at us," Thelonious said.

"I haven't had much sleep," Sky said.

"You want to bump an Oxy?" Thelonious offered.

"You have OxyContin?" Melody Rain said.

"I don't know," Sky said.

"It'll take the edge off you," Melody Rain said, smirking.

"Let's walk," Thelonious said. "You want to come?"

"I want to explore Shakedown Street," Teflon said.

"Sure? We won't be long. We need to score two miracles."

"I don't want to be around you sniffin pain pills. You know it ain't my steez, dog. I'll catch up to you on the rebound. Bye, ladies. Monk, just shout me on the cellie when you're done."

Teflon blended into the Shakedown bizarre. Cutting over an aisle, the other three and the dog escaped the crowded main street. Thelonious forged ahead and the girls followed. They headed toward the South lot. Poor Sky didn't notice the amber crystal that fell from her skirt pocket. The old relic of a crystal, her good luck charm, chipped on the ground, rolling into a discarded Coca-Cola cup like its destiny was a game of cosmic Yahtzee.

Sky also forgot her violin case, covered in *God Bless the Freaks* stickers. The case was picked up in a minute by a Shakedown straggler who thought: sweet zu-zus, ground-score!

'LUDE—*the rock star steez—a message from Thelonious Horowitz*

That was the first time I seen Melody in two years. Think I
believed one word of her story? Stoops. She's a liar. And she
knows what she is. She's cool with it, so in some ways, believe it or
not, I'm cool with it. I can forgive her and still chill with her cause
she's family. To me, everyone in this network, everyone at this
festival, is like family, mos definitely if we've been through some
shit together. You don't have to *like* everyone in your family, but
you better still *love* everyone in your family. Can you understand
that? Just don't think I believed her. She robbed me that night in
the empty warehouse. She probably wasn't alone. She'd nevah
admit it, but that girl has a problem with the H. Betcha she still has
that bench warrant in Texas too. Melody Rain's got mad secrets,
but for real, who doesn't? I mean like whatevs, come on, now.
We're here for the music. The show must go on. And of course all
the headz are gonna shake what the good lord gave them. And at
the end of every song hands will rise high into the air, some will
clap, some will throw a variety of signs, like the hang loose thumb
and pinky \m/ the two fingered peace sign \/ and the three
fingered jammy \\n/ And at the end of every song the crowd's
energy will expand then erupt and explode with screams. Yellin
whistlin yeah yeah we're gonna get down tonight. Like what: okay,
tens of thousands of beautiful open minded young spirits, tens of
thousands of screaming, carousing, sweating souls. Tens of
thousands of spinnin, shakin, bouncing, people—rollin trippin
puffin sippin—peeps escapin, reuniting, comin home, baby, home.
There's no way some old school drama's gonna get in the way of
this. Funk all of that. Nothing could get in the way of this show.

Thelonious led the girls down the grassy hill on the backside of Shakedown Street. They crossed 18th Street into the South lot. Sky walked Bodhi-dog on the leash because of the heavy traffic. They roamed the meaty South lot, toward the distant convention center, venturing to an obscure area of the car park known as the nitrous zone. Two five-foot nitrous-oxide tanks—on the opposite side of the same aisle—stood shadowed by the narrow enclosures between parked cars. Little lines formed at the nitrous tanks, as heads waited for a fix. Some were getting their first dose. Others clutched deflated orange balloons, a look of desperation in their eyes. More heads were scattered about the nitrous zone vicinity, huffing away, fastened upon half-filled balloons. Heads in the nitrous zone were too fucked up to care or notice anything. It could've been 1871, and Chicago could've been burning down for all they knew or cared. Here, in a dark den of the parking lot, Thelonious brought the girls. They found an empty area between a Volvo with Arizona plates and a SUV from Indiana.

"Do you have a book?" Thelonious asked.

Melody Rain had a book in her bag, *The Spirit of Zen*, by Alan Watts, a gift from Sky. The pages were never turned. Thelonious dug in his pants and grabbed a quarter and his wallet. He fetched a dollar bill and a silver NYPL access card. "Roll this." He gave Melody Rain the bill. Thelonious crushed up an eighty-gram OxyContin by pressing it down on the book with the quarter. Using the library card, he ground the powder, and broke off three thick lines. Melody Rain blasted a line up her right nostril and passed the rolled-up dollar to Thelonious. He followed suit, and then passed the bill to Sky. Sky snorted a line, and her nose hairs instantly burned. All three of them had the sniffles.

"Let's do a balloon," Melody Rain said.

"Bad idea. Let's concentrate on tickets," Thelonious said.

"Come on. We're here. Get three balloons," Melody said.

"Aiight," Thelonious said. "One nitrous balloon each."

Thelonious walked over to the tank. The line stood four deep, but moved quickly. "How many?" the nitrous vendor asked.

"Let me get three for ten," Thelonious said, over the *sssssbhhh* sound of gas. "I got two girls waiting for me over there."

"They're five bucks each."

"Come on, bruddah. We're all headz here."

The nitrous vendor smiled, took the ten bucks, and filled up three orange balloons. The vendors that sell the gas are involved in the most lucrative trade on the parking lot. The high lasts less than three minutes and the controlling effect on the mind almost guarantees a desire for a repeat expenditure. The nitrous zone is infamous for sending customers to the ATM. Nitrous vendors receive gas from one of two places. Either they steal it from a hospital, or they buy it from a company that supplies racecars with the booster. No matter where the gas comes from, the product is said to be of a medical grade, the difference being nitrous oxide used in cars is supposedly laced with chemical additives.

Thelonious walked over to the girls. He handed the balloons around. The three started huffing. "What's your name, anyway?" he said, in a deep voice filled with gas.

"Sky," she said, laughing at his deep voice.

"I'll probably forget in a second."

The more gas they inhaled, the more removed they became. They had to sit down before they fell down. All three sat quiet. Sky broke the silence. "I want another balloon."

"I want to go look for tickets," Thelonious said.

"Pretty please," Sky said.

"Hippie crack." Melody Rain giggled. "Wah, wah, wah."

**

Thelonious returned with three more balloons. He passed them around. Melody Rain and Thelonious took a hit and relaxed. Her foot secured the leash of Bodhi-dog, and the retriever lay on the floor, panting. Sky, breathing back into the balloon, went for the fish. Repeatedly, she huffed in, and then exhaled back into the balloon, as if hyperventilating into a paper bag. Eyes fluttering, body twitching, the balloon, a quarter filled, slipped from her fingers. The balloon flew away, releasing the gas like flatulence. It passed Thelonious's outstretched hand. He tried in vain to save it. In the meantime, Sky fell to the floor with her body convulsing like a fish out-of-water. To the outside world, she lay on the floor, spastic. In her mind, an immediate sense of clarity and understanding overtook her. She could see things. She could see a grid. She was being pulled forward and backward along an electric grid composed of luminous red spaghetti filaments. In this electric grid, she could see flashing images. An image from her past surfaced. Keith Lipsiznowaz drawing henna hands with Mayan eyes on her body. Then an image of the now—she saw herself with a balloon the moment before she fell into the fish. Finally, still in flux, she encountered an image she didn't recognize. It looked like Keith staring at her through a window, but she couldn't tell for sure. Then everything moved faster, as if she was a piece of cotton being sucked through a vacuum cleaner. She couldn't tell if she moved forward or backward, but an important secret appeared to be close by. A secret worth dying for. The, big, ultimate, secret, is. A bright image she couldn't reach. She couldn't quite reach the illuminated image and spun in dizzy circles. Things slowed down.

Sky opened her eyes and curled upward.

"You're back."

"I've been here before, Melody."

"*Déjà vu?*"

"*Déjà voodoo* is more like it. Where's Thelonious?"

"He went to get more whippits."

"If I do one more balloon I will figure out the why."

"The why?"

"The why in U.I.R.B.Y."

"Whatever." Melody Rain looked around for Thelonious.

***

Thelonious clutched three deflated balloons. He felt a bit dizzy, and a slight taste of rust lingered in his mouth. Granted, he liked nitrous oxide enough, but still, his original itinerary did not include getting cracked-out in the nitrous zone. You wind up in the nitrous zone if you can't get into the show, or, after the concert, late at night, when you want to take your head to a whole other level. This was his third trip to the same nitrous vendor. He noticed how the vendor looked like the kid Keith that Teflon met. At least they both had the same out-of-control beard, a strand of that brown, reddish, Nordic, sort. Thelonious wished he could sport a beard. His own facial hair grew in patches. His beards never amounted to much, like a winter storm where the snow didn't stick.

The nitrous vendor, with a wad of cash in one hand, grabbed the balloons and began to fill them. "Three for ten, right, brother?" Thelonious asked, offering up a ten-dollar bill.

"Three for twenty," he said. The oldest trick in the book. Get them hooked, then up the price. "And I'm not your brother."

"Yo," Thelonious said, over the *sssshhhh* of the gas. "Keep it real. I got shorties waiting. This is my last trip, word is bond."

He placed the money in the vendor's hand.

The vendor crumpled the ten-dollar bill and threw the money back at him. "Watch out," the vendor said, moving around Thelonious to sell the balloons. The fiending customers would pay whatever the seller wanted. Thelonious didn't catch the ten-dollar bill. He let it fall, bit his bottom lip, and looked around the scene. The throng of people surrounding him looked pathetic. Then a fight broke out in front of the tank. The conflict appeared to be over the gas. One head hogged another head's balloon. The brutes actually came to blows. That's when something snapped in Thelonious. He felt a level of stress ten times stronger than when he lost it on the train heading to see Teflon play ball, when he decided to leave New York to come to the show. The stress released an urge, uncontrollable, dark, impossible not to act upon. He trembled. If his mother saw him, she'd have insisted he took his meds. Instead, he sneered, picked up the crumpled money, and threw it in the vendor's face. "We got ourselves a problem now."

***

Melody Rain and Sky hadn't moved. They looked up at Thelonious. By the fast and disjointed way he walked back, they knew something bad happened. Thelonious held his cell phone to his ear, but since his lips weren't moving, whoever he called must not have answered. Without leaving a message, he put the phone back in his pocket. "So, uh, no balloons?" Sky wondered.

"Nah," he barked. "I shook that feeling. You can too."

"I don't know what you're talking about, Mister," she said. Sky moved her head, and her dreads whipped about. "Nope. Not me. No idea." Sky stood up and spun around. Her skirt expanded, like a balloon. "I can't stand still. I think I have to walk now."

She moved in the direction of the nitrous tanks.

"Looks like she wants a whippit," Melody Rain said.

"Your girl's a wingnut."

"She hasn't slept in awhile, that's all. Now the gas got her."

"Them nitrous vendors fake the funk. We should take-em out. On the real for real. I need to make a phone call to make sure of something." He dug in his jeans and retrieved the cell phone.

Whomever he called didn't answer, but the young rock star left a message along the lines of: yo, stoops, call me, kid. I'm in Chi-town. I know you're here. It's mad important. It's Thelonious.

"Take them out?" she repeated. "You're aggro. Chill."

"I'm not chillin. Ain't no chillin. Not now." Thelonious made another phone call. "Teflon, it's me. You need to find Curtis and meet me in front of the South lot. There's a situation." Thelonious listened and then responded. "Not now, brother, right now." More chatter. "Okay, see you there." Thelonious hung up. "It's going down." He stared at Melody Rain until she looked scared. Even Bodhi-dog yelped. This was not the same kid she remembered, nope, not even close. She wouldn't mess with this kid now, and neither should anyone in their right mind if they saw the uneven look in his eyes moments before he stormed away.

***

In a minute, Sky Tyler returned carrying four balloons.
"We can get all the balloons we want for free."
"How'd you hook that up?"
"I let the nitrous guy stick his hand down my skirt."
"You're not wearing underwear."
"So," Sky said, holding up the balloons.
"Baby, don't go wasting your nectar on them fools."
Melody Rain looked at the encompassing hippie crack scene. She glanced in the direction where Thelonious headed, but he was out of sight. She sighed heavy and turned to her girlfriend. "Sit down next to Momma and give her one of them whippits."

Mikey the taper didn't want his car upstairs on Shakedown Street because he felt the music equipment would be safer in the garage below, an area that was less populated. On the garage floor, atop a comforter, he laid out a bunch of video and audio recording equipment, and tools. The Princess and he sat there since their arrival, an hour already. "I used to have a 75ES, but I had dropout problems from the get-go. It was in the Sony service center as much as it wasn't, so I gave it back before the warranty expired."

"Uh-huh," the Princess said.

"So yeah, I got a new DAT player, the DA-30. Anyway, it won't let me make back-up copies in DAT form because of the stupid Serial Copy Management System, so to defeat the SCMS, I need to take off the top cover, find a certain short jumper wire, and clip it." He described the process like a surgeon, as he carefully took apart the DAT player and made his way to the wire that needed to be cut. "Clippers." The Princess looked down at her nails, lost in thought, or lack of thought, a certain meditation. She was not aware of any meditation, unless it entailed being bored.

"Clippers, please."

"Do you have to do this now?" the Princess whined.

"CLIPPERS."

The Princess looked annoyed. She passed Mikey the tool he asked for, a pair of wire cutters on the floor, equally between the two of them. He cut the wire, as if diffusing a bomb. "Cool," he said, brightening, "I can make perfect clones all day long."

The Princess yawned. She looked around. She heard loud drums coming from upstairs. The people that passed by in the garage, and there were a lot, all seemed to be heading upstairs. She wanted to go upstairs. The Princess did not owe this guy. She hardly even knew him. Connections were made all the time. Connections were broken. If it came down to wiring, if anyone could understand, this guy, this thing, this chauffeur, he could.

"The thing with bootlegs is we're not really bootlegging. The bands want us to record them. They want us to circulate their live music. It creates a broader fan base for them. What bothers me is when they create guidelines for us to follow. Bring your own power, duh! Don't go overboard with equipment, please! Don't tell me what to do or bring. I've been doing this for years. And shows aren't the easiest thing to deal with. I still like the parking lot scene and the vending, but I've come to loathe the traffic, crowds, young punks, and teen drunks. It's all about sound. I've spent thousands of dollars on equipment for the sound. Then I get into the show and because of guidelines they herd us into taper areas, always behind the soundboard. Don't get me wrong, Princess, I love taper zones, but if I can get in front of the soundboard, I'm going for it. Look at my collection, whether I traded for the tapes or recorded them myself, almost all of my DAT archives have FOB not TS on the label. That's Forward of Board not Taper Section—"

"Okay, like, sorry, Bubba," interrupted the Princess. "I have to leave you now."

***

The Princess walked around Shakedown Street. She felt like a piece of jigsaw in the wrong puzzle, like there were a thousand other pieces, but no one and nothing could fit, no matter how hard she tried to connect. It was puzzling, a puzzling game, indeed. She felt ready to sell her body for money to get back to Florida. She would have sucked some to get home, except she'd never put a penis near her mouth. It was an expression. The Princess didn't do that to anyone. No way, like not even. That was something a slutbag like Alicia Goldman did. Anyway, she felt out-of-place at the show. The scene reminded her of back home, at the Pompano Beach pier, Fisherman's Wharf, like total scalawags everywhere. Yet the Soldier's Field event still resembled a party. A different sort of party then she attended back in the Coral Springs suburbs. Parties where they gathered at the home of Alicia Goldman whenever Goldman's parents went out of town, they drank keg beer and made a mess until the cops came at eleven and forced everyone to leave. This Soldier's Field event was different, and she felt terribly out-of-place. Then the Princess bumped into Shore Morris. She was looking at her nails when she crashed right into the bald Asian. The encounter resulted in the Princess falling to the ground, like a burlap sack of potatoes. "Watch where you're going," she yelled. A hand extended and she reluctantly grabbed it.

"Shore Morris, a pleasure," he said. "What's your name?"

"The Princess. But you can call me nothing."

"Ahh, nothing, very good. I like nothing a lot. Very existential," he said. "Still, the Princess is a phat name for a head."

"Who are you calling fat head, Mr. Clean?"

"Clean I will be. Clean done with promotion. Take this, my last flyer. You are cordially invited." He passed over the flyer for the open microphone at six o'clock. The Princess looked at the advertisement, scrunched it, and threw it on the floor.

"Heads don't litter, Missy."

"My head didn't litter." She smirked. "My hands did."

He rocked back. "You don't know what a head is."

"Fine," she conceded. "What's a head?"

"A head's ahead."

"What does that mean?"

"A head is someone that's conscious."

"I'm conscious."

"Are you *really*?"

"Conscious of bullshit when I hear it."

Shore Morris laughed.

"You've never been to a show, have you?"

They looked at each other and they had their moment. Like so many moments in so many relationships. So many watershed moments when the first seed is planted, the first spark connected. It didn't mean anything would grow. It didn't ensure that whatever was created wouldn't break down. The Princess tilted her head to a forty-five degree angle. He wasn't that dirty, considering. And he was built nice. Shore Morris curled his bottom lip over his upper lip. He stroked his baby-skinned chin, as if a goatee grew there. He thought she needed a guide. He could be her teacher. Amidst the organized confusion of Shakedown Street, time stood still until someone bumped into the Princess.

Shore Morris grabbed her by the arm and walked off to the side where it looked safe to stand idle. "The show's a complicated place." They made their way to an old, rusty, receptacle. The bottom of the barrel appeared charred in black. In white paint, on the side of the garbage, the words "HOT COALS" were written. Shore Morris deposited the flyer into the receptacle and walked along the side of Shakedown, his pupil in tow. "Heads can be divided into two groups, wrecking-crew and G-crew—"

"G-crew? Is that some gangster rapper crap?"

"G-crew is more like a state-of-mind, a kind, no chemicals, Save-the-Earth, enjoy-your-being, mean-people-suck, hugs-not-thugs, right-on, brother, kind-of-vibe." The Princess had no idea what Shore Morris was talking about, but he did have nice pectorals. "Then there's wrecking-crew," he continued. "Wrecking-crew constitutes heads intent on making a ruckus. A little bit of anarchy. Out of eighty thousand here, maybe five-percent are pure G-crew, and five-percent pure wrecking-crew. The other ninety-percent of us lie in-between, more toward the G-crew side, but still possessing characteristics of both. Like I said, G-crew and wrecking-crew are more like states of mind than actual clubs or cliques. And everybody has a little bit of both in them. Get it?"

"No," the Princess said. "Not at all. But you can buy me a drink, if you want." She tossed Shore Morris a patented princess smile. She flashed her full teeth and made her blue eyes sparkle.

Wrecking-crew steez

Fifty yards from the American flag, Thelonious huddled with his friends, Teflon and Curtis. They never saw Thelonious so frustrated. "Don't front on me. I know what you're thinking. You think I'm a crackhead. You think I'm upset because the little baby from New York couldn't get his balloon. This is about respect."

"But you were there buying balloons," Teflon said. "You had a choice to say no to their gouging. You had a choice to walk off and continue on with the day. We need tickets, remember?"

"That bearded shiite threw money at me." Thelonious was shaking. "You try me, I'm tryin you! Stoops! That's all there is to it! I ain't going out like that. I don't give two shits about that prick. Fuck that wack-ass motherfucker to my very last breath!"

"Then you get him," Teflon said. "Why do you need us?"

"Because he doesn't work alone," Thelonious said.

"You really want to take out the nitrous?" Curtis said.

"Believe me. A lot of headz in this scene don't like the nitrous gas. It doesn't belong on the parking lot. It'll be all-good. Maybe it's about time someone stepped up and made it happen."

Teflon looked at the surroundings. He raised his hand and threw two fingers into the air, a peace symbol. "I thought all of this shit was supposed to be about peace signs? And music? And love?"

"It's about energy," Thelonious yelled. "They come with darkness. We bring the light. It's Common Sense. Chicago. The Light. Sometimes the light's all shining on me." Curtis and Teflon looked at each other and shrugged. Neither ever saw Thelonious so agitated; however, they were also aware he was a little bit bipolar.

"I don't know, Monk." Teflon's gut said no. He always listened to his gut. Always. "You're not thinking this through."

126

"You walked away from the NBA. That was crazy, son. I haven't said anything because you followed your heart. And I got your back. You watch out for your brethren. You know this, man."

Teflon knew it like he knew a basketball was round. Of course he felt inclined to stand behind Thelonious. Yet the bad feeling lingered. His bellybutton rattled. Something in his intuition insisted. "If you really need me," Teflon said. "I got your back."

"Fuck it, hee-hee," Curtis said. "Let's get gangsta."

***

Just next to the South lot, off of 18th Street, sitting on the grassy top of an incline, an area of Museum Park known as Sledding Hill, on top of this precipice, Chief Black Hawk faced east, into Burnham Bay, into the stirring wind, into tomorrow.

The bumrush

Curtis and Teflon flanked Thelonious. They walked slowly with their heads raised high. They all wore the New York City evil eye. An irate Thelonious looked angrier when he noticed Sky and Melody Rain glued to the same spot. The soundtrack of the area was still laced in *sssshhhh*. There were two tanks, with people scattered about the zone. Thelonious spotted his nemesis, the red-bearded vendor. "Let's do this fast and hard!" Thelonious barreled through heads waiting for balloons and knocked the tank into his opponent. Thelonious, his enemy, and the tank fell on the ground *crash zowie* then Thelonious threw a forearm into his foe's face knocking his mug back *crraack* then Thelonious came down with an elbow right across the vendor's lip *zamm* Thelonious continued the assault *sock flrbbbbb ooooff* until two nitrous runners jumped on him *rakkk kapow* but Teflon and Curtis jumped on the runners when they tried to get into the fray *krunch zlonk ouch whamm klonk zap urkkk zzzzzwap* with the valve open, the fallen tank continued to spill its contents into the air *sssshhhh* until all the gas in the tank exhausted. The red-bearded vendor, and two of his runners, lay on the ground, a bloody pulp. Thelonious dug through the vendor's pockets and grabbed a thick wad of money. "Fuck you, bi-atch." Thelonious crazily spat in the bloody face of his nemesis.

"What are you doing? Why are you taking their loot?" Teflon didn't like this. His mother didn't raise him to be a thief, except it was too late. There was no turning back. This was bad.

Curtis eyed the other tank. "What about that guy?"

Thelonious ran up to the second nitrous seller and bowled the tank over *crash whack zamm* the vendor fell along with a couple of heads waiting for balloons *splatt* a couple of kids fought for their right to a balloon *pow boff* but most of the heads in the area sat by, too stoned to react, the whole scene was dumbfounded as eight people locked in a melee *eee-yow ooooff zowie thunk kayo* the vendor closed the valve on the tank but Thelonious went for it, along the way flipping a head over his shoulders *thunk* he turned the valve on the tank and the gas shot into the air *ssssshhhh* a few ambitious hippie-crackheads ran to the tanks and tried to suck the nitrous from the air. One head almost lost his lip in the frozen spray of gas. When the scene cleared, a bunch of heads lay on the ground, bloody, and in pain. Teflon, Curtis, and Thelonious stood alone hardly scratched. Teflon lost his Yankees hat, that's all. They did it. They cleared the lot of nitrous oxide. Then Thelonious robbed the other nitrous vendor without any qualms. Then all three of them dipped the nitrous zone so fast it was like they weren't even there.

∗∗∗

"Did you see that?" Melody Rain asked.

"See what?" Sky popped up.

She had been on her back in a nitrous space-out.

"That shit was gangsta."

"What was gangsta?"

"I don't think he knows what he just did."

"Who?" Sky asked. "What happened?"

"They looked good, though, especially Teflon."

"I'm getting to go a balloon."

"You do that, Sky," Melody Rain said, sarcastically.

"Om." Sky looked around. "Have you seen Bodhi-dog?"

Thelonious had not been in a scuffle since a gig at Roseland the previous summer, when he kicked some dude in the head while stage diving. This scrap felt good. His blood never pumped like it did when they ran away from the nitrous zone.

All three of them ran like Walter Payton, slicing through aisles, eventually dashing out of the South lot, across 18th Street, and into the garage below Shakedown Street.

They didn't say a word to each other until they made it to the safe haven garage. Then the adrenaline reigned. Adrenaline soaked Thelonious's spirit and flooded the dharma of his sphere with revelry. "The world is ours," Thelonious said, out-of-breath.

"Okay, okay," Teflon said. "But you didn't say anything about robbing them. What was that about? I've never robbed anyone in my whole life, Monk. That is definitely not my steez."

"It just hit me like a lightning bolt," Thelonious said. "Their money comes from poisoning heads. They shouldn't walk away from this parking lot the better for it."

"You know who runs the nitrous," Curtis said.

"Who runs the nitrous?" asked Teflon.

"They'll be looking for us now," Curtis said.

"Trust me. It's all-good. I have a plan. For starters, there's a wad in these here jeans." There was so much money in his back pockets, his derriere looked like a pillow. "I need somewhere to count the cream and divide it three ways. We'll work this out."

Then someone called for Curtis. They turned toward the squeaky voice. On the floor, only ten yards away, sat a rotund fellow, androgynous in appearance. Mikey the taper was on the ground surrounded by video and audio recording equipment.

"What is that?" Teflon asked.

"Custie of mine," Curtis said.

The three meandered over to Mikey.

"Can I use your car for a sec?" Thelonious said.

"What's in it for me?"

"Here." Thelonious dug in his pocket and procured a twenty-dollar bill. Mikey gladly accepted the money and Thelonious jumped into the car with Florida plates. "I'll be out in a minute."

"What's all this equipment for?" Teflon asked, mildly interested. That's all it took to set Mikey off. He went on and on about video and DAT recording, about how he leads a taper tree, with a bunch of branches and leaves, all sending him blanks and postage for a bootlegged copy of the concert. It didn't matter that Curtis and Teflon weren't listening. They wouldn't normally be interested in that kind of stuff, especially under the circumstances.

***

"Let's bounce." Thelonious jumped out of the car and walked away. His pace forced Teflon and Curtis to catch up, after brushing Mikey off with a goodbye. They walked in silence toward the back of the garage. Instead of heading up the stairwell to Shakedown Street, they remained on ground level and walked toward the pedestrian underpass. The pedestrian underpass served as an official entrance into the stadium, a depot for the river of foot traffic that would converge from the tributaries of the Shakedown parking lot and the walkway that led from the Lake Shore Drive pedestrian underpass. Not yet time to enter the show, heads still milled, some venturing toward will-call to pick up tickets, others wandering around the stadium, perhaps to play on the Great Lawn. A vendor with a blue cooler packed with beers picked a good location to sell his wares, as did a girl selling a variety of hemp necklaces. Thelonious bought beers and led Teflon and Curtis to a little grassy knoll in this area, before the underpass, with Soldier's Field hovering behind the tunnel. They settled on a tiny incline, plopping on the grass with grunts. Teflon and Curtis adjusted their necks. As adrenaline wore off, it became apparent that maybe they didn't escape the melee without a bruise or two.

"Six-thousand dollars," Thelonious said.

"I'm not for sale," Teflon said. "I had my boy's back."

Thelonious had a feeling Teflon wouldn't want the money. Besides the moral implications, when Teflon's mother died she left her only son a trust for when he turned twenty. His 20th birthday was a couple of months away. And if you divorced a womanizing All-star basketball player, oh boy, won't that kitty be meowing.

"What should we do?" Curtis asked, hiding behind his dreads. "Should we fuck with this money? You said it's all-good. Even I don't think so. What do you know that I don't, Monk?"

Thelonious couldn't take his eyes off a scalper. The scalper, obvious in nature by his attire, was trying to sell a young girl a ticket. The girl held out three bills, and the scalper shook his head. The girl offered more money by procuring another bill. The scalper took the money, thought about it, then apparently changed his mind. He returned the money to the girl and walked away.

"Thelonious, are you listening?"

"What if there were no more scalpers?"

"You want to roll the scalpers?"

"We can buy the scalpers out." Thelonious looked composed. Serious would be the better word. He didn't shake. He wasn't smiling. His hair did not block his vision, and his firm eyes would've made Phil Helmuth fold in the World Series of Poker

The young girl who tried to buy a scalped ticket walked by the pedestrian underpass. Thelonious watched her as his friends mulled over his plan. "Yo, shortie," he said. "Come here a sec."

Jupiter Healy, a beautiful, bright-eyed believer, lived in the dorms of a local art school, dorms with cages on the windows, dormitories walking distance from Soldier's Field, dormitories where she hung her anonymous poetry inside bathroom stalls.

"How much did that scalper want for a ticket?"

"A hundred bucks," Jupiter said. "Ticket only cost fifty. I offered him eighty. Guess I'll have to miss Oracledang this year."

"Don't go," Thelonious said. "Kick it on Shakedown Street. Keep your head up. Tickets have a way of materializing."

Jupiter smiled for the first time since she left the scalper. "Maybe I will hang." Why not? After all, there was action. Maybe she'd spend her money on a shirt, or a hat, or something cool from the girl selling the patchwork. "Thanks a lot," she called back.

Teflon spoke. "You do realize if you buy all the tickets from the scalpers you'll be making their day. Hello, Monk. You won't be hurting them. You'll be hooking them up tremendously."

Thelonious looked at Teflon and laughed. "Scalpers pollute this scene. They're wick wick wack. Scalpers aren't headz. Headz don't gouge. Headz kick-down. So we hook them up like what? At least for one show we won't have to look at the fuckers."

"What will you do with all the tickets?" Teflon asked.

Curtis knew the answer to that one.

"He'll kick-down miracles."

"Won't be one head not getting into Oracledang."

"It's a good idea, Thelonious," Curtis said. "But what about the nitrous money? This is turning too complicated for me."

"I need a favor, C-love."

Curtis usually wore a smile on his face, but not now. He knew the Falafia controlled the nitrous. Bad enough he already robbed the Falafia, now he was being asked to forfeit his share of the score. Why was Thelonious putting him in this situation? Of course it was a great idea. Take the money you robbed from the nitrous dealers, buy out the scalpers, and give away the tickets.

Brilliant! One problem. Curtis could only think of Geri and her swelling belly. "I'm on my own mission. We're trying to buy land."

"I'll give you your third," he said. "That's two g's. That'll help you and Geri a little bit. Just let me keep Teflon's share."

"Of course," Curtis said. "And I'm sorry, Monk."

"I understand completely, daddy. There's no need to apologize. You earned that cream." Thelonious smiled and the light in his smile changed the whole tone. "Let's not worry. And this one's on me, boys. It'll be my inspired mission. Check it: a one-two, *fakin the funk, the bunk punks, scalpin chumps, they don't belong here anyways*," he busted. "And don't you two worry about the people behind the nitrous. Thelonious Horowitz got it all taken care of."

After Hurricane Horowitz stormed through, the nitrous zone looked as wrecked as a trailer park following a Category Four. The hippie-crackheads already abandoned the area to wander the parking lot like lost souls. Maybe they'd find Shakedown Street. Maybe they'd make it into the show. More than likely, the nitrous heads will stay on the lot, get drunk, and pass out someplace unsanitary. The nitrous zone, once a goldmine, now resembled a ghost town. Still, the bearded nitrous seller remained. People called him Choke. He was an ugly head, in his early twenties, bushy, just a burly man. The burly man, in a nod to irony, hailed from Burlington, Vermont. Currently, Choke took on the collection of the emptied tanks. The five-foot tanks could and would be refilled. The bruised and sore nitrous vendor grudgingly loaded the tanks into the hatchback of a Ford Explorer with Michigan plates.

Two California girls also remained in the nitrous zone. One girl frantically ran about calling the name of her dog, "Bo-o-o-dhi—" The other girl casually strolled over to the man loading nitrous tanks into the Ford Explorer. "You all right?" asked Melody Rain. Choke looked at her and said nothing. "I've never seen anything like that," she said. "Thelonious is cr-a-a-zy."

"You know that kid?" he said.

"Who? Thelonious?" Melody Rain lied. "Not really."

"People I work for will want to have a word with him."

"You're with the Falafia, huh?"

"What do you want?"

"My girlfriend lost her dog."

"That's not all she lost." Choke sniffed two of his dirty fingers. His beard appeared blotched with patches of dry blood. When he smelled his grimy fingers, it made him smile. "Yum."

"Have you seen a retriever or not?" Melody Rain said.

"Can't see much," Choke said, with puffy, swollen eyes. "But I'll tell you one thing, brown mamma. When we find your Thelonious, we're going to be the last thing he sees." Choke loaded the final tank into the Explorer and slammed the hatchback closed.

***

In a Motel 6 twenty miles outside the show, in a dimly lit room with the drapes closed, Camilla sat on a queen bed with her back against the headboard. Her dirty feet stained the clean white sheets. Camilla cracked her knuckles and looked around the room.

At the brown table scuffed with burn marks, near the air conditioner, sat Scruffaluffakiss, a tall, lanky head with a big nose. He sat at the table, sorting money. The pile of green was stacked two feet high. On the floor, a topless brunette watched an episode of *Woody Woodpecker*. And a clean-cut naked teenage boy lay in the bed opposite Camilla. The room smelled like marijuana and opium. Choke, the burly runner, explained what transpired. When he finished the room was silent except for the mocking laugh of the woodpecker on the television. The air conditioner hummed. The drapes shook. Two of Choke's phrases stuck in Camilla's mind, *emptied the gas* and *took the money*. Camilla held a glass pipe, a hammer. She jumped out of the bed. "It's one thing to get shut down by the police. We can't help that. But a fucking head—"

She threw the pipe into the hotel mirror. Both shattered.

"What do you want us to do, boss?" Choke asked.

She looked at her broken reflection in the mirror, her dreadlocks like serpents. "Do?" She opened a drawer in the dresser. Next to the bible, she pulled out a gun case. She opened it on the bed. There was no gun in the case. Its contents contained a needle, and a vile of a clear liquid. "We're going to do what we did in Deer Creek." Everyone looked at each other in fear and utter disbelief. "How many of them jumped you?" Camilla asked.

"Three," Choke said. "But I can only recognize the one called Thelonious. I didn't get a good enough look at the others."

"He's the one who started this. He's the one we want."

"There's eighty thousand people at the show, boss."

"We'll find him," she shouted. "Now everybody out!"

The naked boy and the topless brunette scampered to get their clothes on. They dressed quickly and bolted out the door. Choke followed quickly and Scruffaluffakiss was behind him.

"Scruff, you stay," Camilla said, placing a hand on his shoulder. He obeyed. They stood for a moment and she spoke.

"Do whatever it takes to find this motherfucker," Camilla said. "At all costs, make sure you avoid the feds, and then get your ass back here immediately. Mr. Russo's not going to like this."

Russo's name was not mentioned often. Only a few people knew of Camilla, and even fewer knew of the existence of Russo.

134

Let it suffice for now that Russo was the man behind the woman. Their family wasn't that large, but it loomed big enough. *Los Federales* could only wish to penetrate the scene deep enough to know of Camilla and the untouchable Russo, and to that extent Mr. Unnamable, who was a lot older than these nickel and dime bag kids, and a lot wiser than his young blood soldiers. Let's say Mr. Unnamable, the man behind the man behind the woman, could get a United States Senator on the phone in five minutes; leave it at that. Mr. Unnamable's not relevant here. Russo? Russo comes later. This call belonged to Camilla. What Thelonious did automatically called for the Deer Creek needle. Camilla didn't need approval. In her mind, according to the rules, if she didn't order Scruffaluffakiss to dish out the Deer Creek needle, she would've been wrong, and she would've heard it from Russo. That's how it worked. The funny thing is, without knowing it at the time, if Camilla ever mentioned the name Thelonious to Russo, he'd have squashed the order in a New York minute. Russo would've absolutely issued Thelonious a pass, at least on the Deer Creek needle, if anything.

Los Federales

The man in the FBI windbreaker looked at his troops, a clean-cut group of eight men and women. "A clean sweep of the parking lot," the Captain said. They were holed up at the local FBI headquarters within the city limits of Chicago. "Special Agent Pryor," the Captain said. "What are we concerned with today?"

"LSD only, sir," said Agent Pryor, a redheaded woman.

The Captain continued his speech. "There's more LSD at this one gathering than in all of California and New York," he said. "Special Agent Foxx," he pointed at a mysterious looking man in his thirties with black hair. "What vernacular do we look for?"

"L, doses, tabs, hits," Agent Foxx said.

"Good." The Captain looked at his crew hard.

"Sir," Agent Foxx said. "Is the city providing security?"

"Good question," the Captain said. "The city of Chicago plans to have minimal security for this event. The numbers are at about twenty officers, in uniform. The CPD officers have their agenda, to maintain the peace and snuff out the blatant use and distribution of any narcotic or paraphernalia. We have our own agenda. Pick up your uniform on the way out. Let's get to work, and remember, don't waste time with anything small. Got it?"

"Yes, sir," they yelled in unison.

In the air lived a synergetic moment of reverie.

As the federal agents walked out, they passed the Captain.

"Shirt size?" he asked. He equipped each agent with their undercover uniform, a new tie-dye shirt from the Gap, and a brand new pair of Birkenstock sandals.

Scalping

The scalper stood ten yards from the Will-Call window.

"Tickets? Who needs tickets?" he yelled.

Thelonious zeroed in on him with the eye of a hunter.

"Whatchugot?" Thelonious asked, rolling right up to him.

"Floor seats. Upper deck. Tell me. What do you need?"

"I need you off the lot."

"What are you talking about?"

"I want all your tickets."

The scalper looked Thelonious over.

"Scram, all right, kid." He pushed Thelonious.

Thelonious stepped to the scalper's face. "You see this," he held his cell phone high in the air. "Touch me again and I'll bop you so fucking hard you won't remember what hit you."

The middle-aged scalper looked at Thelonious. The kid's eyes were squinted little slits. His body looked as tense as a donkey's ass during mosquito season. The kid looked for real.

The scalper's name was Chauncey Meck. He used to be a pilot for American Airlines. Meck was an unshaven white-guy in his forties. The devastating event in his life occurred when he got jumped by a group of teens in a Midway parking lot. They escaped with only $200 and left him for dead in a coma. Meck suffered physical and psychological traumas he could deal with only through the uncontrolled flight of a pair of dice and the turbulent landing into the bottom of a bottle. The devastating event in his life should not throw too much sympathy his way. Before the accident, his resume included being a bastard to a beautiful daughter in Lubbock, Texas, and a slight subtle tendency toward pedophilia.

The scalper mulled. "You want all of my tickets?"

"All of them," Thelonious said.

"I have sixteen left."

"I'll give you fifty each."

"I can get more than fifty——."

"Fuck you. Fifty's already above your cost." Thelonious dug into his pocket and whipped out a wad. He counted off $800.

"I ain't got all day."

The scalper saw the money. It wasn't a bad deal. On top of which he'd get the rest of the day off. If he hurried, he could make the late-double at Arlington Park. Meck gathered the tickets from a hip-sack. Thelonious examined them all to make sure they weren't counterfeit. He looked at the venue and date to confirm if they were correct. With some of the tickets he used the burn test. If you light the back of a ticket, a small black smudge appears on the front of the ticket. If there's no black smudge, then the ticket's fake, or if a hole quickly burns through, the ticket's printed on fake paper.

"They're real," Chauncey Meck said.

On Shakedown Street, Teflon nodded. The scene before him, the circus, the fevered revelry, this was the Shakedown Street Thelonious often spoke of. One aisle away, Teflon noticed a bunch of hip-hop heads gathered around an old Cadillac Coupe DeVille. Thelonious said there'd be hip-hop at the show. Meanwhile, the crowded bazaar filled with 420 allure. Out of glass pipes, clouds floated past eager noses. Every ten feet they walked into a wall of secondhand smoke. It wasn't always so smoky, but around twenty minutes after four, according to Curtis, Shakedown Street steamed.

"You want a goo-ball?" Curtis asked.

"I think I'll pass," Teflon said.

Curtis stopped a sister walking around Shakedown Street carrying a basket of goo-balls. "Three bucks, two for five," the young lady petitioned. Curtis purchased two, began eating one, rolled another in a napkin the vendor gave him, and pocketed it.

"You don't seem worried about our actions," Teflon said.

"Thelonious said he had it covered. I trust him. Don't you?" Curtis threw a chunk of his goo-ball in the air. The goo-ball seemed to pause before falling, and then he caught it in his mouth.

"What's in that thing you're eating?" Teflon asked.

"Want to know a headie secret, hee-hee." Curtis danced around Teflon. "The secret of making ganja goo-balls." Teflon watched the dreadie trickster. Curtis began to slap his thighs and sing like a bluegrass banjo player. "*Simmer-it-down, simmer-it down, simmer-your-clippings to the butter turns green.*" The last word, like the tossed goo-ball, seemed to hang in the air. Curtis clapped his hands. "What comes next relies on the chef." He dropped back into bluegrass mode. "*Cocoa crispies, oats, and sunflower seeds, coconut shavings, peanut butter, and dried cherries*—yee heew—" he started to slap his thighs again. "*Toasted walnuts, honey, and chocolate from a dove, vanilla, marshmallows, and lots and lots of LOVE*, hee-hee-hee."

"Sounds good, actually," Teflon said, smiling

"Here," Curtis broke him off a piece. "Try it."

Teflon munched the goo-ball and nodded.

***

***

"There's my nacho-mama, hee-hee."

Back at the booth, industry prospered. Geri, for the first time, did not have a needle in her hand. Instead, she held a wad of money. Her wares were selling as fast as a sale at Old Navy the day after Thanksgiving. Curtis and Teflon walked behind the vending booth to *The Jedi*. Curtis kept his pipe in the car and the boys wanted to 420 outside, sitting on the back bumper. As they smoked, two Southern girls walked up and began to look through a rack of dresses. The girls addressed the area, no one specific.

"Y'all hear someone closed down the nitrous zone," said one of the gossips. "And not the po-lice for once neither."

"Yup—some heads rolled right on through and emptied all the gas. If you ask me, it's the best thing for this place too."

"Is that right?" Geri said. "Took out the nitrous zone?"

She remembered Teflon running up and blabbering about Thelonious needing help, not now, but right now, were the words. She looked back at Curtis. Old Curtis wore a look-of-guilt, his shifty eyes as culpable as a dog's after being busted for eating the cat's food. Geri stepped over to Curtis and Teflon. She grabbed her man by the ear and yanked him toward the front of the car.

"Teflon, you mind clerking for a minute, *papi?*"

"Yes, ma'am."

He hopped off the trunk and occupied Geri's chair.

Geri deposited Curtis on the hood of *The Jedi*.

"Is there a secret you'd like to tell me?"

Curtis went deep into his unconscious repertoire of faces and surfaced with the "look-of-love." His eyes resembled those of a begging dog, a dog who really wanted a bite of steak, even though his bowl already overflowed with Kibbles N Bits. "Don't you give me that stupid look," Geri said. "You know who runs the nitrous."

"It's all-good, baby. Besides, I got more money for us."

"What? You took their money? That's not all-good. Where's Thelonious?" Geri lightly slapped her boy across the cheeks. "*Oye*, what the fuck are you guys thinking? You're crazy."

Cell phone conversation between Teflon and Thelonious

4:45 PM

Teflon: Where you at?

Thelonious: I'm on L.S.D.

Teflon: LSD?

Thelonious: I'm on Lake Shore Drive looking for scalpers.

Teflon: Word—how's it going?

Thelonious: I got like seventy tickets. I'm running out of cheddah.

Teflon: Come back to the car. Curtis has some cream for you.

Thelonious: He does? Why?

Teflon: He feels bad about taking the money. He wants to give it back to the scene.

Thelonious: Curtis needs the money. That's his steez. Geri and him have a bun in the oven.

Teflon: True, but Geri sort of yelled at him.

Thelonious: You still wit them?

Teflon: I'm at some hip-hop cipher.

Thelonious: On Shakedown?

Teflon: The next row over. You know, Monk, people are talking about what went down.

Thelonious: Word travels fast on the lot. No worries. You know me, son. I have a plan. I'm not stupid. I got this one, bro.

The clean-up men

Behind black glasses, shrouded in a hoodie, hands in the sweatshirt pocket, Scruffaluffakiss walked through the South lot bent on one thing, finding the kid who thought he could clear the lot of nitrous oxide. The kid that cost his bosses thousands, the kid from New York, the kid named after the piano player. In his hand, he held the gun case. One custie came up to him thinking he had glass for sale. The reaction? Scruff mooshed the kid in the head, and then continued to walk the South lot. Very rarely did he go to a show. He hung at the hotels. Sometimes, when there was more than one show at a particular venue, campsites were set up so the heads could party. At these gatherings, Scruff sometimes popped up. He arrived in the middle of the night and looked for spun out lot lizards that couldn't sleep. He lured them to one of his comrade's tents with pharmaceuticals, and then he had his way. But he never ventured inside the festival. To Scruff, the concert existed for custies, and teeny bopping groupies. He hated the show.

There were two of them, Scruff, and Choke, the nitrous henchman, the man who could recognize their target. Choke also wore dark glasses and a hoodie, even though it wasn't cold. They walked along the South lot, side by side, quietly. When Choke identified the target, he would leave. Those were the orders. Choke would pin recognition on the target, and then they'd separate like a 7-10 split. If only they could find their target. They'd find the target. No one wanted to hear Camilla. No one wanted to get Russo involved. They'd find the target all right. They always found the target. They would walk the South lot, Shakedown Street, and then the garage below. Then they'd do it again. And then they'd do it again if they had to. Scruff and Choke were on a mission.

Out of the port-o-potty, feeling Smurfy

Into the blue port-o-potty to pee into a pit of Hades—a fellowship of feces—Thelonious stared into the cauldron filled with vomit and urine and used tampons. He winced like a lifelong carnivore drinking wheat grass for the first time. What an odor! Worse than stink bomb, worse than chicken pee. And so dark the kid could barely see. He used his cell phone for luminosity. Then he whipped it out and began to pee. Again he tried to make a call, and again the cell phone went directly to voicemail. Tension as door of neighbor opened and *snapped* shut like firecracker. Too private for something so public. And the sweat built atop his brow. Sweatshop, coffin, sardine, claustrophobia, as his neighbor pissed with the force of a racehorse. This time he would leave a message. "Where you at? I know you're in Chi-town. Something went down at Oracledang. You need to hear this from my mouth. Whatevs. It's all-good. Holla at your boy, Monk." He wiped the sweat from his brow as his neighbor's pee reverberated through the chamber of stink. That's it. Back into daylight he burst out of the doodoo coffin slamming the plastic blue door, *SLAP*, two hands together—onward and upward trudged Thelonious Horowitz.

La, la, la, la, la, la / la la la la la.
He walked along the South lot, smiling, yeah.
The show, like a lotus, was in full bloom, yeah.
The sun shined down on the South lot characters.
Destination: Shakedown—on the way, smile
at the girl with the butterfly wings. Oh, yeah,
as beautiful as a supermodel, right?
One girl wore a Twister board, wrapped in vinyl.
One girl wore a jacket made of Uno cards.
And one guy wore a jacket made of maple
leaves. Hence an interesting crew of foliage.
A couple wearing shirts and pants stitched from palms.
Girl with ivy wrapped up her bare legs and arms.

Look at Thelonious as he walked along Shakedown. His head shook, his shoulders and arms shook; his whole attitude had Parkinson's. Like his steps had their own theme song, *bom chicka bom bom*. The key to having fun is being funky. He strutted over a discarded pack of Camel Lights. Accidentally, he kicked a bottle of Heineken under a van, the green glass twirled like a break-dancer, *bom chicka bom bom*. Ain't it funky now? He walked past a gallery selling blotter art. Autographed images of Leary and Babbs over perforated sheets of acid with Alex Gray graphics, *bom chicka bom*.
Completely elevated, Thelonious ventured *further* on Shakedown Street, feeling very aware and inspired. Five paramedics ran toward the corner. Another one bites and another one bites.
The dust on a Southern car caught his eye. The fat red laces on a pair of Adidas caught his eye. He caught a brand new price tag hanging off a pair of Birkenstock sandals. Thelonious

looked up to catch a poseur Federal agent. Thelonious knew a phony when he saw a phony. He caught everything, even his own reflection in the window of a Subaru Outback. He caught the New York plates and nodded, and he even caught the town, Rye.

...LOST

"What's shaking?" Geri asked.

"I need a skateboard," Thelonious said.

Geri opened the trunk and Thelonious rummaged through the dirty and cluttered car. After an archeological dig excavating clothes, bootlegged DVDs, and an assortment of books, he found an old Keenan Milton skateboard, from the skate label Chocolate.

Thelonious nodded when he saw the fallen skater's deck.

"A Keenan, *n-i-i-i-c-e.*"

"Anytime, *papi.*"

"Where's Curtis?"

"He's cleaning up balloons."

"Heard about the nitrous, huh?"

"You're crazy. Don't you know who you're fucking with?"

"It needed to get done."

"What you're doing is right on." Geri grabbed her friend's hand. She looked up at Thelonious. "And the miracle thing." She nodded and her almond eyes moistened. "You're transforming a regular show into history. You're creating the myth, *papi.*"

Thelonious took a sip of beer, more than a sip, a gulp.

"I don't know about all that. I just want everyone in this place to hear some good music, but I know where you're heading with all this, and I refuse. You need the loot. I won't accept it."

"Too bad." From a backpack on the floor, Geri produced a stack of tickets. "We spent the money. It's like an investment." She handed the tickets over. "There are a few less scalpers now."

"How did you get these so quick?"

"You know Curtis," she said.

"Your man is the Magi." Thelonious bit his bottom lip and his eyes gleamed. He sorted though the stack of tickets. There must've been at least thirty. Some of the passes had black smudges, the test for authenticity. "That boy never ceases to amaze me."

"You're on your own from here, *hermano.*"

Thelonious straightened up, arching his back and chin.

"I've been on my own for awhile, *sista.*"

"Well, try not to get lost."

"Too late," he said, smiling. "Love you, Geri."

Thelonious jumped on the skateboard and that was that. Love you, Geri. She smiled and felt warm. Family love was special love. At the time she didn't know those were the last words she'd hear from Thelonious. Could she have heard any better three?

I see you, Thelonious

Thelonious maneuvered his way through the crowded Shakedown Street aisle. When he had room, he jumped on the skateboard and headed toward the stairwell leading to the garage. On the way, he landed a one-eighty kickflip in front of a pack of girls, then he licked his finger and slapped himself in the ass. Check him out. On total fire. In the garage below, he filled the chamber with echo after echo of ricocheting ollies, flips, and nose grinds.

When he made it to the street, he tried to land a nollie halfcab heelflip off the curb and he ate it. He bounced to his feet.

Watch out world, here cometh Thelonious.

"There he is." Choke pulled on the sleeve of his comrade.

"Is that him?"

"That's him all right."

The two henchmen stood on one side of 18th Street, shrouded in hoodies and dark glasses, fresh from patrolling the South lot. Thelonious stood on the other side of the street, holding a skateboard in the air like a trophy, hollering and hooting like a cowboy. "Are you sure that's our guy?" Scruffaluffakiss said.

"I'd recognize that fucker anywhere."

Scruff took a good look at the kid. He studied the obvious features. Skin tone, a shade of white, not unlike vanilla soymilk; height, a stubborn 5' 9"; weight, 150 pounds; hair color, a dyed black; hair style, a messy, longish Caesar, growing over the ears; sneakers, Adidas Gazelles; pants, baggy JNCO's. Scruff, with the catalogued mind of a digital camera, stored the images in his head.

Thelonious jumped on the skateboard and traveled down 18th Street, toward Lake Shore Drive, in search of more scalpers.

He was flying now that he had a skateboard.

"Fuck. I didn't get him with my camera," Choke said.

"I got him," Scruff mumbled.

He gripped the gun case with the Deer Creek needle.

KC McGovern and Keith Lipsiznowaz could not resist the lure of Shakedown Street. Who could refuse the noise and the clutter? Who could deny the mad energy of this gathering, of this festival where the freaks come out all day long? O' Shakedown, O' Shakedown! Youth shined on Shakedown Street. The South lot must wait, the South lot could wait, because the South lot looked barren compared to this urban oasis, to this heart of town.

"Let's look at the crystals," Keith said. He knew about rocks and wanted to show off. "You can tell a crystal miner by the clothes they wear. They're stained with red marks." Keith attracted the attention of the vendor selling crystals. "Did you mine these stones in Arkansas?" The vendor looked at Keith and nodded.

"I like the bookends with the Saturn rings," KC said.

"Agate slices," Keith noted.

"They're pretty."

"Their rings take me to the Kundalini gong."

"They take me to a painting in the Whitney."

"What painting?" Keith asked.

"Arthur Dove's *Ferry Boat Wreck.*"

The art of flirting. Keith played the Ross Geller geologist-monkey part to perfection, while KC lent a subtle charm to the often-crude role of Culture Whore. They loved every second of it.

"So how do you know Thelonious?" KC asked.

"I know his buddy Teflon. Thelonious gave me a weird vibe. He seemed a little reckless, irresponsible, maybe oblivious."

"Are you shittin me?" KC rose to his defense. "You should see Thelonious on stage. That kid's a true rock star."

"This vendor is a rock star. Look at his crystals." Keith picked up a stone. "This one's a tabby. They're short and flat with notches on one or both of the flat sides. Tabbies are my favorite." He put down the tabby crystal and picked up another. "This is a laser wand or scepter crystal. They're long and look like something Superman's dad would mess with. Those are record keepers over there. They have pyramid shaped heads." Keith noticed a chipped amber quartz crystal. He picked it up and immediately had déjà vu. "Where did you get this amber quartz?" he asked the vendor.

"Someone kicked it down."

"Really?" Keith said.

"You can have it. It's too chipped to sell."

Keith quietly put the rock in his pocket while the voices inside his head spun around like lotto numbers about to be drawn. *Sky? Could it be hers? The one I gave her? It is hers! No way? How?* Keith fiddled with the amber crystal inside his pocket. The pointy chipped edge of the rock pierced his finger. He put the finger to his mouth and sucked on the cut appendage. *Look for Sky. No, stay with KC. You came here for Sky. I'll find Sky later. Sky needs you. Sky hurts me.*

"What?" did KC say something.

"I want to sell some books, rockhead," she said, smiling.

***

Do you know someone who for whatever reason is unable to get to a book? If so, try Books on Wheels, a program brought to you by KC McGovern, a Friend of the Library. Yeah KC's car with the American flag and her bookstore were on the South lot, but she also had a bookstore in her backpack. So while Keith snuck away to the Muslim oil stand, KC stood in the middle of Shakedown Street, handing out flyers, and trying to sell books. As it were, other heads trolled Shakedown handing out literature, the Krishnas and the Zendiks. The Zendiks, from what KC could put together in a brief chat with one of their booksellers, belonged to a gypsy-commune they liked to call an artist-sanctuary. They solicited donations in exchange for the *Zendik Arts Magazine*, and they also pushed the literature of their community founders, Wulf and Arol Zendik, two revolutionaries of some sort. They seemed cultish. Lunar, the young man whom KC chatted up, lived on their farm for six months. KC concluded her conversation with Lunar by kindly declining an invitation to the farm. The Brooklyn girl couldn't get past an image in her mind of the Zendik closets being filled with black Nikes and schedules of looming comets.

The Krishnas, wearing long flowing robes, also combed Shakedown. They solicited donations for one of their many books with the phrase "self-realization" in the title. The Krishnas, at their Shakedown base, also offered up a free hummus concoction.

KC's work differed from the Krishnas and Zendiks. Her stories weren't didactic or inspirational. Her stories entertained with simple fictions consisting of make-believe characters. Her lies were as true as any truth that claimed not to lie. So *Ms. Daisy Doolittle and Her Crew of Wascally Wabbits* wouldn't win a National Book Award? Of the stories in the collection, although a few were worthy of publication, none would come to be nominated for a Pushcart Prize, or appear in any "Best Of" anthologies. The book she spent a thousand hours composing could probably land her a literary agent, or maybe win a contest, or even catch the eye of an editor at a small press, but a major publishing house, no way. KC knew it. She did not have any visions of grandeur. She was only twenty years old. Unless lucky, and right on the Zeitgeist, she knew she had to live more, experience more, and write ten-times more. Nonetheless, she wrote a book. This constituted her dream. KC stood firm on Shakedown Street, and every time someone made eye contact with her, which happened often since she looked like a beautiful redheaded goddess, she began her spiel. You like to read?

Frankincense from the wise man

On the edge of the Muslim vendor's table, a burning sagebrush smudge filled the air with a thick smoke. Spicy, clean, deeply relaxing, jarring, yet immediately familiar and comforting, the pungent odor of sage—nothing like pot—gave the parking lot and Shakedown an extra dimension of character. Maybe Keith would buy Sky some gum resins. Incense sticks you could get at a 7-Eleven, but only a handful of places in the most exotic cities sold gum resins. Gum resins burn the heaviest smoke with the deepest aromatic potency. The only way to light the resin is with charcoal. He'd buy the frankincense, of course. Thousands of years ago its value equaled gold. It was said to protect the spirit forever. Its smoke was believed to carry prayers to the heavens. Besides, frankincense was Sky's favorite. Maybe he'd buy her the frankincense oil. Maybe he'd buy some sage. He really should buy something for Sky, after all, she was the reason he came to Chicago. Sky liked to burn sage, especially when she moved into a new house. She burned it in every corner of every room to cleanse the air of any foul spirits lingering from previous occupants. Keith looked at the plastic applicator bottles that held all the essential oils, and he decided to buy Sky Tyler a vile of frankincense oil.

In a vending booth next to the Muslim oil stand, stickers, displayed on oversized cardboard poster boards, were also for sale. They sold for three dollars, or two for five. Keith wandered over to the stickers. In a minute, KC rejoined him there.

"Are you ready to jam at the concert?" Keith said.

"I'm here to sell books. Who'd you come to see?"

"Me? I don't have a ticket for the festival. I don't even know whose playing. One of my yoga students said that Radiohead is headlining Oracledang this year, but I don't care too much."

"I heard thirty huge headlining bands are playing in six hours. All types of music too," KC explained. "Funk that. It'd be nice to see the show. At least I'm working. Why are you here?"

"I'm here for bumper stickers. They give me wisdom."

She looked at the Californian. She liked that he taught yoga. The fact he knew Thelonious's friend gave him brownie points because a friend of a friend was a friend. She also liked guys with beards, they seemed raw and savage, and that always appealed to her. Yet she didn't understand why Keith was at the festival. She figured he was only kidding about not having a ticket. Then she read the bumper stickers and her mind became filled with insight into the nature of the characters that attended music festivals.

THOSE WHO ABANDON THEIR DREAMS WILL
DISCOURAGE YOU FROM ACHIEVING YOURS
SUBVERT THE DOMINANT PARADIGM
KILL YOUR TELEVISION
REHAB IS FOR QUITTERS
PIMPIN AIN'T EASY
MILITANT AGNOSTIC—YOU DON'T KNOW EITHER
VISUALIZE WHIRLED PEAS
ENJOY YOUR BEING
QUESTION REALITY
SURVIVE SOMEHOW
FAIL TILL YOU SUCCEED
BE GOOD FAMILY
INQUIRE WITHIN
YOU GET WHAT YOU GIVE
TELL THE CHILDREN THE TRUTH
WHY BE NORMAL?
FEEL THE FLOW

On a skateboard, Thelonious moved around Museum Campus quickly. He found one scalper near the North entrance of Soldier's Field, by the JFK monument. He encountered another in the Children's Garden, in the recreation area that resembled a miniature golf course. Also, by the Field Museum with the big Roman pillars, he found another scalper there. He flushed out one by the merry-go-round, near the Shedd Aquarium. And behind the museum, in the shade over by the ancient Mexican god statue, the wide-lipped statue that looked like Teflon. He eliminated another scalper there. Also, by the tunnel that connected Grant Park to the city, the pedestrian underpass to the north, there he found two scalpers. Thelonious came across a couple of hustlers selling bunk tickets, and they didn't even argue when he ripped up the fake tickets. He found a couple of more scalpers on Lake Shore Drive. Thelonious took it far. He took it to the streets. They weren't going to be any on Shakedown Street. Scalpers didn't hang out in the headie preserve. When all was said and done, he had 111 tickets.

Rock stars

Although the open microphone didn't start until six o'clock, KC wanted to relax in the vicinity of her stuff. Keith Lipsiznowaz followed her like a lost dog. They walked along Shakedown Street, and then headed through the garage below. In the poorly lit garage, Keith mentioned to KC that he was looking for a friend, and that he could only hang out a little longer. By talking about Sky, he felt in some way that qualified as looking for her, as if the exertion of energy toward speaking about a person would have a reaction to attract that person. Eventually, they made it back to KC's belongings. Her neck and upper back hurt from being in the car for so long, and she asked Keith if he knew of a stretch that would alleviate the pain. He suggested the Sanskrit name of the Half Spinal Twist, the *Ardha Matsyendrasana*. KC was impressed, as Keith hoped she would be, until he directed her into a pretzel configuration. All right, take your right foot and place it over your left leg, next to your left hip, great, now turn around and place your right hand behind you, align your right hand next to your right butt cheek, your other right butt cheek, good job, now take your left armpit and secure it snugly against your right knee, there you go, now let's twist those shoulders. Let's twist the night away. She obeyed until it hurt, but Keith could see this so he guided her into the Lotus Pose. She stayed in the cross-legged lotus pose until a customer came along and KC had to play bookseller.

The customer turned out to be a writer of sorts, currently a student of a prestigious writing workshop in a nearby state where corn was as abundant as ink. The customer, if he could be called that, since technically he had no intention of supporting the bookseller or the self-published book, instead wished to debate the merits of her book, even though he never read it. Was it a collection of short stories or a novel? Who was the central character? Was it Daisy Doolittle? Who were the Wascally Wabbits? What did they want? How did they plan to reach their goals? Do they struggle? Is there trouble? Resolution? Do the characters change? Why self-publish? There's no credibility in self-publishing. KC listened to the critic's concerns, and then smiled. She explained her book was a collection of interrelated short stories modeled after Denis Johnson's minimalist classic *Jesus' Son*. There existed a central character, and yes, her name was Daisy Doolittle. Daisy Doolittle could be described as a contemporary American chick with an anarchist's soul, a soul burdened by the lackadaisical drive of a suburban slacker. KC admitted the character and her friends were loosely based on the journals of the indie burlesque pinup group the Suicide Girls. The grad student never heard of the Suicide Girls, probably because he lived in Iowa. In answering the rest of his inquiries, KC, with a bright smile, did say, yes, she understood the mechanics of a plot, but no, she wouldn't reveal any details. He would have to buy the book for that info. KC concluded that she understood she was a novice writer not good enough for major publishing houses, but writing hijacked her dreams many moons ago, and by self-publishing she breathed life into a listless dream. The critic, to her surprise, dug into his pocket and produced ten dollars. He wanted her to sign the book, and even gave up his e-mail address if she wanted a reader for the future. She invited him to the open mic, but the scholar, although a head, declined because quite frankly he didn't go for slams. KC didn't bother to explain to the scholar that what they were hosting wasn't a slam, but since the event occurred in a parking lot, she figured it would've been moot to persuade him to the contrary.

When KC turned back to Keith, she found the yoga instructor upside-down in a head-stand pose. His shirt covered his face. KC bowled over laughing. "What are you doing?" she asked.

"I want you to have this," he said.

Keith wiggled his hips until an amethyst tabby crystal fell from his pants. He caught the rock, and then tumbled gracefully out of the *sirsasana* pose. Keith held his lucky amethyst. He owned the rock for awhile and felt a sudden urge to give it to KC. He still had the chipped amber crystal that belonged to Sky in another pocket. Keith handed the amethyst over to the writer, and then he smiled and bowed his head. KC's skin again turned burgundy. "Purple's my favorite color." She took the rock. "It's so regal."

"Well, you're a rock star," Keith said.

"Nah." KC dug into her cooler and grabbed a Red Stripe. She popped it open with a lighter. The cap flew ten feet and landed on the ground with a twang. "Lee and the dudes in Hurricane Clout are rock stars. The bands at Oracledang are rock stars." She picked up the litter and placed it in her pockets. "I'm a receptacle."

"If you're a receptacle, I'm a piece of garbage."

KC smiled. She looked at the tabby crystal and rubbed it for good measure. She couldn't suppress the scandalous thought that popped into her cranium. The thought said, before the day is through, the crystal won't be the only thing I'm rubbing, baby.

"What are you potskying around with over there?"

"Frankincense," Keith said, playing with the vile of essential oil for Sky. "The stupid lid's on too . . . tight—" He used all his strength to open the cap. When the vile opened, he spilled half its contents on himself. "Shoot." He reeked of frankincense.

KC laughed. "You smell good, ya rockhead."

Doobie doobie doo

Bodhi-dog didn't intend on running away from Sky. *Rere she row?* Normally, when Bodhi-dog wandered, he heard Sky's soft voice and returned immediately with smiles and pants. This time Bodhi-dog wandered too far. Nothing looked familiar. *Rut row.* Bodhi-dog already missed his master. The loyal pet hoped she wouldn't be mad. How could she be mad? After being in the car for so long he was at the show, he couldn't help but wander.

Bodhi-dog, a little retriever from San Francisco, made it to Oracledang, and it was bigger than anything he ever saw. So much to sniff—*rhut's ris rover rere?*—it's a burrito, Bodhi. *Rhut ra-route ris?* That's a roach from a spliff, put that down, dog. Come on. Get that out of your mouth. Where do you find these things? There were so many places to go, through cars, open spaces, and then more cars. Bodhi-dog zigzagged through the parking lot. *Rere's rye raster?* He wandered aisles, crossed paths, moved *further* away from the defunct nitrous zone. Other dogs followed him only to be called back by whatever syllable they responded to. Bodhi-dog looked saddened, but he continued wandering through the South lot until he smelled the faintest trace of a familiar spice— *rankenrense*—his ears perked up. *Rye row rhat rell!* Bodhi-dog barked a little bark of joy! He followed the scent and broke into a gallop. *Rhat's rye roner's rell!* The smell of his owner became stronger and stronger. A barking Bodhi-dog connected the odor to a human figure. Then Bodhi-dog ran toward the figure and leapt.

***

"Whoa." Keith fell on the ground. "Whoa there, puppy."
Bodhi-dog stood on Keith's chest and licked his beard.
"You got a new friend," KC said.
Keith rubbed Bodhi-dog's nose until the retriever sneezed. Then the fluffy animal and the scruffy human rolled on the ground, all over a pile of books. KC liked the way this Keith boy played with the dog. It showed exuberance she hadn't seen in him. She fancied a yoga instructor from California to have a playful nature. KC liked young-at-heart guys, guys who were in touch with their inner child, guys unlike her ex-boyfriend Dickie. Eager to join in the fun, she rubbed the dog's belly. "You're absolutely adorable."
"Thanks."
"Not you, lummox." KC tossed her hair. "The pup looks adorable. You? You look like an Oscar Meyer hot dog, you swine."
"Swine?" Keith began to tickle KC's ribs.
"Stop," she yelled.
KC felt unable to control the splash of tickle juice that wet her bones. All she could do was retaliate, and soon they were both on their backs, rolling around the makeshift bookstore. Bodhi-dog's ears perked up, and the animal also jumped into the fray. In a minute, all three sat panting, and KC read the dog's nametag.
"Bodhi-dog, area code 415."
"San Francisco," Keith said, still out-of-breath.

KC grabbed her cell phone and dialed. The phone rang three times before an automated machine answered with a pre-recorded message. "Looks like the phone number's disconnected."

The winded yoga teacher stroked the retriever's chin.

"I wonder if anyone's looking for you."

***

"Bo-d-h-h-i-i-i—" Sky scratched her dreads. "Where are you, Bodhi?" Sky and Melody Rain walked around the South lot.

They whistled. They yelled.

Sky scratched her leg. "Oh-my-God, what did I do?"

"You have a nametag, no?" Melody Rain lit up a smoke.

"It's my old telephone number."

"It's all right. Don't worry about it."

"Don't worry about it," Sky said, starting to cry. "Are you kidding me? I was doing nitrous instead of keeping an eye on Bodhi, and you're telling me don't worry about *it*. I lost my dog!"

"We'll find him, lighten up." Geez, he's just a stupid dog, no need to fuck up Melody Rain's head. "I have an idea. Why don't we split up? We both have cell phones. We'll cover more ground."

"Think so?" Sky scratched her arm. "I don't feel so good."

"You're fine. The OxyContin's kicking in, that's all."

Sky didn't know where to go except in a direction away from Melody Rain. Should she walk around the South lot and canvas every aisle up and down? Or walk side to side across the lot row by row? Sky never felt so bad in her life. This felt worse than the time she gave her baby up for adoption. It felt worse because she swore to herself that she would never lose another baby. And Bodhi-dog qualified as her baby. After she abandoned her child, Sky made a promise. She put the promise in her safety deposit box. She locked the promise in her heart. Yeah, she always found false comfort in the insecurity that she was too young to have a child, too poor, too hungry. There were too many things to accomplish before a family came into the picture. She wanted to Save this, Abolish that, and Stop the other thing, even though she knew deep down they were dreams, and the baby she abandoned was real. What good was she if she couldn't keep this promise? She'd be no good. No good at all. Where did Bodhi go? Sky wiped her runny nose on her arm. She bit her lower lip. Her jaw moved side to side.

"For the most part—it's been straight," Teflon said.

"Good," Keith said. "I hoped our paths would cross."

"Figured I'd peep the mic. I remember shortie saying come through by the flag. There's nothing like making music."

"Do you want to perform?" KC asked.

"What's that smell?" Teflon flared his nostrils.

"Frankincense," Keith admitted.

"Do you have two mics?" Teflon asked.

Teflon was a little stoned and distracted.

Keith pointed at 18th Street.

"Isn't that your friend on the skateboard?"

Teflon looked, nodded, and then yelled out.

Thelonious skated over to the bookstore. He tried to land a nollie-backside nose-slide one-eighty off a car's bumper and ate it. Filled with energy, Thelonious bounced up and walked to his friend. He gave Teflon a hug. "I see you found the open mic."

"Finish your mission?" Teflon asked.

"I have to give them away now," Thelonious said.

"You two need tickets?" Teflon asked.

"Tickets for what?" Keith inquired.

"For Oracledang, stupid," Thelonious said.

"I don't have a ticket," KC said. "I'm not here for music."

"Stoops. It's all about the music, Kerou-wack. You'll see." Thelonious grabbed three tickets from his pocket and handed them out to Teflon, Keith and KC. "Enjoy the show," he said, smiling.

"No wa-a-a-y." KC hugged Thelonious.

"Thanks for the miracle, dude," Keith said.

"It's what I do," Thelonious said.

"Thank you, Monk."

"So, what time's the open mic starting?"

"In forty-five," KC said. "Shoot. I need a signup sheet."

"I gots work to do," Thelonious said. "Teflon, sign us up."

"No doubt."

"Yo, isn't that Melody's friend's dog?"

"I thought it was the same dog," Teflon said.

"Do you know the owners?" Keith asked.

"She's girlfriends with my friend Melody Rain. I forget her name, but I'm not surprised the spunion lost her dog. Last time I seen her she looked like she was going to suck some for nitrous."

Keith shook his head in disgust. The yoga instructor never entertained the notion that Bodhi-dog might've belonged to Sky. If he had, this information would've put the thought to rest. Sky Tyler was not the type to "suck some for nitrous." Not his Sky.

"Yo, I really have to bounce. I'll peep you guys soon." Thelonious skated down the South lot, back toward 18th Street, and Shakedown Street. "WHO NEEDS A MIRACLE?" he yelled.

"He seems a little kooky," Keith said.

"It's a long story," Teflon replied.

"It always is," KC said, examining the ticket that Thelonious kicked down to her. Then she looked at her watch, it read 5:22. "Shit. I wonder where the heck Shore Morris is."

Something's shaking on Shakedown Street

The derrière of the Princess. They found the disco bus and she was getting down on the good foot to old classics like "Give It To Me Baby," by Rick James, "Double Dutch Bus," by Frankie Smith, and "Ain't No Stoppin Us Now," by McFadden and Whitehead. The Princess didn't know the names of the songs or the singers who belted them. Shore Morris of course knew the answer to all three. If the Princess wanted to know, he would've issued a reply. But she didn't tear herself away from the disco bus to ask. And he didn't charge the dance floor to tell her. Instead, he limply watched from the side and waved as the Princess threw her arms in the air, knocking her butt against the thighs of those other heads who took advantage of the danceteria on Shakedown Street.

Shore Morris had no desire to groove at the disco bus. It had been many shows since such an urge filled him, not since his rookie days. There were more serious matters to attend to than frolicking at the disco bus. Speaking of which, why didn't the Princess ask him about the disco bus? At the end of the night, the crowd at the disco bus is the last to be dispersed by the police. When the cops come through, and the red and blue lights tear up the night sky, and George Clinton tears the roof off the sucka, and heads bang on the patrol car, that's when the disco bus earned its name. Shore Morris knew this. He was there; he saw it with wrecking-crew eyes. He could explain the disco bus, if she asked. But when the Princess walked over to her guide, after the deejay put on Donna Summer's "Bad Girls," she had something on her mind. "What's with these Bob Marley wannabees?" The Princess winced at a dreadie. "Dreadlocks are like, ugh, so disgusting."

The late afternoon sun shone. There looked to be some clouds in the east, possibly a storm. Either way, it appeared a long way off. Then a group of three dreadies walked by. The Princess rolled her eyes. "If you ask me, everyone wants to be the same."

The Princess walked away from the disco bus in search of a beverage. Shore Morris followed, trying to carefully explain the history of dreadlocks, going into detail about the fringe cultures that wear their hair in dreads, from the Sadhus to the Maoris to the Rastas to the Baye Fall Muslims of Senegal. He patiently explained the grooming techniques of dreads. The Princess passed a couple of vendors selling soda, beer, and water, out of coolers. Her mind focused on something else, and when her mind was fixed on having something, obviously she tended to get it. Then an overeager man wearing Birkenstocks and a tie-dye T-shirt stepped right up to her face. "Do you have any L, doses, tabs, or hits?"

The Princess pushed the solicitor to the side.

Shore Morris, knowing the solicitor was in fact a Federal agent, definitely liked the Princess now. "You don't like dreads but do you know about Jah Rastafari?" he asked, keeping up with her.

"Yeah, Marley yells Jah, and everyone yells Raster Ferrari."

"It's Rasta, sweetie, like pasta," he corrected. "Rastafari is closer to a cult than a religion, but it's more of a philosophy than a religion or cult. It's quite interesting but a little bit complicated—"

"Everything's complicated with your cranky butt. To me this is just a concert. And like I really really really want a smoothie. Where's the Jamba Juice stand? Is there no Jamba Juice stand?"

"Do you want to learn something or not?"

"Not," she sneered. He looked upset and she felt bad.

"I'm trying to teach you—"

"Okay, okay, go on."

"Forget it." His patience exhausted.

"Come on, tell me."

"You wouldn't understand."

"Try me, Mr. Seriouso."

The Princess folded her arms ready to listen.

***

Shore Morris and the Princess sat on the side of Shakedown Street. They each nibbled on a veggie burrito. They also carried bottles of water. The Princess wanted to eat a Chinese platter or a kebob, but since she wasn't buying, Shore Morris, a vegetarian, insisted on the burritos. Same thing with the water, the Princess wanted a mojito from a Shakedown bar vendor, but Shore Morris, who didn't drink, would not enable such a thing. So they sat and chewed their food slowly, and they continued to debate, as Shore Morris tried to explain Rastafari to the Princess. He began a long lecture, of course littered with constant interruptions, covering the concepts and histories of Babylon, Zion, Psalm 68, verse 31 of *The Bible*, King Solomon, the Queen of Sheba, the colonization of Africa, the Diaspora, Ethiopia, Lij Makonnen, Haile Selassie and his politics, Ras Tafari, the Rasta lifestyle and dogma, philosophy like I & I, then Jamaica, Kingston town, and finally reggae music.

"Enough," the Princess said, flatly.

She didn't want to hear it anymore.

"Fine." Shore Morris rose. He had more important things to do anyway than hang out with a suburban princess. He had an open mic. Why was he even wasting his time with such a little brat?

Shore Morris led the Princess to a garbage pail. They dropped off the veggie burrito wrappers and held on to the bottled waters. This was it. They could take each other or leave each other; he was too serious for her nerves, and she acted way too stubborn for his patience. That's where they stood when another man in a tie-dye shirt and brand new Birkenstocks approached them.

"Do you have any L, doses, tabs, or hits?"

"Ugh," the Princess said. "Like, fuck-off."

This girl was a classic. He should lighten up. Maybe she'll teach him something. "Listen, Princess. Why don't we do something fun. Let's go to the Great Lawn and play Frisbee, or let's go shopping." Ding, ding, ding, the magic word was shopping.

Now the man was talking.

"Okay," the Princess said, with a sparkle in her eye.

They found a vendor selling Guatemalan clothes. While the Princess busied herself looking at purses and scarves, someone skirted by on a skateboard and slapped Shore Morris in the back of his shaved head. Shore Morris turned to see Thelonious.

"Who's this hippiecrit?" the Princess said. "A friend?"

"Meet the Princess. Thelonious and I go back a few."

"Are you an impostafari like these other people?"

"What a bitch." Thelonious kissed her on the cheek.

"Get a haircut, dude."

The Princess turned back to the Guatemalan clothes.

Thelonious raised his eyebrows in shock. He wasn't used to being told off by a girl at the festival. Then he remembered why he stopped when he saw his old friend. "Shore Morris, you know everyone in this scene. It's very important. Have you seen Russo?"

Shore Morris pulled Thelonious to the side.

"What do you want with Russo?"

"A little business, that's all. Have you seen him or not?"

"Stay away from those guys, if you know what's good."

Thelonious dropped the skateboard. What did he expect? Whatever. No big deal. Besides, he had a lot of tickets to give away.

***

The Princess beamed with beauty and smile. She jumped up and down, and her princess curls danced on her princess shoulders. She pinched Shore Morris on his fair arms, legs, and buttocks. She spun in circles, with her arms stretched out. She even landed a cartwheel. Right there on Shakedown Street, heads applauded her, and she took a princess curtsy. A fine and good Princess, in the best princess mood; she was in splendid princess form. "Tell me. What's in it for your friend to give out tickets?"

"What's in it for him? Good karma, of course."

"Karma," the Princess said, laughing.

"Yes, good karma."

"Can we come back to planet Earth?"

Amidst the thousands of heads wandering Shakedown, a completely naked man walked by nonchalantly. The Princess almost choked on a cough. "Did you see that, Shore Morris?"

"Naked guy. Usually he stays at the Rainbow Gatherings."

"Is that some sort of gay thing?"

"Not quite."

Shore Morris again began a detailed explanation to the Princess, this time about Rainbow Gatherings. The lecture covered scouts, Rainbow Council, camping in National Forests, the First Amendment, the main circle, "A" camp, rainbow warriors, and different kitchens like Granola Funk, Nic at Night, Joy of Soy, and the Confusion State Freeway. The Princess nodded, even though she didn't understand. All she knew was that they just received a free ticket to the show. So they happily continued with their walk. At one point her cellphone rang and Ray Ray Rodriguez's name popped up on the screen. She smiled at the thought that Rodriguez must've been all right, but she didn't answer the call. Later on, when the Princess checked her voicemail, Rodriguez mentioned something about the charges being dropped, on account of his defending himself on the grounds that the Florida State trooper had no videotape to prove any assault occurred. In the meantime, the Princess grabbed the arm of Shore Morris. It stood almost time for the open microphone, and they would go together. The Princess patted the new Guatemalan purse she wore around her shoulder, a gift from her new patron and friend, Shore Morris.

***

Shore Morris and the Princess finally made it back to the South lot. To the Princess, the American flag made the area look like a used-car dealership. Shore Morris introduced her to KC, who was happy to see him with a girl because somewhere in Indiana she began to have her doubts about the well-built man that never came on to her. Teflon and Keith were a few yards away, playing monkey-in-the-middle with Bodhi-dog. They tossed a tennis ball, back and forth, while the dog tirelessly tried to catch it.

Shore Morris and the Princess stood next to the Dodge Ram that belonged to KC's neighbors. Shore Morris left his bag inside their van. Like a dummy, he'd locked himself out of KC's car earlier. The owners of the van were wandering around. They said they would leave the van unlocked so he could get his belongings.

The door of the van slid open and Shore Morris disappeared into its belly. He stuck his shaved head back into the Princess's field of vision. "Hey, Princess. Come in here a sec."

"I don't think so," she said.

"I have a present for you."

The Princess sucked her teeth, grabbed his hand, and rose up. The van looked cluttered with road trip stuff. She cleared an area of clothes and sat on an old mattress. Shore went into his bag and grabbed a worn paperback. "Thanks," she said, with a twist of sarcasm. "What, no diamonds?" Still, the book represented a nice gesture, so she kissed him on the cheek. Shore Morris blushed.

"Thank you for letting me be your guide." He kissed her cheek. "And thanks for letting me buy the burritos." He kissed her on the neck. It was totally innocent, with both of them laughing. Then the beast burst loose and shined in both of their eyes.

She lunged at him, kissing him, sucking up and down the slope of his neck. Shore Morris raised her arms, and off came her shirt. Kisses on her chest. Off with her bra, kisses on her breasts.

Long, full kisses on her hardening nipples, under her breasts, on her stomach. Gusty winds stirred their passions as they fell on the ratty bed. Somewhere along the way, they lost their pants, and closed the van door. He took off her panties and turned around, positioning his head near her bellybutton. His beastly kisses moved closer. He flicked her switch with his tongue, and then backed off, moving all the way around her valley, slowly, letting her simmer. He kept up, around her valley, below the spaghetti patch, around and around, and then, ahhhhh, on the switch, mmmmm, all over the switch. He flicked her switch good. Meanwhile, her hands groped in his underwear. She found her way, and a shot went through him, a warm rush at her first touch. She took off his undies and maneuvered him closer, wanting to give back. Then she took him in, ohhhh, a hot stream ran along his linings. He slowed, flicking her switch, and then going down her valley, in long, slow, motions, down and up. He opened up her canyon with his finger and looked for the uptown spot. He found the spot and his finger settled there. One of his appendages joined him. Two fingers blew up the spot, it was peace. Oh oh oh that's it, she had to stop what she was doing, that's it mmmm don't stop don't stop, his tongue worked the switch, and his fingers blew up the spot, ohh right there don't stop oh ohh yeah, yessss, yesssssss. She went back to her task, ferociously. He started to build. Oh, yeah, she could tell. She felt the building shake. It was going to blow. It was coming. The building, building, building, building, building, building: ohhhh, yessss, mmmm, ohhh, oh, ohhh. These beasts moved fast and they were conditioned to go multiple rounds. For the record, not surprisingly, the Princess won the dance four rounds to two.

Melody Rain walked up the Shakedown Street bizarre. She wanted to mingle. She wanted to find a 420 and puff. She didn't want to look for Sky's dog. Melody Rain came to the show to party. She didn't come to baby-sit. And she definitely didn't come to Chicago to play dogcatcher. With one eye on the lookout for Bodhi-dog, and the other on the scene in front of her, she saw a familiar face. Look at crazy Thelonious. What was he up to now?

Thelonious ran in a circle. He held tickets in the air.

"Who needs a miracle? Get your ice-cold-gooey-miracle."

She walked up to him and pinched his butt.

"You so crazy, boy."

"One for you," he handed her a ticket.

"Great," she hugged him. "I needed a miracle."

"And one for your hottie friend."

"Actually, Sky lost her dog," she said, taking the tickets.

"Where is she?"

"We split up to look."

"You left her alone. She's spun."

"She's all right."

"Well, my peeps found the dog."

"Where?"

"In the South lot, see the American flag."

"Great," she said, with a snake in her smile. She looked at the two free tickets to Oracledang. "You know, I've been thinking, Thelonious. Maybe you and I should reconnect." Her eyelashes fluttered and then she stared at him with soft brown eyes. He saw the look before, that inviting look enabled their pheromones to communicate at a dirty rate of ninety-nine cents per second.

"I'm tempted."

He bit his bottom lip and his eyes darted to the side.

Then a couple of older heads approached Thelonious.

"Are you the one giving away miracles?"

Thelonious tore himself away from Melody Rain.

"I am," he said.

"We tried to catch Phish last night."

"What happened?"

"We came up with nothing."

"It's a family affair," Thelonious said.

He handed over two tickets. "Kick-down so you can get-down." They hugged Thelonious and walked away glowing.

Melody Rain stared at Thelonious and felt a wave of guilt. Guilt to her was a temporary feeling. Truth felt like an annoying itch. "I accidentally told the guy with the nitrous tank your name."

"You did what?" Thelonious shook the hair away from his eyes. He slapped himself in the forehead. So they knew his name. It wouldn't help them find him. At least not before he straightened it out. But time moved against him. "You're a real rat, Melody Rain."

She touched his shoulder. "It just slipped out."

"I don't have time for you. Go get your homegirl's dog."

Without argument, she moved away from Thelonious. When she turned around to look at her old lover, she noticed him glued to a cell phone, holding a finger to his ear. If she didn't know better, Thelonious looked frustrated, maybe even a little scared.

To the rescue, here I am.

Melody Rain didn't smile when her glance fell on Bodhi-dog. The animal sat at the feet of a dude with a beard. She didn't smile when she saw a redheaded chick talking to the dude with the beard. When she noticed Teflon, Melody Rain more than smiled, she squeezed her thighs together and moistened. Teflon sat Indian style, ten pages into a book he borrowed from KC, *The Fire from Within*, by Carlos Castaneda. Thelonious said heads at the show liked the same author his mother adored. He finished *The Eagle's Gift*, and now he consumed the New Age writer's work like candy.

"I hear ya'll found a dog," Melody Rain announced.

"Actually, your dog found us," Keith said.

"Um, actually, it's not my dog. It's my friend's dog, okay."

"You two should've been more careful," Teflon said.

People were beginning to show up for the open microphone. KC busied herself constructing a signup sheet. Keith sat on the ground and played with Bodhi-dog. How come the girl who came to claim the dog didn't even acknowledge the animal? You would think she would've showered the dog with love. Also, you'd think the dog would've jumped on her like it did on the yoga instructor. Instead, Bodhi-dog stayed near his side, allowing Keith to rub its belly. The yogi wanted to mind his own business, except, he didn't like the girl who lost the dog. To his yogi, it seemed like a serious boo-boo. How could someone have let that happen?

"Where's your girl?" Keith shouted. "The dog's owner?"

"My girl?" Melody looked at Teflon. "I don't have a girl."

"Then where's your friend?" Teflon asked.

"You're no fun," Melody Rain said.

"Your friend must be worried sick," Keith said.

"Yeah," Teflon said, looking at the dog. "Call shortie up."

"Okay, okay," Melody Rain said.

Dazed and confused

Sky Tyler straggled and roamed—a rover of the meaty section of the parking lot, the long middle. She strayed across aisles, like a lost cat, down rows she stumbled, calling her dog's name. She asked the occasional head if anyone had seen a golden retriever. This was a festival, so of course people offered to help. Soon, the middle of the South lot echoed with the word *bodhi*. Off the lips of many, in different tones and ranges, the word enlightened the air and could've been fairly meditative, if accompanied by a didgeridoo. Not that Sky could've noticed. She looked a mess. Her eyes burned, and they turned all puffy and red. Her nostrils felt more stuffed up than ever. Not so much from crying, more from sniffing the OxyContin. And the itching and scratching. Like a flea bitten dog, Sky couldn't stop *The Itchy and Scratchy Show*. If her violin teacher Mrs. Mellors was there, she would have looked at Sky, sucked her teeth, and said concentra-shone, Ms. Sky, concentra-shone. Why did Sky miss that violin lesson? How long ago was that? Four months? Three days? She had no idea. Somewhere along the line, her days morphed into a daze. Her daze needed a y to function, and an s for that matter, but an e is so close to an s, one could simply stretch the e out and mold it into an s. The y was her problem. Oh, yes, y to z, so close, neighbors, even. Why was she there? Why did Melody bring her only to leave? The y was the key. You. I. Are. Be. Why? Why did she lose Bodhi? Concentra-shone, Ms. Sky, concentra-shone. U.I.R.B.Y. Why can't she catch that z? She should catch some z's. Let her dreams work it out. Is my phone ringing? "Hello."

"I found Bodhi-dog," Melody Rain exclaimed.

"You did?"

"And I got us tickets."

"Huh?"

"We're at Oracledang. Experience *it*, Sky."

"Where are you?"

"The front of the South lot."

"Where's that?"

"There's a flag, an American flag. See it?"

Sky looked around. The fog in her eyes lifted, and there shined the light, like the San Francisco sun breaking open a cloudy Bay Area day. "I do see it." Sky hung up the phone. "I'm coming."

The proudest monkey

KC McGovern finished the signup sheet for the open microphone and posted it to a clipboard. The clipboard rested on the trunk of her car along with one of her favorite possessions, a Betty Boop grip-pen. The pen had an image of Betty Boop winking, with a graphic that read "100% pure." KC usually wore it clipped to her shirt, where a winking Betty Boop hung inches from her pale Irish breasts. A few heads already signed up for the open microphone. Teflon inked his name, and also his buddy's: Thelonious and Teflon. He thought the chicken-scratch scrawl linked the two of them together like Nice and Smooth. KC's signup sheet had columns for the performer's name, as well as their skill. The open mic order would be selected by KC, not necessarily in the order of those who signed up. She wouldn't want to bring three rappers up in a row, instead she'd throw in a storyteller or a guitarist or a comedian, someone to make the jam more eclectic.

"The dog's owner is on her way," Melody Rain said.

She still never once acknowledged Bodhi. "I can't believe you lost your dog," Keith said, raising his voice. "Don't you have compassion? You're a woman! Where are your maternal instincts?"

"Who the fuck are you?" Melody Rain said.

"My name's no one. I'm like you, except I'm responsible."

"I'm not no one. I'm filled with the beauty of Jah."

"You're filled with something," Keith said.

"Jah guides me." She poked him in the chest.

"Jah guides nothing."

"I don't worry about nothing."

"Worry about looking out for your family."

"I knew we'd find the dog. Jah provides."

"Aiight you two, chill," Teflon said, stepping in. He aggressively shot Keith a raised-brow expression that said I may want to nest with this bird, so let's not ruffle any feathers.

"Keith? Is that you?" Sky Tyler arrived and walked straight over to her puppy. "There's my baby. I missed you." She kissed Bodhi-dog and then looked up at Keith. "Dude, talk to me."

As soon as Keith heard her voice, he turned into whipped cream and his brain went meow. Sky came upon him suddenly and without warning. It was like seeing a cockroach in his peripheral vision. His head jolted to the side, he saw the roach that he knew was there, yet he still flinched. He couldn't help it. Except Sky Tyler was not a cockroach. How could Sky have fallen from Keith's radar screen so fast? KC and her sunshine man. Could that be the reason? He came to the show to find Sky. He was obsessing over her like never before. Because of KC, a girl he knew for one hour, he forgot the most important person in his life so far. Was that even possible? How could Sky have fallen off his radar screen?

Everything flowed backwards.

Radar spelled backward spells radar.

"Keith." Sky waved her hands in front of his face.

"What a foola," KC said.

A Brooklyn foola spelled backward is a Californian aloof.

"This is Keith," Melody Rain said. "What a dum-dum."

Dum-dum spelled backward translates to mud-mud.

And like a car in the swamps, Keith and his alter ego ~ Keith, when in the presence of Sky Tyler, seemed stuck stuck.

He looked around. KC smiled, Melody Rain shook her head, Bodhi-dog panted, Teflon nodded, and Sky looked as smug as can be. Keith did the only thing he could think of. He ran.

Bodhi-dog bolted after Keith. Sky Tyler trailed Bodhi-dog. Melody Rain rolled her eyes, shook her head, and walked after Sky. Kristen Chastity frowned. "What was that?" She circled her index finger around her ear. "Cue the Loony Tunes soundtrack."

Teflon rubbed his face with his big baller hands. He pulled his tight cheeks down, a tic he sometimes did when he searched for the right thing to say. He wanted to defend Keith, but he found the task extremely difficult. "Word. Must be some Californian shit."

"Whatever. I got an open mic to put on."

***

Standing near the back of KC's car, holding the signup sheet for the open microphone, was a tall, scruffy man in a hoodie. He studied the names on the list. Two names jumped off the page: Thelonious and Teflon. The chicken-scratch scrawl told him just about everything he needed to know. Scruff placed the clipboard back on the car, approached KC, and tapped her on the shoulder.

"What do ya want?" she said.

"What time does the open mic begin?"

"I'm sorry," she said. "Like in fifteen minutes."

"Fifteen minutes."

"Would you like to perform?"

The scruffy man ignored the question and walked away.

She came from Atlanta. She looked pale and worn and tired. Her head was a nappy nest of locks. Her armpits were hairy. The woman didn't plan on coming from Atlanta. She hailed from Portland. A year ago, she and her old man were seeing some shows in the South, and she was popped outside the Fox Theater for smoking a joint. There was a group, her old man included. They all ran. She got nabbed. Eleven months in a Fulton County jail. Bail? Her boyfriend bailed, that's who bailed. After serving her time for smoking a joint (and resisting arrest), she met a group of heads in Little Five Points, and caught a ride to Oracledang. Afterwards, she will walk along Shakedown Street with a sign saying Portland. She will catch a ride to Humboldt, and it will be close enough. "I need a miracle," she yelled. Her arm was raised high with one finger up. Thelonious slowly crept by and slapped a ticket in her hand.

***

A sister walked along Shakedown Street, hailing from Hawaii, sun bleached, with long strawberry locks, and dimples. Her bag was robbed while on a bus getting to the festival. She had no money, only friends. They were family. They styled her out and took care of her head. But she needed a miracle to get inside. Thelonious spotted her and heard her plea. He went up to her from behind, tapped her shoulder. When she turned around, there was a ticket in her face. "Thank you, brother." She hugged him tight and long, her face beamed a thousand thank-yous, her feet were already dancing.

***

A brother stood off to the side of Shakedown Street. Short, with curly blond hair, still in high school, from Dayton, Ohio. He didn't have a job or money. His mother was an alcoholic who went out to bars on Tuesday nights, bringing home different guys every other week. He couldn't live at home for the summer. So he caught a ride to Oracledang with some heads he knew. He didn't have a ticket, but he had a heart, and a sign, cardboard, written in black marker: **I need a miracle**. Thelonious walked up to him, looked him in the face, and whipped out a ticket. "Enjoy the show." The kid from Dayton meets a young lady inside the concert. He stays on tour all summer as a result. He follows her to Denver because she attends college at Naropa, and he ends up studying glassblowing, apprenticing in Boulder. During the Colorado winter, she becomes pregnant and has a miscarriage. The two tour again next summer, selling glass, and eventually they move to upstate New York.

***

A sister walked along Shakedown Street with a warm finger in the air. "It's my first show, and I need a miracle." Thelonious ran up to her, grabbed her by the waist, and spun her around and around. When they stopped, he went down on one knee, produced a ticket from his pocket, and presented the lady with her gift. Then he ran off, leaving her dumbfounded. She didn't have time to thank him. But she could be counted on in the future. And she recognized him as the dude by the grassy knoll. The dude that told her tickets had a way of materializing. Every show Jupiter Healy attends, she buys an extra ticket and gives it away, remembering her first show and the miracle she received from the dude with the crazy, wild, black hair.

***

Two gutterpunks, in from Kentucky, too pierced, attractive, and dirty. They hitchhiked to Chicago, working in strip clubs along the way. They had tread marks on their arms, holes in their stockings, tattoos on their necks. Thelonious gave them six tickets. He told them to do what they would: sell or give away all six, sell four and use two, use two and give away four, use two, give away two, and sell two—the choice was theirs. They split the tickets, three each. One girl sold two, scored a fix, and entered the show. The other, inspired by Thelonious, gave away two tickets. The girl that gave away tickets had a baby daughter, almost two, outside of Branson, Missouri. She didn't see her child in a year. Inside the show, she calls her mother and asks if her daughter was yet walking. Within a week, she travels home for the first time in almost twelve months.

***

As Thelonious walked around, he kept seeing familiar faces. He thought they belonged to people he knew, yet he never met them in his life, same headie face, totally different person. After a bunch of shows, a lot of heads look alike. Especially the heads with freshly shorn scalps after shaving off dreads. Then Thelonious walked past himself, the eighteen-year-old version of himself, with blond dreadlocks. He could've sworn on his life he walked past himself. They made eye contact, and after turning around, the figure disappeared into the crowd. Shakedown Street was crazy! Before he let himself get worked up about the possibility of seeing his double, before he wondered if parallel worlds could exist on the Shakedown crossroads, he surrendered; when you come face to face with magic nothing changes. But Thelonious did *see* himself, on the crossroads in the middle of Shakedown, where the main aisle and row meet. In the middle of the cacophony and chaos you can make a deal with the devil and return with a new version of the blues. So? Thelonious let it all go. He was on a separate mission.

***

"Who's got my extra?" He was curly haired and bearded, a mountain rat who worked winters at a Whistler ski resort in British Columbia. Summertime rolled and a Canuck was on the road. At Oracledang he ran into a girl that he met at a festival during the previous summer. They couldn't see the embers of their love for each other. She needed a ticket. To help, he wanted to trade some BC nuggets for an extra. Thelonious kicked-down, telling them to puff-out headz inside the show. Inside the concert, they ignore their assigned seats and move to section 420, all the way up, on the left side of the stage. Together, they smoke out everyone in the section. During one headlining band, they hold hands, and before the night is over they kiss. They're married in the wintertime.

***

A straw colored dreadie, with a septum nose-ring. He looked like a scarecrow, and went by that name. He needed tickets for himself, his nacho-momma, and their six-year old boy. Scarecrow grew up in Queens, New York. Both of his parents were blind and he resented them. After getting in trouble for shoplifting he went on the lam and landed on the West Coast, where he hustled. He coined the term 1.3 street, referring to the pinched sacks of weed he sold to college kids on 13th Street in Eugene. Scarecrow possessed an ounce of mushrooms; cubensis, little mushrooms with orange caps. He wanted to trade. Thelonious kicked-down tickets and told him to spin some heads out inside the concert.

***

A couple from Boston, two adjunct professors from the Berklee College of Music. They had two extra tickets for the next festival, Channel Roadjog, in Deer Creek, Indiana and they wanted to trade two tickets for Oracledang. Thelonious kicked-down two tickets and instructed them to give their extras away at the next show.

***

"Cash for your extra-a-a," yelled a dude from Athens, Georgia. His girlfriend and their two friends walked around Shakedown Street, wrecking-crew style, passing around a handle of Jim Beam. They were drunk, a little loud, all under twenty years old, and needlessly angry. No one could get in the way of the powerful dark energy that wrecking crew brought. The teen drunks had money yet they were looking for only ten-dollar tickets. Thelonious kicked-down four and told them to buy headz a few shwills inside the show.

***

Thelonious had a ticket for any head that held a finger in the air. He didn't have time to find the neediest. He had a lot of tickets and was determined to give them away before the open mic started. For the first time in awhile, Thelonious felt eager to get on the mic. He wanted to sing. And then there would be an amazing festival filled with energetic music to dance to. Thelonious wasn't even worried about repercussions relating to robbing the nitrous dealers. He still had a plan to make all of that go away. If only he could find someone who knew where Russo was—he tried to make another phone call. No luck. In the meantime, he soared on inspiration. Whatever spirit he lost in New York, he regained while he gave out miracle after miracle. He personified the wind blowing out birthday candles. He represented a shooting-star soaring across the Shakedown sky. He was three coins tossed into a headie fountain, a genie in a bottle of Oatmeal Stout, and a leprechaun at the end of a rainbow gathering; Thelonious, he that delivered the wishes.

Why am I running . . . remember your koan . . . what happens when you run and chase at the same time? You get nowhere . . . **move by standing still** . . . nothing changes when you run . . . **move by standing still** . . . I'm a slave to the spider . . . **be here now** . . . why am I running? There are things you run away from . . . **be here now** . . . the mind is a tree full of chattering . . . **be here** . . . monk . . . **now** . . . keys . . . why am I running . . . spider monkeys. This is hopeless . . . double the effort . . . why am I running . . . there are things you run away fro—disengage the thinking mind mid-sentence . . . **move by standing still**. You are not your body, you are not your mind; you are something supreme, you are something divine . . . **be here now** . . . I forgot Sky . . . forget Sky . . . **be here now** . . . why am I running? What happens when you run and chase at the same time? You get nowhere . . . **be here now** . . . the mind is a powerful tool, but a terrible master . . . **be here now** . . . the mind is a tree full of chattering . . . **be here now** . . . nothings . . . **be here now** . . . nothings . . . why am I running . . . remember your koan . . . what happens when you run

Goose in the bottle

In an animated frenzy, Keith ran east. Like the Road Runner kicking up dirt, *mheep mheep*, like a little rodent, like Speedy Gonzalez, *Andale! Andale! Arriba!* When Keith stopped, he ran far. He came to a halt atop the plateau known as Sledding Hill. There, he fell to his knees and stared at Soldier's Field. It looked like a UFO landed right in the middle of Chicago. The contemporary New Age palace was a possible escape route, like a one-way ticket on the mothership, one way to get the funk out of Dodge.

Bodhi-dog came upon him first. The animal licked his face. Sky Tyler knew Keith long enough to take him as he comes.

"What's wrong with you, dummy?" she said, out-of-breath.

Sky kneeled down. Her head blocked the sun and her sandy dreads acquired a yellow aura. They hugged. Something gave birth inside the hug. It felt right. A lot of something lived and died in one long hug. He didn't plan on saying it. "I love you."

Melody Rain made it up the hill. She didn't like the scene at all. She looked down at the two of them with her arms crossed.

"What's going on here?"

Sky stood up. Keith felt like a loser.

He stayed on the ground.

"What are you doing here?" Sky asked Keith.

"I got your e-mail. You sounded weird."

"Sky's fine." Melody Rain put her arm around her.

Keith stared at the flattened grass on Sledding Hill, crushed and brown from season after season of sleigh riders. If the lawn ever considered a revival during the summer and spring, the mountain bikers made sure the play was about them. The flattened grass on Sledding Hill would never find the peace it needed to grow. Was nature trying to tell Keith something? If so, he missed it. He wanted to roll down the hill. Maybe his head would roll so hard and fast as he tumbled down the hill, his obsessions would fly out of his ears, and when he came to a stop, he wouldn't care about nothing. If Keith were lucky, he'd roll down Sledding Hill, eventually land in Lake Michigan, and drown, taking his chances in the next world, the fool that he felt like. He had neither the desire nor the courage to be there, and he prepared to throw in the towel.

"Are you fine, Sky?"

"Sky's fine, don't you worry none."

"To tell the truth, I'm tired," Sky said.

"Why don't we take a nap before the show, baby?"

Keith watched Melody Rain with caution. You know what? Why should he cave? He could battle. Keith knew Sky better than her own divorced parents did. He definitely knew her better than this Melody girl. And he knew his own intuition. And his intuition smelled Melody Rain, and the girl reeked of trouble. Keith stood.

"Stay inside the bottle, Sky. Please, if only for the now—"

"Shut up," Melody Rain said. "The girl's tired."

"There is no bottle, Keith." Sky scratched her scalp. "You know that. Besides, Melody saved my life, dude. That's all there is to *it*. Do you know what that feels like? The girl saved my life."

Sky couldn't look at Keith anymore. She turned away.

"Come on. Let's take a disco nap, babe." She held Sky by the arm. "Let's go. We'll rest before the show." They turned toward the South lot, the way they came. Melody Rain looked back. "Come on, pup." Bodhi-dog looked at her, then turned to Keith. The retriever tilted his head, his ears perked. He followed the girls.

***

As soon as the girls walked away from Sledding Hill, the voice roared. What are you doing? Don't let her get away. Don't let the bad girl win. Keith couldn't help but to follow Sky because in his heart he knew Melody Rain would abandon her, and oh swami, was he right. So there he stalked, thirty yards behind. He followed them back to their car. From his perch one aisle away, he watched as Melody Rain opened the car door for Sky. Shortly after, she walked off in the direction of Shakedown Street, her pace indicative of her desire to leave. When she walked far enough away, Keith went to Sky, venturing right up to the shotgun window. Bodhi-dog noticed him first, raising his head and ears up off the backseat. Sky's eyes were still closed. A smirk colored her face with a little smile. Keith stuck his face up to the car window. He tapped the glass and Sky's eyes opened. When she saw his face jammed against the window, she jumped. Where did she see him jammed against the window like that? Sky experienced the faintest *déjà vu*.

He walked around to the driver's side door and sat behind the wheel. She spoke in a whisper. "I'm sorry I walked away—"

"*Shhhhhh.*" Keith put his finger to his lips.

"She left me again. I'm just so confused—"

"You don't have to explain."

"You came for me," she said, half-asleep.

"I won't let anything happen to you, Sky."

"You say nothing. *It* happens," she said.

"What is nothing? Is that *it?*" Keith asked.

"I can't explain *it,*" she whined.

"We could never communicate right."

Sky sighed. "You have to experience *it.*"

"Sky?" Keith didn't care. "I'll always love you, no matter what—" "And I'll always love you—" "—But I think *it's* time."

He couldn't do anything for her. She needed to rest. Maybe he could give her something, but there was nothing he could do. He understood now. To him *it* had been love, a form of love turned into obsession. For them, this love had not been enough, but it represented something. Now it was time. It was time to move. Keith went into his pocket and grabbed the chipped amber crystal he earlier stumbled upon at the vendor's stand.

"Sky, look what found me."

Sky smiled weakly. Her eyes fluttered like moth wings. Her head dropped like an anchor at sea. The nods were a dead giveaway of her fadedness. She was done. "I'm so tired," she mumbled.

"Do you remember Watsonville?" Keith asked.

"The strawberry fields." She was falling asleep.

"Go to the fields." He held her hand and squeezed. Sky squeezed back until the last ounce of energy left her body. Then he placed the chipped crystal in her hand and kissed her forehead. She fell into a deep and well needed sleep. Sky would not wake up in time for this show. She would rise again, just not in time for this show. And when she wakes, her dog will be there. Keith thought about staying. He sat still, not a tense muscle in his body. He looked at Bodhi-dog. "It's time." Keith smiled at the pup; the pup smiled back. He rubbed the dog's nose until the dog sneezed.

Then Keith left the car and took a breath. There were no voices. He experienced nothing. And that was fine because *it* felt like an orderly bright nothing, a yabba dabba doo nothing, a free nothing. He didn't have to move to get as far as he ever did.

Keith looked around the South lot and found the American flag. "*It's* time." He spoke to no one. And that was cool.

Karma hits

Melody Rain headed toward Shakedown Street, without a worry in the world. She had two tickets in her pocket, a nice buzz, and a spun girlfriend asleep in the car. She had money in her pockets from the glass they sold, and the festival started soon.

Her intention was to do a lap around Shakedown. Then, who knows, maybe look for Teflon. In the meantime, she strolled ten paces behind a tall dreadie kid with a nice physique. She admired that young ass. The blond dreadie looked familiar. From the back, he resembled a young Thelonious, as she remembered him. He wore the same silhouette as Thelonious, and a silhouette is not unlike memory. Then something fell out of the kid's back pocket, a baggie. Nobody in the vicinity saw what happened. She picked up the baggie and looked around. Ground-score! Melody Rain never found ground-score. It felt good to find ground-score, like discovering treasure, or coming upon an Easter egg, or a lost item in a scavenger hunt. Except it wasn't ground-score when you knew where it came from, it was stealing. Melody Rain didn't know the difference, and that would be her ultimate demise. She picked up the baggie and walked between two cars to secretly examine its contents. Inside the Ziploc, lay an un-perforated piece of white cardboard the size of a bank check. She put the cardboard in her hand. Whether the sensitive pores of the hand, or the electric charge of the chemical, when Melody Rain held the LSD, she knew what she was holding. Her hand tingled and turned numb. A jolt ran up her arm. She actually felt a little scared. It was a lot. Testing acid was not like testing cocaine. She couldn't lick it to see if it was real, unless she wanted to get spun, which she didn't. It wasn't like marijuana. There was no odor. But when holding a lot of acid, the *charge* she felt convinced her of its authenticity. She didn't want to hold it any longer, and she didn't want to rub it. And she definitely didn't want to find the kid that looked like a younger Thelonious and return it to him. This was finders keepers ground-score. It belonged to her, and she wanted to sell it. This was good karma, as Sky would say. She'd sell the doses and call them karma hits.

***

Melody Rain walked along the Flea Market of the Absurd, along Shakedown Street, into the heart of headie Zion, the ultimate artery. She joined the cacophony. Her lips, full and wet, opened, and her tongue ran along the roof of her mouth, pushing off her top teeth the syllable *doe*, and then her tongue coiled back, hissing the syllable, *ses-s-s-s*. A soft hand fell on her caramel shoulder.

"You have doses?" a female voice said. "I want a lot."

Melody Rain looked at the custie and nodded.

"I have three-sheets."

"Let's go for a walk."

They wandered two aisles over, to a lane more reserved than Shakedown Street. "What kind of doses are they?"

"Karma hits," Melody Rain said. "Like white blotter."

Melody Rain chose a spot between a SUV and VW bus. She looked over the young woman in a tie-dye shirt and Birkenstocks. She thought about asking for $200 a sheet because this girl looked like a real custie. The going rate was $150 a sheet.

Crouched between the two cars, Melody Rain took out the baggie. The custie examined the acid, while Melody Rain rose up and smiled. Then the custie put the LSD back in the bag, and smiled back. Then she came at Melody Rain with Ju-Jitsu. She grabbed her arm, threw it behind her back, and thrust her against the side of the VW bus. "FBI," Agent Pryor said. "Don't move."

"SIX—" Melody Rain tried to yell six-up, a code among heads for the police. She hoped somebody would free her, wrecking-crew style. Except Special Agent Pryor whipped out a Taser and zapped Melody Rain limp. Special Agent Foxx, her partner, swooped on the scene. To anyone who didn't know better, Melody Rain blacked-out, apparently drunk. Her arms were wrapped around two heads for support. Some heads understood the truth, but who'd interfere? No one knew Melody Rain. You had to watch out for your own family. Wasn't that what all this family talk boiled down to? No one tried to help as the agents carried Melody Rain down a set of stairs into the garage below. In the back corner of the garage sat a U-Haul truck. Two unmarked station wagons, also belonging to feds, flanked the U-Haul. Special Agents Foxx and Pryor dragged Melody Rain to the back of the U-Haul. Agent Foxx slid open the back of the truck, and deposited Melody Rain into her new container like a bag of dirty linens.

***

Melody Rain's eyes were closed when she felt something cold and wet land on her shoulder. She thought it was a drop of rain, a cold December rivulet, a San Francisco tear. Melody Rain must've been resting in Golden Gate Park, on her favorite hill. She was lying down, it felt cold. She had to be in the park, right? What about the moaning? Were those moans? No, no moans, that's just the soft panting of the dogs, the dogs that run around the hill.

She was lying on the same hill where she met Fraggle. The same Fraggle she partnered with when robbing Thelonious at an abandoned warehouse in the East Bay. Fraggle, poor Fraggle. Fraggle rocked the crack rock. Fraggle rocked the needle. Fraggle, dead Fraggle, the first R.I.P. in Melody Rain's world, his death the first rip in her heart's lining. The same rip that let in the darkness of her demons. A darkness illuminating one bird in the sky, Melody Rain's white-bird the only light in the dark San Francisco sky, her demon-bird, the s-shaped heron. She kicked her legs, helplessly. Another drop fell on her, this time heavier than rain, more like bird dung. Her thoughts crystallized as the dizzying effects of the Taser wore off. She wasn't in San Francisco. No. The cold she felt wasn't the memory of a December night, but the chilly floor of a truck, and she wasn't alone in this truck. She remembered the karma hits and the federal agents. A moan she thought originated from a dog reached a climax, as another globule of what landed on her face. As it dripped over her lips, she knew what befell her. The girl gasped. What Melody Rain saw destroyed all remnants of her womanhood.

When KC stepped to the microphone, she looked out at the crowd, swaying her head and body to music only she heard, as if Janis Joplin lived in the wind. On the mic, she kept quiet for so long, she looked pensive. KC merely admired the crowd, maybe a hundred deep. There were all types of heads, some with guitars around their shoulders, others with rolled loose leaf paper in their hands, some stood, others sat. She swayed, smiling gently.

KC played off the mood, going into a little poetic ramble, as host she could do it, she earned it. "I'm always trying to explain to people that I'm a receptacle. I receive what's around me. I receive what's around me and react accordingly." She held out her hands as if she could grab the stars and play jacks. "I'm very sensitive to energy. I feed off of people, places, and things. You could say I feed off of nouns. You could say I'm a verb." At this point in KC's poem, Keith Lipsiznowaz walked to the front of the crowd. "Lights, camera, ACTION." KC noticed Keith and improvised something. "Act, don't think about acting. An idea for a story is not a story, write the story." KC looked him dead in the eye. "He found trivial all that was meant to charm him and did not answer all the glances which invited him to be bold—James Joyce." She let the quote hang in the air, then smiled at the yoga instructor, and looked back to the rest of the crowd. "I'm a blackboard. When I come across you, you are my chalk, my lesson, my teacher." She looked at Keith. "You're an eraser, so we can start over. I'm nothing, except a verb, because a verb takes action. CONJUGATE ME." She spread her legs, opened her arms, stuck out her chest, and tossed her head back. The crowd, including Thelonious and Teflon, gave her a nice ovation. "Thank you. My name is Kristen Chastity McGovern, and I have a book for sale." She had to plug the book. "Next up is a good friend. Welcome to the stage Shore Morris." Only a tepid round of applause followed because no one approached the mic. KC yelled. "Where ya at, Shaw Morris?"

Shore Morris heard his name and quickly jumped out of the Dodge Ram. He tied the string to his khaki shorts and carried a backpack across his shirtless shoulders. The Princess, still topless, poked her head out of the van. If she saw the frazzled mess her curls had become, she wouldn't have come outside for a week.

"Break-a-leg, baby," she said, waving him off.

Shore Morris skirted the outside path up to the microphone. He maneuvered through a couple of bearded heads sitting on the floor, their legs wrapped around djembe drums like the instrument was a lover. Most of the crowd formed in front of the microphone placed directly behind KC's car. The set-up was simple, two microphones attached to skinny fifteen-foot black cords plugged into a karaoke machine. Meanwhile, center stage, Shore Morris dug into his book bag, and surfaced with a stack of papers eight by eleven inches. He had a long poem he wanted to read, a tome knocking the power of American corporations. Surprisingly enough, he did not lecture, did not preface what he was to say, did not ramble. For this one, he jumped right on in.

Ellipses . . .

Keith hung like a pair of pressed pants returned from the dry cleaners. He hung with arms folded, waiting to be worn, barely protected by some plastic wrap. Yeah he felt crisp and free of wrinkles, but he also felt starched, and that made him uptight. His wrap made him feel plastic. He knew KC would see right through it. So far she didn't even acknowledge his presence. And that figured. Nothing came easy. Nothing came too easy, but at least he felt stronger now. He could wait. He had time. Or so it seemed.

KC occupied herself with a head that bought one of her books. Keith didn't want to interrupt the conversation, but how long could he wait before waiting became a little ridiculous? The book customer didn't want KC to sign the book. The reader asked if she would trace her hand on the first page, the hand that created what followed was what he wanted marked. KC grabbed her favorite Betty Boop pen clipped to her shirt, and obliged the customer. "Well," she said, to Keith, "if it isn't the running man."

Her snipe wrinkled him a bit. "Hey."

"So, what's up?" she said, half-listening to Shore Morris.

"I'm just thinking—"

"Should I care?"

". . . have you ever thought about an ellipsis?"

"Have I ever thought about an ellipsis?" She took a good look at Keith. In the late afternoon light, he looked soft and vulnerable, even beautiful. The beard made him look wise. The yoga trained posture and toned body made him look strong. But the look in his eyes did it. The light brown in his hazel bubbled like magma under the earth's crust ready to form rock. And behind the light brown in his eyes, behind the hardening rock, there glowed the faintest trace of yellow, like a mist, like how the universe must have looked before it found creation. He had her attention.

"Whattabout it?" she said, heavy on the New Yorkese.

"An ellipsis goes on and on. Three little dots, incomplete and eternal." He knew he had her attention. And he knew he acted like an idiot when he ran. And he didn't know what came next, but he could continue. "Our lives are an ellipsis. . . . We figure out our dots, figure out where to direct them, what to do with them. . . ."

KC tested him.

"Shit out your dot, plop, let it fall, that's it, period."

"Or collect enough dots and eventually get an impression." He felt determined to make his point. It seemed like an important truth "Connect the dots, form a reality, something solid, so you think, but when broken down, your reality is still a series of fleeting dots . . . an impression of a fleeting transition within a matter of time." He smiled. "Sometimes the impression is beautiful—"

"—Monet's *Sunset in Venice*—"

"Sometimes it's ugly, like when I ran. But *it's* an illusion."

"Maybe I'm real, Keith."

"I know."

"Do you? Do you know?"

"I do. Just *it* gets tricky sometimes."

KC thought about Shore Morris. She should cut him off.

"Silly wabbit," she said. "Trix are for kids."

Keith laughed. Then he looked at the stage.

"You need help selling books?"

KC took a good look at him and smiled.

"Why not, ya rockhead."

Classical ending

"We're Americans." KC indeed cut Shore Morris off because he really could go on forever. She pointed at the flag and added sarcastically, "we rule the world. At least right now we do."

"We are Americans," Shore Morris agreed.

179

"We are the world," KC said.

"And we love America too—"

KC looked at the restless crowd. They were ready for the next performer. "I'm pretty sure everyone's getting in tonight. I know I got a miracle from the miracle man. And now he's out here in the crowd. He wants to come up and do a little something with his boy, so let's hear some noise for Thelonious and Teflon."

Teflon marched front and center, while Thelonious followed, nodding at every pair of female eyes he caught in his field of vision. The crowd split before them like Moses parting the Red Sea. One person didn't move as they approached. He was tall and scruffy and Teflon didn't like the way he looked at all. The scruffy man had a glow, but not a luminous glow. His glow appeared dark, like the moon during an eclipse. Only Teflon could *see* this, but not with his eyes. Was Teflon just *seeing* things? He ought not to be so stupid. Then time almost froze. Everything moved in a disjointed manner as they split up to walk around the man. To Thelonious, the dude in dark glasses and a hoodie loomed as a detour, a mere obstacle on the way to the microphone. And then: "OUCH."

Thelonious put his hand on his ass. He turned around to see the back of the scruffy man's head disappear above the crowd. Other heads continued to pat them on the back as they walked up to the microphone. Everything sped up. "Something bit me."

"You aiight?" Teflon asked.

"I'm straight. Some sista must have pinched me."

***

Get on the mic, get on the mic mic! All hyped, they grabbed two mics. Thelonious jumped up and down like his Adidas had pogo sticks in the heels. Teflon threw his hands up. They didn't bust a yo and the energy they created was a bitches brew.

The Princess, alive and glowing, stood next to Keith, off to the side by KC's stand. She whispered in his ear. "That's the guy who gave me a free miracle ticket for the show." She applauded.

A warm wave ran through Thelonious. *"Pick up the pen pen, speedy like phen phen, balance with Zen—"* Teflon took the next verse. *"Tend to bend the line, one mind, It's all-good and Plenty—"* "420—" crazy Thelonious back on the mic. They went at it line for line, freestyling, no beat, strictly a cappella. They batted the flow back and forth, like they played badminton. The crowd reacted positively by throwing up their hands. And the abstract rapper said: *"Keep your head up, maintain, recognize, represent,"* while Thelonious yelled, "*peace out, whatevs, we're at the show, pitch-a-tent.*" Thelonious began to feel a little dizzy. Teflon approached him and they locked their arms around each other's shoulders. "Yo—let's get classical on this joint." Teflon looked at his buddy, practically his brother. Thelonious began to sweat profusely. A bit off, he still knew where Teflon wanted to go. They wrote the hook only a couple of days ago while listening to Giuseppe Verdi's "La Donna e' Mobile." Thelonious's lyrics, Teflon's idea to lay them over the opera track from *Rigoletto*. Both of them carried the rhythm of the classical song in their rhymes. "*Gang * stas * con * tempt * ible*" they sang at the same time "*Bit * ches * just * men * strual*" both of them smiled wide "*We're * dusted * as * hell*" the slow pitch totally perfect "*And still * intel * lec *tual.*" What kind of crazy operatic world were these New Yorkers creating on the South lot? Whatever they were up to, everyone thoroughly enjoyed it, but no one more than the two tenors. The light in their smiles could've powered the city. They were having the time of their lives up there on the microphone. If Thelonious didn't have pure adrenaline flowing through his veins, he would've felt his legs weakening. They nodded at each other, and the nod said one more time from the top. At the same time they sang the first line, someone began to play the jingle on an instrument. They sang the next line and the musician stole their attention. Was that Curtis playing a vacuum cleaner? Yes, that was Curtis, and yes, he was jamming a vacuum cleaner. Thelonious smiled at his Florida brethren. With music, the performance elevated. Everyone in the area yelled along to the lyrics or banged the rhythm of the song on a drum, guitar, car hood or trunk. They tried to sing the hook one more time except Thelonious fell to the floor while reciting the first line. *Gang * stas * con * tempt—*

***

Now Thelonious could handle his drugs and alcohol fine. He never fell out. Not Thelonious Horowitz. He was not that guy at the party who yawned or slurred or stumbled around like a nincompoop. Thelonious was crazy for life, and crazy for talk. When he opened his mouth, what came out was usually worth the air it took to compose the statement. Thelonious burned like a rocket's chamber during blast-off. He burned like a Roman candle.

When he fell to the floor in the middle of the classical music skit, he did not know what hit him. He never realized it was sabotage. He didn't think of the scruffy guy, or the Deer Creek needle. He didn't think of Russo. He never realized this was the payback for the nitrous. He didn't think anything. He didn't even have time to panic. He simply

fell. Maybe he thought one *oh!* before being cut from his consciousness, that's it. When it came, it came like that. He fell.

He fell
like the
blade
of a guil
lotine—

off with his

head.

Of course, unconsciously, Thelonious tried to reason with death. Time out. What happened? Could he get a do-over? Whatever he did must be a mistake. Death didn't want to listen. Maybe there was something death needed? Something Thelonious had in his possession that could interest death? Hmm? Thelonious knew death took no bribes. That didn't mean the kid wasn't going out without a fight. Death would not roll over Thelonious Horowitz like freshly tarred gravel. No way, death would have to struggle to take him. Thelonious epitomized a warrior. Death would have to take on the mask of a joker and trick him. Death would have to tickle his symphony into gradual crescendo because it wasn't that easy to take Thelonious Horowitz away forever.

***

Teflon Jones dropped to the ground.
He grabbed Thelonious in his arms.
"What's going on?" he yelled. Thelonious felt as hot as the sun. His body temperature rose so suddenly. "Get a doctor." Teflon looked around at all the dazed heads. They crowded the fallen rapper not sure what to make of the scene. Was it part of the performance? If so, the foam forming on the convulsing kid's mouth looked awfully authentic. If any person in the area had a

single doubt as to the legitimacy of the scene, the grave tone of Teflon's voice squashed any suspicions. "Someone get a doctor."

"Get out-of-the-way."

Keith and KC maneuvered through the crowd.

Thelonious's seizures slowed into muscle spasms. His body temperature dropped. He looked seriously off. He had a discolored tongue, blue lips, and his skin turned clammy and cold. In his hand, he clutched the microphone. Teflon held his buddy's head up. "Stay with me," he pleaded. He took the microphone from the hand of his friend and placed it on the ground. Teflon looked at Keith and KC. "What the hell just happened?"

***

Most of the heads at the open microphone scattered.

An ambulance closed in on the scene, its sirens heard along Lake Shore Drive. There would be cops, questions, and there lay Thelonious, on the ground, not even moving. KC, Keith, and Teflon stood over him. Curtis hid an aisle away. There was nothing Curtis could do. He didn't have any tricks up his sleeve for this one. He did know one thing, embedded into his code of survival. He had no intention of being around when the cops showed up.

So Curtis walked off, or better yet, he disappeared.

The Princess, cuddling up to Shore Morris, stared at the listless body. "I've never seen a dead person," she said.

"We don't know if he's dead," Shore Morris said.

What transpired next went down fast. An ambulance blew through the lot. The paramedics whisked Thelonious to Mercy Hospital, on Michigan Avenue. They came and left within a span of three minutes. Since Teflon was not blood family, the paramedics wouldn't allow him to accompany the body to the hospital. The police stayed behind to conduct interviews, begin the filing of the report, all the usual. The five witnesses, Teflon, Shore Morris, the Princess, KC, and Keith, were all interviewed separately. Everyone told the truth. The incident came out of nowhere. He was singing one moment, and then he fell. Their stories corroborated. It appeared drug-related. These things happened at festivals. After thirty minutes, the cops left, telling the heads they were free to enjoy the show, whatever that meant now.

"You all right?" Keith said. He put his arm around Teflon.

"Something's fishy." Teflon remembered the scruffy man. He didn't tell the police about it because he just now remembered.

Did this have something to do with that man?

'LUDE—*the rock star steez—technology fails Thelonious Horowitz*

Check it! I know that nigga Russo from middle school. We were in
the sixth grade together at Dalton before I got kicked out and went
to Trinity. Russo and me used to trade baseball cards, Mattingly for
an all-Gooden, that kind of crap. Then his family moved to France
or wherever the Russos moved and that was that. Five years later, I
ran into him at a show in Philly, at the Spectrum, all grown up and
headie, running nitrous around the lot. Half that tour I rode with
them and we raged. Two sixteen-year olds, pimpin, hotels in every
city, nice ones too, like Hiltons, and our pockets were full like
what. Along the way we went through Detroit where the kids we
worked for bought mad tanks of gas. I met the Falafia cats that
tour. I know the scene! It's not my steez, but I know it. You think
I'd really fuck with the Falafia's nitrous money if I didn't have an
ace in the hole? Come on. I got Russo's digits right here in my
cellie. I called him five times and left two messages telling him the
dilly. His phone bounced right to voicemail every time I called. He
would've been pissed, but he wouldn't try to kill me over six lousy
grand. He'd have understood about the scalpers too. I didn't figure
on him not answering. And I sure as hell didn't figure on them
coming at me so hard so quickly. The Deer Creek needle! The only
thing on my mind was music. Whatevs, I'm at Mercy hospital, son.
Even though I'm unconscious and can still think straight, it doesn't
look good. Peeps don't come back from the Deer Creek needle,
and to tell the truth—stoops—I'm more than a little scared.

Teflon marched out of the South lot. He stared at Shakedown Street. Should he look for the tall scruffy fucker? The scruffy fucker had something to do with this. Vengeance longed for control of his legs because someone had to pay. Pay in a James-Brown-big-payback sort of way. This was the Law of the Talion, an eye for an eye, a tooth for a tooth. Yet Teflon Jones didn't walk toward Shakedown Street. He needed motion, but instead of walking toward the crowded festival scene, he walked away.

Did that really happen? Why? What if Thelonious was okay? What if it was something he ate? Maybe he had a weird reaction? Should he find out how to get to the hospital? Should he call Thelonious's parents? Why was Teflon even in Chicago?

Well, there stood colossal Soldier's Field. He dug into his jeans, grabbed the miracle ticket, crumpled it into a ball, and threw it as far as he could. The wind carried the ticket an extra thirty yards and it landed on the Great Lawn. Forget about the concert.

Teflon headed toward Solidarity Drive, a peninsula of a road leading out to the Adler Planetarium. The path could've led anywhere, for he had no real destination. At one point he passed a group of kids waiting for a bus. They looked away as he passed, recognizing him as the basketball player from ESPN who walked away from the NBA. Teflon could hear the slanderous remarks. That's him. The crazy one. The one who walked away from millions. The one whose mother killed herself. Not once was he recognized at the show. He almost forgot about any potential repercussions from the press conference. What did it matter? Thelonious was sick. Teflon walked on, also sick.

On Solidarity Drive, he didn't notice the homeless guy on the wooden bench. He didn't see the group of tourists in high-watered pants. In the harbor, yachts swayed; boats with Chicago names like *Chelios* and *Rene Douglas*. Teflon didn't see these things. He continued oblivious, head down, as he walked along the road.

The world absolutely bombarded him with sound. All he could do was listen to the world's spiel, even if it only sold one thing. Like the panting jogger. In the hollowness of exhausted breath, Teflon heard death. And in the swarm of hummingbirds that flew out of a tree in Grant Park, in their shrillness, Teflon heard death. In the *screeching* of brakes on the red Gray-Line Tour bus, there lived death. Death loomed everywhere. In the rustle of leaves, in the sounds of sneakers scraping along the concrete sidewalk, in the oscillation of a grass blade, underneath the wing of a bumblebee, and in the z-zz-z-z motion of a fisherman's cast. He intuitively felt Thelonious would die and he was too scared to currently head over to the hospital. What if his intuition was right?

After six, the Adler Planetarium appeared closed, and no one lingered. Teflon walked around the outside of the big dome museum. He settled on the grass, with the city of Chicago at his back. He reached the end of the road. Here, he looked east into the lake. The skies looked gray. There was a nasty storm coming. It looked like "the nothing" from *The Never Ending Story*. The wind gave him chills. A gull gawked, and the only sound was the gentle repetition of the water that brushed against the rocks. Why his boy Monk? Teflon's chest heaved. Blinded by teardrops, he rubbed his eyes. When Teflon regained his focus, he was no longer alone.

***

"Who are you?" Teflon asked.

"Chief Black Hawk," the Indian said. "I am your ally."

"I don't have allies."

Teflon looked at the leathered Indian sitting cross-legged in full-warrior regalia. Was he hallucinating? Did this have something to do with that crazy goo-ball Curtis gave him?

Chief Black Hawk turned to the west, toward the city skyline. "Turn to death when things are unclear," he whispered.

How did he know his mom used to say that? On those dark nights when Teflon awoke in a cold sweat from the shadow nightmares. He walked into his mother's bedroom (his dad on the road shacking up). He woke her up, Mom, it's the shadow again, and she let him sleep in her bed where she talked to him about death. She told him to think of the shadow as death, and to turn to the shadow when scared or confused. Teflon never spoke of these conversations. He trusted his mother. When he thought about death, he never felt scared. She wouldn't try to scare him. Of course, later, the psychologists equated the shadow with his father, and they were probably right, but that didn't mean his mom was wrong. He was eleven when the shadow nightmares kept him up at night, fourteen when his mother killed herself with a suicide note that read "The shadow knows!" As he stood face to face with death, dealing with the loss of Thelonious, Teflon remembered what he learned a long time ago: in many ways, death was a friend.

"Death is always present," Teflon said.

"Accept that and live freer," the Indian whispered.

"I'm a warrior." Teflon clenched his fists.

***

Teflon sat alone. He thought of his mother. His mother had a special gift. She could perceive things with an intense awareness, just like the Carlos Castaneda books talked about. Maybe her awareness was too intense, and she couldn't handle it, and that's why she killed herself. Teflon's mother used to talk to him about being a warrior. The warrior's path was laced in loneliness, she would say, even if it was filled with power of unimaginable quality. Maybe she couldn't handle being a warrior. Maybe the path wasn't for everyone. What if Teflon also had the gift? He understood he could *see* things. Except he knew he could live with it because he felt no desire to explore it. There was no Indian. No shadow. There was the NBA, and his best friend, in the hospital. There was also the scruffy fucker. If Thelonious did indeed die, the scruffy lunar man better watch out, because Teflon would use all his resources to set the situation straight.

Teflon turned away from the "nothing" storm in the east. He headed back towards the city, where he belonged, determined to see Thelonious in the hospital, no matter what the outcome.

Dancing bears

Back on Shakedown Street, Curtis popped up in front of Geri. A second ago, he wasn't there. When Geri heard his voice, she didn't flinch, just like she didn't flinch when a gust of wind jostled the hair on her neck, or when a customer had a question.

"You breaking down?" Curtis asked.

"I don't want to break down." Geri sat in her chair, working on sewing a pair of patchwork pants. Six bears were currently stitched on. It did indeed look like the bears were dancing. "There's been a lot of work. Big city, lots of custies," Geri said. Her almond shaped eyes, soft and black, looked vulnerable. Their forecast called for an 80% chance of precipitation. "Let's not break down." Curtis moved behind her to rub her shoulders.

"You heard, huh?"

"It travels fast."

Curtis kissed Geri atop the head. Her hair smelled like sandalwood and sage. "You sold a lot, Geri." The display didn't look as cluttered as when they set up. The metal racks weren't as packed with hangers. The table not so stacked with clothes.

"I want to keep going," Geri said.

"What are you up to?"

"Four thousand. How about you?"

"I sold out."

"Well, that's the end of it then."

"That's the end of it."

"Curtis, I want to move to Asheville."

"We can go wherever you want, baby."

Geri rose and gave Curtis a hug. They hugged long and tight. The two dreadie heads looked like two royal palm trees, entangled, forever rooted as a part of their environment.

"Are you going into the show?" she asked.

"I don't know. I like the lot when it starts to clear."

Population wise, the South lot cleared. Shakedown would soon transform into a shell of its current metropolis, as most heads entered the stadium for the concert they came to see. Curtis bent down and put his ear against his partner's belly. As Geri cried, Curtis heard nothing. What did he expect to hear? They both knew it was too soon to encounter signs of life, but with certainty they also knew life existed in there somewhere. He lifted his partner's patchwork shirt and kissed her on the stomach. Then he stood, moved a dread away from her face, and kissed her on the lips.

Geri wiped the tears from her eyes.

"It's starting to clear, isn't it?"

"It's starting to clear."

I know, you walk

The stadium opened.

All entrances, all directions, all lots, through all underpasses. Thousands trickled into Museum Park, many walking along Shakedown Street before pouring into Soldier's Field. These heads arrived for the music, and not the scene. Shakedown Street was always extra crowded right before and right after showtime.

The sounds of Shakedown Street filled the Chicago winds. The normal discordant chorus now mixed with a low gossip. You get a miracle? You think the miracle man's got any more miracles? Dude, you didn't hear what happened to the miracle man?

Curtis walked away from the cacophony because he didn't want to listen to the crowd, or take part in the clutter. He walked away from Soldier's Field, deep into the South lot. No one saw Curtis, or approached Curtis, for he could make himself invisible like nothing. This would be his last concert. Did Curtis come all the way from Florida to walk around a parking lot? That's what this scene boiled down to, walking around a parking lot. And consumerism. Everyone was selling something. How was this different than anywhere else? He wouldn't miss it. Soon there were no more heads, only a plethora of cars, and Curtis still walking. He thought about Thelonious. Was the sacrifice worth it? At some point he and Geri would go to the hospital, but not until Curtis found peace. He did find some peace while looking at the cars. The different license plates on the different cars proved a network existed, connected everywhere. There wasn't a state in the union not represented in the parking lot. There was unity. And the dirtier the car, the further it traveled to get to the show. All the plates, all the heads, all states, blue, red, it was definitely worth something.

Shout outs

A 1998 Subaru Outback, University of Ithaca sticker, New York plates, blue and white lettering, the background over graphics of city skyline, Niagara Falls, and mountain-line: The Empire State. And Curtis could hear Thelonious. *New Yaawk New Yaawk, it's my motherfuckin town, Westchester's up, Staten Island's down, Manhattan in the middle, with Brooklyn below, Queens to the right, and this is called the show.*

***

A 1984 Volvo 240, silver, with Massachusetts plates, blue and red lettering over white background: The Spirit of America. Again, Thelonious was in Curtis's ear. *Gettin wicked, can I kick-it unrehearsed, took ya eighty years to lift the fuckin curse, Boston's in the house, New Year's in Worcester, kickin it in Lowell, with an alcoholic rooster.*

***

A 1977 VW Westphalia, olive green, black curtains on the back and side windows, Oregon plates, blue lettering over blue hues graphic of big green Douglas Fir and mountain backdrop. *Home of the cubensis and mad glassblowers, barter fairs on the Kesey farm, drunk-drivin lawnmowers.* Curtis will miss his brethren, if it was so.

***

A 2001 Chevy Suburban, dust on the windshield, a crumpled Wendy's bag leering out of the window; Georgia plates, black lettering over white background with peach graphic: On My Mind. *Special love to the ATLiens and Athens kids who know what a party's all about, stormin thru the South, we're a force, we're Hurricane Clout!*

***

A 2004 Nissan Sentra, white, with Colorado plates, white lettering over green background. *It wouldn't be a party without Colorado in the house, right Denver, right Boulder, that's right.* Curtis walked on and on, while the cars went on and on. . . And on and on and on. . . .

'LUDE—*the rock star steez—a message from Thelonious Horowitz*

There are really only two things missing. One, what's the dilly with the three deejays in Hurricane Clout. How's it possible to keep shoutin about peeps that ain't even in-the-house? Anything's possible—aiiight—stoops if you don't think so. Those are my niggaz. They're up in my steez. So you ain't seen em here, it's all-good. So they always sound grouped together. Those peeps are as different as can be. Trust—if this stayed in New York, focusing only on me, bet your bottom dollar Chopshop, Lee, and Diamonds gonna be in the house. It's like that, and that's the way it is! Wha-a-a-t—Definitely My Crew—we're runnin the Shiite. The other thing missing? What crazy adventure befell Thelonious Horowitz on his high plains drifter, Steve McQueen, Terry Southern, easy ridin, on the road mission from New York to Chi-town? *Nada nada nada, not a damn thang.* There ain't always high drama out there on them seas. You know I took a train, one-way, one hundred and ten ducks, wasn't a kewl Amtrak train with a kewl Amtrak name, like the Crescent or the Meteor, nah, they had me on the Lake Shore Limited, nineteen hours just chillin with your boy blasé. No shorties to kick it too. Slept ten hours. Drank a coupla shwills in the bar car. Oh, and I wrote a song, or part of an untitled song, on a cocktail napkin. I could-a named it Last Song, whatevs, it's in my pocket, someone will find it. One-way ticket? I always travel one-way. You never know what will happen after a show. And if I die, will you care? You really think you'll miss me when I'm gone?

LAST SONG (lyrics T. Horowitz)

My eyes are bloodshot / Haven't shaved in weeks / Could use a
few adjustments / Work out all the tweaks / I drink too much / I
smoke too much / I don't fuck enough / I'm so out-of-touch / I
don't know where I'm goin / Don't know where I've been / Don't
remember anything / Don't remember sin / It had something to
do with gin / There might've been some tonic / Might've ate
some pills / The problem is it's chronic / Don't know where I'm
going / Don't know where I've been / Don't remember anything /
Don't remember sin / I have no idea what's going on / no idea
what's going on / I have no idea what's going on / no idea what's
going on / I have no idea what's going on / no idea what's goin on

KC, Keith, Shore Morris, and the Princess walked out of the South lot, across 18th Street, into the Waldron garage. At one point, they stood to the side to let a U-Haul truck pass. Two white station wagons followed the truck. One of them almost hit Keith while he stared at the U-Haul, distracted by a cry he thought he heard from the truck. No one else heard it. The garage looked empty and tired in amber florescence. That's how KC described it in one of her Mead notebooks (she meant fluorescence but she misspelled the word) while she waited for the completion of another group sidebar. The Princess wanted to sneak into the car she drove to Chicago in, the car with Florida plates, the vehicle that belonged to the taper. Mikey the taper had an umbrella, and the Princess wanted an umbrella very much since it really looked like rain, and because the stadium was outside, her hair could get wet, and there'd be no telling what she'd do if that happened. But the door to the car was locked, and before she could throw a hissy fit, Shore Morris promised that if it rained, they'd find a dry spot, maybe in a corporate box, cause hells bells if they wouldn't let him into a corporate box, because those boxes were for anyone who wanted to sit in them, at least at any show he would attend. When they exited the garage in the rear, they found themselves near the pedestrian underpass, the same place Thelonious, on the grassy knoll, conceived the notion of eliminating the scalpers. The open space once housed a few vendors, but now it was showtime and the underpass served as the main depository into the Southern entrance of Soldier's Field. The synergy of the crowd, like a magnet, sucked the four into its deluge and pushed them under the bridge where all were awed at the colossal stadium before them. American flags, raised high on poles, highlighted the magnificent promenade. The flags were lined in two rows, one row of flags in the foreground along the steps of the entrance, and another row of flags atop the stadium itself. The American flags blew mightily in the wind. Yeah, the air smelled like rain. Indeed, a storm crept in from the east. It didn't matter. Rain or shine, the air sizzled with an anticipating chatter for what awaited all beyond those golden stairs leading into the stadium. The girls had the tickets. Holding each other's hands, they ascended the golden stairs together. They only broke the chain upon approach of the ticket collector. Then along with tens of thousands of other people already inside the colossal stadium, four more heads entered the Oracledang music festival.

THE END

AUTHOR'S NOTE

This novel, although a work of fiction, depicts a wonderful world that over generations has been very real to hundreds of thousands of people. Although we're aware of the scene's flaws, and of the novel's flaws, this story ultimately needs to be told. During the five years of composing and revising *Headz*, almost 60,000 words have been deleted. Many anecdotes did not fit into the narrative arc of this compact and crowded novel, but still feel relevant and entertaining. Consequently, we've created a website, www.headzthenovel.com, dedicated to sixty deleted scenes and bonus features. If you enjoyed the story, we invite you to visit the website to learn more about the scene and the characters in this drama. Finally, over the years of learning the ins and outs of this enduring counterculture, and composing and publishing the book, there are too many people to thank. Therefore, to all my friends, family members, muses, fellow writers, professors, artists, musicians, and to the publisher of this press. You endlessly provide inspiration and give me the strength to persevere. For that, I am eternally grateful.

ABOUT THE AUTHOR

J.J. Colagrande was born and raised in New York before settling in Miami. He has been a contributing writer for the Miami Herald, Miami New Times, 944, Closer, and the Sun Sentinel. J.J. currently works as a Guest Lecturer at Miami Dade College and a freelance writer. His fictions have been published in Carve, Big Bridge, Mary, Facets, and many more.

3590593

Made in the USA